r Sir Ga

nsh

in

A MURDER AT ROSINGS

A MURDER
AT ROSINGS

Annette Purdey Pugh

HONNO MODERN FICTION

First published in Great Britain in 2021 by Honno Press
'Ailsa Craig', Heol y Cawl, Dinas Powys, Vale of Glamorgan,
Wales, CF64 4AH

1 2 3 4 5 6 7 8 9 10

A catalogue record for this book is available from the British Library.

Published with the financial support of the Books Council of Wales.

ISBN 978-1-912905-35-5 (paperback)
ISBN 978-1-912905-36-2 (ebook)
Cover Design: Isabella Ashford
Text design: Elaine Sharples
Printed in Great Britain by CPI Group UK

For Rhiannon

1

The old gardener had always considered the glasshouses at Rosings to be his own peculiar domain. He expected his time there to be ordered by himself and him alone, free from interruptions by kitchen maids, under-footmen and the like, with their inappropriate demands for out-of-season fruit and flowers. He did not, in any circumstances, expect to see his mistress there.

However, the voice he heard that morning was undoubtedly hers. It reached him with all the deep resonance of the bellow of an in-season milch-cow. 'Dudgeon!'

The old man dropped the clay flowerpot he was holding. It broke into a score of pieces, scattering soil and geranium cuttings. He swore and bent down to retrieve his plants before there was any danger to the delicate sprouting roots. Their distinctive smell filled the small warm space.

'Dudgeon! Here! At once!'

He took a few steps and peeped out from behind the door. He saw a flurry of burgundy near the rhubarb patch. Her ladyship appeared to be dancing back and forth, waving her arms indiscriminately. He hesitated. Could she have lost her wits? She had been in a poor humour for the last two or three years, ever since her nephew had made that most unsuitable marriage. For a moment, the gardener was tempted to slink back into hiding.

'There you are, Dudgeon! Thank God. To me, now, to me!' She turned and started to run back towards the green door in the wall which separated the fruit and vegetable garden from the formal area. A day of wonders, indeed, thought the old man. Not only was his mistress in his vegetable garden, and quite unaccompanied, but she was running! He stared for several moments, until he became aware of her distant voice still calling.

The old man had no option now but to lumber in her wake, losing his cap to a rogue gust of wind, and nearly stumbling several times, as his fustian trousers, which were over-long, caught under his boots.

Puffing, he came upon her on the other side of the door, near the coleus bed. She was pointing down at a shape among the plants.

'You see, Dudgeon? I cannot rouse him, though I have made several attempts.'

The gardener edged a little closer to the object in question. His sight was not always as sharp as it had been formerly, and the day was still early and the light poor. He could see now that it was a man lying there, and not just any man. His black clerical garb was unmistakeable.

'Why, it's the rector, your ladyship.'

'Exactly so. But he cannot be roused. Is he unwell, do you think, Dudgeon? Or has he perhaps taken strong drink?' Lady Catherine was frowning her disapproval, as if she suspected her last surmise to be the correct one. She sighed, impatiently. 'I cannot have this, Dudgeon. Not in my gardens. It will not do.'

The old man shook his head in agreement, a wave of annoyance passing over him as he saw the broken leaves of his carefully tended plants. It was not unusual for the clergyman to be seen in the gardens and park of Rosings. He often walked there as he composed his sermons, frequently stopping to ask questions of Dudgeon and the under-gardeners. He was, by all accounts, re-planting at the parsonage in a style closer to that of the great house, an aim which Dudgeon found inexplicable.

The gardener knelt down and shook the immobile form. 'Rector! Mr Collins!'

The clergyman remained still, and the old man was gripped by a sudden chill. He glanced up at Lady Catherine, who was looking down intently, breathing a little too fast so that her jowls shook a little.

'I do so fear, m'lady, that...'

'Turn him, Dudgeon. We cannot be weak-livered.'

They stared at each other. Though they were both familiar with death, neither was willing to invite it closer by naming it.

Reluctantly, the gardener pushed at the rector's shoulder and hip, so that he rolled onto his back, breaking more of the plant-stems. Then, with an involuntary curse, the old man leapt up and retreated a few paces. 'I must apologise for my language, m'lady, but...'

'He has a knife in his chest, Dudgeon.'

'He does, m'lady. I have never seen the like of it. And he a clergyman and all!'

She clasped her hands as if in prayer. On the other side of the wall, a blackbird was singing. Eventually, seeming to rouse herself, Lady Catherine turned to the old man.

'You will escort me to the house, Dudgeon. The magistrate must be sent for without delay. That such a thing should happen in *my* garden...'

The old gardener dithered a little at her side. He longed to be back in the familiar warmth of the glasshouses.

'W... will you take my arm, m'lady?'

'Thank you, Dudgeon. I feel I must.'

Together, they made a rather slow progress towards the big house, Lady Catherine more shaken than she liked to admit, and the old man worrying constantly that his trousers would catch under his heel again and cause them both to slip.

2

Robert Archer was a good-looking young man. He knew this not from personal vanity but because he sometimes overheard young (and, more often, not-so-young) ladies talking about him when they thought he was out of hearing. The knowledge helped him to gain confidence, as did his own more certain conviction that he was proficient in his chosen trade of wheelwright.

He had moved to Hunsford from Canterbury about ten years previously, on the completion of his apprenticeship, helped by a small legacy from an uncle. The premises he rented were near enough to the high road to attract passing trade, as well as the day-to-day work for the local farms and estates, and he was now pleased to employ two apprentices of his own, as well as a daily woman to keep his cottage clean and prepare the meals. All in all, he was well satisfied with his life.

This satisfaction had been increased two years before, when the local magistrate, Sir John Bright, had appointed Archer to the post of village constable. Although no salary accompanied the position, it gave the young man some status in Hunsford, while the quiet nature of the village meant that his duties did not keep him often from his workshop. He might be asked on occasion to assist a keeper when a poacher threatened violence, or to apprehend thieves and pickpockets at the village fair, but generally his duties began and ended with the quieting of brawls outside The Three Crowns.

That morning, in the September of 1806, Archer was at work

with his lathe, enjoying the peace of a sunny autumn day and the smoothness of the wood under his hands. From time to time, his mind wandered to the other side of the village, where a young woman had recently been employed to assist in the draper's shop. For so long, Archer's attention had been devoted to building his business and reputation; now, perhaps, he could allow himself some distraction. The girl had been introduced to him after church the previous Sunday. He had learnt that she was a niece of the draper and that her name was Sarah.

He pronounced the name to himself a few times as he turned his lathe. He considered it a very pleasing name for a young woman, especially for one with features as pretty as hers. He remembered how she had blushed slightly when he had suggested that they might perhaps meet again the following Sunday. He knew very little about young women, but surely that had been a good sign. He found himself anticipating the next Sabbath quite eagerly.

The barking of his dog, Peter, roused him from his thoughts. He went out into the yard, where Sir John Bright was dismounting from his grey gelding.

'Good morning, Sir John. What can I do for you?'

The magistrate's face was serious.

'I'm afraid I must steal you from your work, Robert. You will ride with me to Rosings, immediately. There has been terrible mischief afoot there, and I need my constable to assist me.'

'Certainly, Sir John, but what...'

'Immediately, Robert! Go saddle your horse now and I'll recount what has occurred as we ride. There is no time to lose.'

Archer was left with no option but to lay down his tools and abandon his lathe and workshop in a most untidy way and make his way at a run over to the small paddock where his mare was standing sleepily in the early sunshine. He gave a silent prayer of thanks that she was not in a skittish mood and hard to catch, though his fingers became clumsy with haste as he fumbled with the bridle. He was aware of Bright's gelding tossing its head with impatience as they waited near the gate. Eventually, sweating a little and red in the face, he was mounted and trotting in the wake of the magistrate, who had set off as soon as Archer had put his foot into the stirrup.

When Bright told him of the murder of Mr Collins, Archer's first thought, unworthily, was that the Sunday service he had been looking forward to would probably not now take place. He frowned as he wondered how long it might be until a new rector were appointed. Apart from the Sabbath, there were few occasions in his week when his path might cross that of Sarah's. Lost in gloomy meditation, he cantered along the lanes at Sir John's side, taking little notice of the meadows and woodlands they passed. However, Sir John's voice recalled him to the task in hand.

'Before we arrive at Rosings, I wish to inform you as to how I would like to proceed with this case. It appears to be most unusual and unlike anything I have come across in my time as magistrate here, though of course I have only the information I was given by the messenger. I have a feeling that we are going to require the utmost ingenuity to uncover our murderer. Have you heard of the Bow Street Runners, Robert?'

'I have indeed, Sir John. A carter from London was talking of them to me just the other day. It seems they are greatly to be feared by felons of all sorts.'

'That is my understanding, Robert. They were founded by Mr Fielding, a magistrate like myself, and I have heard something of their methods. When it is not obvious as to who is the perpetrator of a crime, they use investigation and questioning to uncover him. No stone is left unturned.'

'And you intend to use this method at Rosings?'

'I do. Investigation and questioning. Those must be our watchwords, Robert. I am fortunate in that I have a distant relationship to the de Bourghs, so that it will not be improper for me to address some questions to the family, although I can claim no real closeness to them. I shall rely on you to question the servants in similar fashion.'

'You mean to question the family, Sir John?' Archer had a sudden appalled vision of Lady Catherine in the dock at the County Assizes. 'Surely this will turn out to be the work of some vagrant cutpurse, probably now long escaped.'

'I would you were right, Robert. That would indeed be the best outcome for all concerned here, because the alternatives... Anyway, I would ask you to humour me a little longer, just until we are sure that there is no other explanation. Will you do that?'

'Of course, Sir John.'

'Good. We shall of course need to visit Mr Collins' wife and family in their turn, but we'll not intrude on their grief while the body is, as it were, still warm... Now, we approach the gates of Rosings. I have given orders to the messenger that we must view the body in situ before it is moved. I have also furnished us with paper and pencils, so that notes may be made if necessary. Investigation and questioning!'

Side by side, the two men passed through the ornate iron gates and rode their horses at a trot towards the imposing spread which was Rosings Park. It was the largest dwelling for many miles around and, house and gardens alike, was kept in perfect order by a regiment of servants. Unaccustomed to approaching from the front, Archer was painfully aware, not only of the clatter of their horses' shoes, but also, suddenly, of his own heart's beat. At first, only the chimneys were visible above the mature oaks and chestnuts which lined the long drive; they stood out, starkly white against the blue sky. All too soon, however, the massive façade was before them, and Archer's spirits began to sink in earnest, just as they had when, as a boy, he had ventured to swim in a river which had swollen to unforeseen depths.

3

The morning room at Rosings was, as intended, full of light at that time of day. The pale green walls were adorned with pretty, rural scenes, and a bowl of autumn roses graced the occasional table. Lady Catherine's face, however, betrayed the darkest of moods. On the opposite side of the room, her daughter Anne wore an expression of frightened bewilderment. Next to Anne, the elderly lady who acted as part companion, part nursemaid, regarded her anxiously.

'This is too much, Sir John, indeed it is,' said Lady Catherine. 'For that man to lie there still, after these several hours! It is more than I can bear.'

'I understand, Lady Catherine. I can tell you that the body of the unfortunate Mr Collins is even now being taken back to the parsonage. However, it was most important that my constable and I should see the exact place and manner of his death. You know Mr Archer, of course?'

Lady Catherine glanced over at the constable, who was standing some paces behind Bright. 'Of course I do, Sir John. I know all my tenants. Though he seems over-young to be constable. I have thought this ever since you appointed him.'

'He is young, yes, Lady Catherine, but he has made a thriving business for himself, and is well respected in the village. His strength and level humour stand him in good stead when dealing with lawbreakers.'

'Very well. I shall respect your judgement. Now, how do you

mean to uncover the killer of poor Mr Collins? It is not, I think, the work of some sturdy beggar.'

'Indeed, Lady Catherine, I do believe you are right. I took the liberty, on arriving here today, of showing your butler the... weapon with which he was despatched. It appears it has your family crest upon it.'

'It does. I recognised it at once, despite the blood which disfigured it. It is a paper knife, one of several in our possession. There are two or three in the library and at least one in my writing desk. What can it mean, Sir John?'

'That is what we must find out, Lady Catherine. It seems that it was well sharpened. Is this usual practice?'

'Certainly. My late husband was most particular about such matters. Letters must be opened neatly, and the pages of books slit with the utmost precision. I have striven to keep up his high standards.'

'Of course. And I am assured that there have been no thefts at Rosings in recent months. My own records and those of my constable can confirm this fact.'

'Indeed not! We have never suffered theft in this house, not in my living memory. On the estate, perhaps, sometimes – a pheasant or some apples – such losses, though reprehensible, are suffered by most landowners I believe.'

'When Archer and I were examining the... the rector, it was found that his watch had fallen from his pocket and had become damaged when he fell. In consequence, we can say with some certitude that he suffered the assault at half-past ten yesterday evening.'

Lady Catherine shook her head in perplexity. 'The poor man was given to strange wanderings at times. He liked to say he was clearing his head. I do believe that the sudden prodigious increase in his family was something of a shock to him. Three small children can be a trial to anyone, and especially in a household of modest means. He was pleased to heed my advice as regards his marrying, and Mrs Collins is a sweet woman indeed, but it did all come upon him so suddenly, poor man.'

There followed a few moments of silence as everyone reflected upon Mr Collins and his unfortunate family. At length, Bright took up the conversation again.

'You asked me how I mean to uncover the perpetrator of this terrible act, Lady Catherine. I intend to use the modern method of investigation and questioning, which means that my constable and I shall attempt to talk to all your household in the hope that each tiny scrap of information gathered may help to complete the entire picture.'

Lady Catherine looked a little confused. 'You will talk to *all* my staff, Sir John?'

'Yes, Lady Catherine, and to yourself and Miss de Bourgh, with your permission... and Mrs Jenkinson, of course.'

Anne de Bourgh suddenly brightened. 'Don't you see, Mamma? It will be like a jigsaw puzzle!'

Lady Catherine's frown deepened. 'I fail to see how any of *us* can contribute to your investigation, Sir John. Nevertheless, you must do as you must. You are the magistrate.' She glared at her daughter, who promptly lost any sign of animation. Anne's companion, Mrs Jenkinson, patted her arm comfortingly.

'Thank you, Lady Catherine. Now, I would wish my constable to commence by speaking to the junior members of your household staff.'

'Very well. I shall summon a footman to escort him below stairs.' She turned towards Archer. 'You will treat them gently, Constable. I do not wish them to be upset in any way. The smooth running of Rosings must not be disrupted further.'

'Yes... No, my lady.'

Archer's face was pink as he left the room.

There was another brief silence after the door closed behind him. Bright paced a little, coming to rest before the window which overlooked the rose-walk.

'Mr Collins has been a regular visitor here for some years, I understand?'

'Since granting him the living, I have been pleased to invite him to dine with us several times each month, yes. He has been something of a protégé of mine, and in return, I have received the utmost respect from him. He is – was – a most obliging young man.'

'Is that the general opinion among his parishioners?'

'You should put that question to your constable, Sir John. But, yes. I have heard nothing but good of the young man. He was by all accounts an inspiration to the living, and a source of great comfort to the dying. I shall be hard put to replace him; hard put to it, indeed.'

'And you know of no-one who might have borne him ill-will?'

'Indeed not, Sir John.'

Bright shook his head. 'This is all most inexplicable, Lady Catherine. It has neither rhyme nor reason. If it were not for the weapon, I should be content to conclude that Mr Collins was the unfortunate victim of some random felon, now escaped. However, as you and I agreed earlier, such a person could not have been in possession of the paper knife. Theft might explain such possession, of course, but what thief would simply take a paper knife and nothing else?'

'What thief, indeed?' said Lady Catherine.

'Now,' continued Bright, 'as to the assault itself, were you aware of any disturbance yesterday evening? Unwarranted shouting, for example?'

'Certainly not. I retired to my bedchamber at about nine o'clock, as is usual when we have no guests. My daughter did likewise.'

Bright turned towards Anne de Bourgh. 'And you, Miss de Bourgh, you heard nothing unusual?'

Anne turned her anxious gaze to her mother, who glowered at her, and then answered in a nervous rush. 'No, Sir John. I spent some time at my prayers, of course, and then I studied my Bible a little. I have for some time been committing to memory some verses from the Book of Proverbs. Mr Collins has assured me that this is a most valuable activity and... Oh! Please excuse me.' Her small face crumpled, and the tears started to fall as she turned away from Bright and ran from the room. After a few seconds, the elderly Mrs Jenkinson hurried a little stiffly in her wake.

'Your daughter is most affected by Mr Collins' death, I think.'

'Of course, Sir John. She is a young lady of the utmost sensibility.'

'I'm sorry if I have caused her grief by my questioning... Now, I must say just one more thing before I leave you to your mourning, Lady Catherine. I am most anxious that neither you nor Miss de Bourgh walk the grounds unaccompanied. Until we uncover this most foul of felons, I cannot know what danger may exist here. This morning, for instance, you were walking alone. Is it usual for you to be abroad so early in the morning? It was just after half-past six, I understand.'

Lady Catherine regarded him sternly. 'Magistrate or not, you are presumptuous, Sir John. I was over-heated this morning, and sought the cool air. That is all. Now, I am weary. I must ask you to leave.'

4

Mary Bennet was alone in the parlour at Hunsford Parsonage, her book unread in her lap. She could not help but hear the sounds coming from the room next door, where a woman called Mrs Creech was washing, dressing and laying out the body of her cousin, Mr Collins. Mary opened the book in a bid to block out the images the sounds conjured, but the letters blurred as she stared at the page.

When her father had suggested that she accompany him to Kent, she had immediately tried to find some excuse not to go. Her mother was in Newcastle, visiting Mary's sister Lydia, and Mary had been finding that the sudden quietness at home provided her with the opportunity to make real inroads into her Greek grammar. Mrs Bennet was expected to be away for some months, and Mr Bennet, as usual, had been content with the company of his own books.

However, only two weeks into their sabbatical, Mr Bennet had announced after dinner that they were to go to Hunsford the following day. 'I have urgent business with Mr Collins. It will be a pleasant diversion for you. You are too much at home, Mary.'

Mary was horrified. 'But Mamma is always expecting me to go with her to Meryton, Papa. I have to spend hours in the company of people I do not wish to see! Now that Kitty is so often with Jane or Lizzy, I have no peace from this visiting... I have progressed so well with my Greek these past weeks.'

'Nevertheless, child, I must insist you come to Hunsford this time. Greek has been with us for thousands of years so far, and I assure you that it will not disappear if you leave it alone for a week or two more.'

'But, Papa...'

Mr Bennet held up his hands. 'Peace, now, Mary. You will one day have your own establishment and may then order your time as you wish. Until then, you must allow me to guide you when I can.'

Mary frowned. 'My own establishment, you say. With some clerk of Uncle Gardiner's, I suppose.'

'That possibility has been mentioned, yes. Your uncle has very kindly suggested that you might find one of his clerks agreeable, if only you would take the trouble to journey up to London. The world needs clerks just as much as soldiers, you know, and probably rather more than it needs grand gentlemen.'

Mary regarded him sadly. 'I would have married Mr Collins, you know, Papa, if only you had told him as much. All your troubles would then have been over. You could have pretended that Lizzy was unavailable, couldn't you? She was much taken with Mr Wickham at that time, as I remember it. I was next in line. But you didn't think about me. No-one ever does.'

'Your mother was in charge of all that, my dear. I had no hand in it. However, I was unwilling for *any* of my daughters to marry Mr Collins... although it would certainly have had a sobering effect upon Lydia... But now, off you go to make ready. I want to get started without delay tomorrow morning.'

Their first few days at Hunsford had been just as Mary had feared. She had been obliged to admire the Collins' three daughters, although the eldest was but four years old, and the youngest just an infant-in-arms. On her first afternoon there, she had made the mistake of playing the piano for the two older girls and had only managed to escape when the nurse had proclaimed that it was time for tea and bed. On each day after that, she had had no option but to repeat the performance, so that she longed even more for the tranquillity of Longbourn.

Her father, meanwhile, had spent much of the time in discussion with Mr Collins; occasionally, their raised voices could be heard from the direction of the study. Mary was grateful that the children were too young to question this. Their mother, Charlotte, still not recovered from the birth of the youngest, was in bed for much of each day, so, she, too, was unaware of their differences.

When her cousin's body had been brought into the house, Mr Bennet, visibly shocked, had very soon shut himself away in the study, leaving instructions that he was not to be disturbed. Thinking now about those heated exchanges, Mary could not escape a deep sense of shame. She wondered if her father's conscience was equally troubled now that Mr Collins was dead.

5

Archer was relieved to be in the more familiar surroundings of the servants' quarters. He was frequently called on to carry out repairs to Lady Catherine's fleet of carriages, and it was not unknown, on a cold day, for him to be offered meat and drink afterwards in the warmth of the servants' hall. It seemed that her ladyship was generous in the treatment of her staff, and encouraged them to be generous in turn. He was reminded of this as he spoke to the boot-boy.

'I sleep in here, sir.'

The boy was indicating a kind of partitioned alcove off the boot-room. Archer could see that it was furnished with a small bed and even had a wash-stand with basin and ewer. In many other great houses he had visited, he knew that the lowly boot-boys very often had to lie down for the night among the boots and shoes they cleaned, with only a rough blanket and a horsehair pallet if they were lucky.

'It seems very comfortable, George.'

'I am more comfortable than I was at home, sir, as I don't have to share my bed with my brothers. It's warm, as well, for the great kitchen is just the other side of the wall.'

'You are very fortunate.'

'Yes, sir. I am told that Lady Catherine herself ordered the building of this room for the boot-boys when she first became mistress here.'

'And you have been employed here for how long?'

'Nine months come Michaelmas. I have hopes to be trained as footman one day, if I grow sufficient tall.'

'You are how old?'

'Thirteen, sir.'

'Now, George, do you understand why I am speaking to you? You know of the dire event which took place here last evening?'

'Yes, sir. Everyone is speaking of it.'

'As the constable, I am concerned to know if anyone here saw or heard anything – anything at all – which might help us to discover the felon who carried out this awful deed. Now, you are well placed here to observe comings or goings through the door to the stable yard. What time did you complete your duties last night?'

'Margaret brought me the servants' boots and shoes as usual after nine o'clock, sir. Lady Catherine advises most of the servants to retire by that time – unless she is entertaining, of course. It is the work of about two hours to clean them.'

'So you retire later than many of the other servants. Did you see anyone entering or leaving in those two hours?'

'No, sir. Mr Harries is most particular that the doors be locked and barred before ten. Though...'

'Though?'

'Though I have heard as how people can get out through the door to the orangery. It has the key in the lock.'

Archer could imagine why some of the younger servants might want to enjoy the hours of darkness away from the strict rules of the Rosings household. However, in view of the lad's age, he did not pursue the matter further. Though a sudden thought did strike him. 'Were any of the boots or shoes dirtier than usual?'

'One of the kitchen maids ain't too particular where she puts her feet when she gets sent for eggs, sir. Her boots are always bad to clean. Most of the house servants stay round the house, so theirs are easier. Miss Anne and Lady Catherine and Mrs Jenkinson, now, they walk a lot in the garden and pick up mud like nobody's business.'

'When do you clean their boots and shoes?'

'They're brought to me at half-past five in the morning, sir. Margaret takes them back up as soon as I am done with them – though she was not well today, and Jane had to do it.'

'So, nothing out of the ordinary, then.' Archer had half-hoped that the boy would suddenly recall an exceptionally muddy pair of boots, perhaps with a smear of blood, so that he could have triumphantly hauled some villainous footman into the presence of Sir John. But it was not to be. He sighed. 'Good. You have spoken well, George. I've no doubt you'll progress if you continue in your present path.'

The boy beamed. 'Thank you, sir.'

In the passageway outside the boot-room, Archer made a few brief notes on the paper Sir John had given him, then went on towards the glass-paned door which led to the kitchen and servants' hall.

He had always found the housekeeper, Mrs Flowerday, rather intimidating. She was dressed in sternest black, her steel-grey hair tightly bound. She pursed her lips in obvious disapproval as he entered the room.

'Ruth and Sally are our kitchen maids, Mr Archer, and young Maggie here is a maid-of-all-work. Please let me know when you have finished with them, and I shall instruct our house maid, Jane, to come to you.'

'Thank you, Mrs Flowerday.'

Archer nodded to the housekeeper, who lingered for a while

as if she didn't quite trust him, or the three young girls before him, to behave appropriately. This despite the fact that he had already interviewed the two scullery maids without mishap, if fruitlessly. He breathed a sigh of relief when she finally made her way towards her parlour.

'I'm sure you've all heard by now of the wicked events of last night,' he began.

'The murder of poor Mr Collins!' exclaimed Sally, wide eyed with horror and fascination. She was the taller of the two kitchen maids, as thin as Ruth was plump. She had a sharp look about her, and Archer felt that very little probably escaped her notice. Ruth seemed perhaps more trusting and docile. Maggie, the maid-of-all-work, was simply a little girl. Looking at her, Archer felt it would have been more appropriate for her to be sitting on a stool at her own fireside, wearing a white pinafore and fondling a doll. She had a small pinched face and wispy hair; her work-apron reached almost to the floor. She was perhaps nine or ten years old.

'Yes, that's right.' Archer tried to sound reassuring. 'I'm here just to ask you all a few questions. No, there's no reason to be afraid,' he added, as he saw Maggie's face whiten. 'Sir John Bright, who's the magistrate, has asked me to see all of you in case you have some information which could help us find out who committed this terrible deed. Now, did any of you hear or see anything unusual last night?'

'What would be unusual?'

'Oh, anything out of the ordinary. Someone shouting, for example, when everyone would normally be asleep.'

Sally shook her head and Ruth followed suit. They were both gazing fixedly at Archer and, young as they were, he felt a little discomfited.

'And you, Maggie?'

'I ain't done nothing!' There were tears on her cheeks now, and she was screwing her apron into a tight ball in front of her.

'Of course not, Maggie,' Sally reassured her. 'No-one thinks that any of us have done anything. She's only been here a month, Mr Archer. Misses her mum something rotten.' Sally turned to the little girl. 'We'll see you right, Mags. Mr Archer's a nice man. I've seen him lots around the place.'

'You was in the cart-house last week, Mr Archer.' Ruth had found her voice at last. 'I seen you when I went over for the eggs.' She was blushing deeply.

'May I ask what time you all went up to bed last night?'

'We all go at nine,' said Sally, 'that's unless there's guests for the morning. Then one of us stays up late to tend the fire. They want an early breakfast if they're out shooting.'

'You too, Maggie?'

'She goes before the rest of us, Mr Archer,' said Ruth, blushing even more. 'She has to be up extra early every day to help Jane with the fires and the slop buckets.'

Archer looked at the little girl and found it hard to imagine her carrying the heavy buckets of coal in the chill of the early mornings. The slop buckets didn't bear thinking of at all. He reflected for a moment on the nature of a junior servant's life, something which hadn't bothered him particularly before.

'What'll happen to us all, Mr Archer?' Sally asked. 'We won't be safe in our beds, not with a murderer on the loose. And to think it's happened at Rosings, of all places! Mum wouldn't have ever sent me to work here if she'd known!'

Little Maggie began to weep in earnest, prompting Ruth to put a motherly arm around her. Archer felt his orderly investigation slipping away from him.

'I'm sure there's no danger to any of you, as long as you keep to your normal routines. You're not often on your own, are you?'

The girls all solemnly shook their heads.

'And you share sleeping accommodation?'

'Ruth and me share a room with the scullery maids, two to each bed. Maggie sleeps with Jane and Margaret in the room next door. We all have good mattresses too, Mr Archer, so we sleep well. The mistress is particular about that.'

'That sounds very good to me. You can look after one another, can't you? Now, I think we've just about finished. Remember to tell Mrs Flowerday if you do think of anything that might be useful, and she can pass it on to me. You've all been very helpful.'

He could hear the two kitchen maids giggling behind him as he went to find the housekeeper.

*

Jane, the house maid, had a face that was ruddy and pock-marked. She was easy in his company, speaking so freely that he found it difficult to question her in the way he intended. As she raised her hand to adjust her cap, Archer saw that her fingers were ingrained with coal-dust. He wondered how many fires she had laid that morning.

When they spoke of the discovery of the rector's body, she dropped her voice to a hoarse whisper.

'Her age, Mr Archer! That's what ails her ladyship.' Seeing Archer's confusion, she tutted at him. 'In women of her age, lady or not, the blood will run extra hot, with the only remedy being the fresh outside air. You will remember your own mother at that time of life, I feel sure.'

Archer, who had left his mother's care at twelve years old to take up his apprenticeship, was still nonplussed. However, the house maid was obviously anxious that she did not lose this opportunity to spread a little gossip.

'I overheard the two lady's maids talking – I tell you in confidence, you understand, Mr Archer – Miss Pearson, that's her ladyship's maid, she said as how Lady Catherine has taken to leaving the house at all hours of day and night, and night, especially. That's when the blood is hottest. In truth, I know not why the Lord has chosen to afflict womankind in this way, indeed I don't. We have all that other trouble in our young years, and then this... I await it with much trepidation, I tell you. I'm not so young as I was, Mr Archer, though a house maid, still. I have not the refinement for parlour maid, you see.'

Archer, who was aware of the blood running hotter in his own face, hastened to steer the conversation back to the rather less uncomfortable matter of Mr Collins. 'This... as you say... this would be the reason Lady Catherine was in the gardens today, so early as to be the first to discover the poor rector?'

'Indeed, Mr Archer. And such a shock she must have had. It doesn't bear thinking of, and him and his family such favourites of hers, such favourites. She's been the soul of goodness towards them ever since Mr Collins became rector here.'

'So I understand... I must say, Jane, that her ladyship seems very well liked by the members of her household with whom I have spoken.'

'Oh yes, Mr Archer. You know, folks who don't know her always say she's proud and unpleasant – my own mother was one, dead set against me going into service here – but, as I said, she didn't know her. She's a good mistress and no mistake, as long as we do our work well and know our place. Knows all our names and makes sure we're comfortable here. It's not every mistress you could say that of.'

'Certainly not... Ah, Mrs Flowerday, you wish to speak to me?'

Archer stood up as the housekeeper entered the room.

'I'm afraid I must steal Jane away to her duties, Mr Archer.'

'Very well. I believe our interview is at an end, anyway. Thank you, Mrs Flowerday – I am grateful to you for allowing your staff time to speak to me.'

He was aware of the housekeeper's eyes on his back as he made his way upstairs.

6

'We have precious little to advance our investigation!'

Bright and Archer were seated on a bench outside The Three Crowns, having procured a meagre meal of bread, onion and hard cheese.

'No, Sir John. I fear that all my questioning has simply revealed that no-one knows anything about the murder, but that nearly everyone *could* have had a hand in it. It seems that the small door to the orangery is always available at the turn of a key, mostly because her ladyship feels the need to walk out of doors at all times of the night.'

'I think you are unacquainted with the ways of women, Robert.'

'I left my home at an early age, sir, and my master was unmarried. I have not lived much among women.'

'Well – and I can recall my own dear mother having this need for cool air – you must merely think of this nocturnal perambulating as a human manifestation of that time when, if we were talking of cattle, say, the old house-cow would need to be sold off as barren.' Archer felt his face colouring yet again, as the uninvited picture entered his head of Lady Catherine penned up at the Michaelmas fair. 'Meaning no disrespect.' Bright eyed him slyly, scarcely suppressing a smile. 'And I don't really mean to make light of the matter. It caused my mother some distress, as I understand, though I was not supposed to know anything about it.'

'I see your meaning, sir. It is all most frustrating even so.'

'Indeed it is, Robert.' Bright swallowed some ale. 'And although this ale is good, the fare is poor indeed.'

'I'm sorry, Sir John. I fear our village hostelry cannot match those of Westerham.'

Bright shrugged. 'To return to the matter in hand, it appears that anyone at Rosings – from Lady Catherine down to the boot-boy – could, if they wished, have taken a paper knife from the library, exited by the orangery door, and accosted Mr Collins. It would not be so easy for someone to enter the house from outside to commit the deed – unless they were let in by an accomplice. And why go to all the trouble of breaking in just to take a paper knife?'

'Why kill Mr Collins at all, sir? It is all so inexplicable.'

'Perhaps his sermons were too long!'

'At times, yes, Sir John... But I see you tease me.'

'I apologise, Robert. I resort too readily to jesting, I fear. But would you say that Mr Collins was well liked in the village?'

Archer hesitated. 'He was perhaps a more serious man than the late Mr Vaughan, his predecessor – that gentleman was often to be found at the inn here, drinking ale with his parishioners – but Mr Collins was ready with guidance and comfort where necessary. I have heard none gainsay this, though...'

'Though?'

'He was a man who thought much of himself, sir. He talked often of his preferment at Rosings and of his close acquaintance with her ladyship.'

'That was my impression, on the few occasions when our paths crossed. However, he *was* unusually favoured by Lady Catherine, it seems.'

Bright pondered for some moments on what he saw as the

rather strange relationship between Mr Collins and Lady Catherine de Bourgh. Presumably, she was simply a lady who thrived on flattery, of which Collins had provided an everflowing spring. He sighed and tried a different approach.

'And you yourself can confirm that no strangers of note have been seen around the village in the past few days? The landlord here told me as much while pouring our ale.'

'I am unaware of any strangers, sir.'

'Hmm... a puzzle indeed, just as Miss Anne suggested... You will remember, Robert, that she likened our method of investigation to fitting together the pieces of a jigsaw puzzle. A most apt analogy, though I fear her mother was disapproving.'

'With all respect, she seems a lonely kind of young lady, sir. Not much given to mixing in society.'

'That is my opinion exactly, and not helped by her mother's choice of companion for her. Mrs Jenkinson would, if anything, be over-old to be companion to her mother! I understand, though, that Miss Anne received a most unwarranted injury to her sensibilities when her cousin, who had been intended for her, made an injudicious and impetuous marriage to another.'

'That young woman was, I think, a relation of Mr Collins.'

'Indeed she was, Robert. However, if Miss Anne had been inclined to murder, I imagine she would sooner have stabbed the young woman in question than that lady's blameless relative... I'm sorry, I jest again. I cannot think Miss Anne capable of killing anything larger than a wasp. Besides, she was most affected by the death of Mr Collins and ran from the room in tears when I was questioning her, which made her mother most displeased again.'

'We must hope that the upper servants and ground staff have useful information to offer us, sir.'

'Indeed, and I must tell you how grateful I am for your support today, Robert. The establishment at Rosings is so large that my method must fail completely were it not for you.'

'I am happy to act in the role appointed me, Sir John. However, so many of the servants merely state that they were asleep in their shared rooms and have nothing to say to me at all.'

'I have found the same. It seems that, unless Lady Catherine is entertaining guests, all the staff are early to bed on her instructions.'

'I have seen most of the lowest ranks, excepting the between maid...' Here Archer consulted his notes. 'Margaret, who is indisposed, and the chamber maids. I have talked to none of the footmen, of whom there are four, nor either of the lady's maids.'

'You are most methodical. We'll see the footmen and lady's maids together, Robert. In my experience, such classes of servant occasionally may feel they are superior to a mere constable. As a modern man, sometimes the English system of class and rank annoys me greatly.'

They finished their ale in companionable silence, and Archer was about to call for the horses when a female voice greeted him. Looking around, he was startled to see the draper's wife and her niece.

'Good afternoon, Mr Archer. It's a beautiful day, is it not?'

'Mrs Smith... Miss Smith!' He fumbled nervously with his notes from Rosings. 'It is a... lovely day indeed. You are both well, I hope? And Mr Smith?

'We are all in excellent health, thank you. We are glad of this opportunity to take the air as we deliver some samples of cloth to the Browne sisters at The Grange.'

'I am pleased to hear it.' Although he longed to keep the pair in front of him for as long as possible, Archer was finding it difficult to suppress a feeling that frivolous talk was somehow inappropriate on such a day. It was clear that the Smiths had not yet heard of the murder of Mr Collins.

He glanced at Sir John, who smiled at the two women. 'You must introduce us, Robert.'

'Oh... forgive me... I have no manners. May I present Sir John Bright? This is Mrs Smith, and her niece, Miss Smith.'

'I have heard your name, Sir John. You are the magistrate.'

'Indeed, Mrs Smith, and I think my wife is well acquainted with your excellent drapery establishment. She says it is far better than anything Westerham has to offer.'

'You are kindness indeed, sir.'

'And you, Miss Smith, are you visiting your aunt?'

Sarah blushed prettily. 'I am recently arrived, sir. I help my aunt and uncle and am training to be a seamstress.'

'You will never be without work. Most ladies of my acquaintance rate fashion very highly – don't you agree, Robert?'

'Er... yes.'

Mrs Smith smiled. 'We will not keep you from your business, Sir John. I trust we shall see you at church, Mr Archer.'

Archer could think of no appropriate reply, so said nothing. As they watched the pair make their way down the road, Bright clapped Archer on the shoulder.

'Struck dumb, my friend? I think that young lady has taken your fancy.'

'She is most agreeable, sir.'

'And it doesn't hurt that she has gold curls and cornflower-blue eyes! You have good taste, Robert. You must learn to talk more to the ladies, that's all. You are altogether too serious.'

'It does not come easy to me.'

'Well then, you must practise. It's time you found a good woman to be your wife... Now, we must return to Rosings.'

7

Mary Bennet stood nervously in the doorway of the small reception room at Hunsford Parsonage and stared at the body of her cousin. In death, Mr Collins had acquired a dignity which he had sometimes lacked in life. Mary looked at his hands, tastefully arranged to hold his Bible, and thought of the occasions when he had been ready to discuss matters of interpretation with her. Apart from her father, he had been the only person of her acquaintance to take her studies at all seriously.

She thought of the evening, less than a fortnight ago, when he had announced that he was taking her father and herself to dine at Rosings with Lady Catherine de Bourgh. Mary had looked forward to this event with much trepidation. She remembered all too well that strange day when Lady Catherine had come to Longbourn to see Elizabeth and had left in a very poor humour without paying her mother the courtesy of saying farewell. She had feared that there must be some sort of punishment planned for Mr Bennet and herself, though she could not imagine what.

She had been placed at the table next to Miss Anne de Bourgh, who looked timidly at Mary without speaking. Mary was, in a way, comforted to note that the young lady was not handsome at all, but small and pale, and that she picked at her food with little sign of enjoyment. On the other side of Anne, the old lady, Mrs Jenkinson, fussed over her constantly.

'So, this is your third daughter, Mr Bennet.' Lady Catherine had been examining Mary through a pair of lorgnettes. 'She is remarkably plain.'

Mr Bennet frowned. 'She is very studious, your ladyship. She is at present learning Greek.'

'Improvement of the mind is important, certainly, for one who has neither looks nor fortune. I take it she has no prospect of marriage?'

'That is a matter not yet settled.'

'I would imagine that she has very little chance. Little, indeed. If you so wish, at some time in the future, I could place her for you with a family. I have a talent for so doing. You will no doubt be anxious to safeguard her against that time when Mr Collins inherits your estate.'

'I am much obliged, your ladyship. I will be sure to call for your assistance the moment I suspect my life of slipping away.'

Lady Catherine had looked at him sharply for a moment but was reassured by Mr Bennet's open and innocent expression. 'Now,' she continued, 'I understand your wife is currently in the North with the daughter who ran away with Wickham.'

'Indeed. My daughter Lydia Wickham approaches her second confinement, and Mrs Bennet has travelled to her assistance.'

Lady Catherine sniffed. 'No doubt all your married daughters will produce a prodigious number of children, being unaffected by the refinement which regulates families such as my own... As to that, Mr Collins, how does your wife now? It is many weeks since I have seen her at Rosings.'

Mr Collins had coloured a little. 'She is still most frail, your ladyship, though she was mentioning to me just today that, if only she were strong enough to come to Rosings, her spirits would be lifted.'

'What says Dr Grace?'

'He advises that she continue to rest undisturbed for much of the day and has ordered that beef tea and chicken broth be given alternately.'

'If she continues in this fashion, Mr Collins, I shall send to my own physician, Sir Richard Price-Jones of London.'

Mr Collins clasped his hands together. 'You are beneficence itself, Lady Catherine.'

After dinner, Lady Catherine had proposed that Mr Collins and Mr Bennet join her at the card table, with Mrs Jenkinson being brought in to make the fourth. The latter was very reluctant and took some time to arrange a rug around Miss Anne's knees before leaving her side. Seated near her in front of the fire, Mary wondered what it was that ailed the young heiress, and why Lady Catherine's physician could not do more to cure her.

'Do you have a tutor, Miss Bennet? For your Greek?'

Mary had been startled by Anne's sudden question, since she had spoken not at all during dinner, but then, neither had she.

'That would be my dearest wish, Miss de Bourgh, but no. We did not have even a governess when we were growing up. I attempt to teach myself Greek by study alone.'

'I should have liked to attempt Greek. I fear that my governess thought subjects like that too taxing for the female brain.'

Mary was surprised to find herself warming to the frail creature at her side. 'You would find it a most rewarding language to study, just as I have. If you wish, I can advise you as to which of the grammars are most suitable to the beginner. Your library here will surely hold them all. Oh, Miss de Bourgh, you are so fortunate! And Mr Collins would help you, I am certain. On the occasions when he has visited us at Longbourn, I have found him to be most ready to assist me in matters of scripture.'

'I too, Miss Bennet. He is always most patient and kind.'

They had both glanced over to the far side of the room, where Mr Collins was listening intently to some pronouncement of Lady Catherine's, and then smiled at each other, which surprised both of them in its spontaneity.

Mary had, for all her life, been compared unfavourably with her sisters. She had neither Jane's beauty, nor Lizzy's clever tongue, while her younger sisters' animation made her seem dull indeed. She had accepted at an early age that she was destined to be overlooked, and any attempts to put herself forward were generally not welcomed. Strangely, considering the young lady's exalted position, she felt that she had found something of a kindred spirit in Anne.

'Do you live most of the year here at Rosings, Miss de Bourgh?'

'We are in town for a short part of the season only. I have not been presented at court, as I am not sufficiently strong. My mother sets great store by clean air and country walks, so, yes, we are usually at Rosings. Since my father died, we have been quiet indeed.'

'You have a very faithful companion in Mrs Jenkinson.'

'Yes, she is most attentive. She has been by my side since I was about six years old.'

'She is someone else who would, perhaps, help you to begin a study of Greek. It is so exciting, Miss de Bourgh – just think of all the wonderful literature which will lie open to you once the language is mastered, not to mention the Gospels!'

'Treasure indeed, Miss Bennet, though I do not think Mrs Jenkinson would be able to assist me.' Here, Anne lowered her voice a little. 'She is... not educated, you know. She is a distant relative who came to us after falling upon hard times. I fear that she cares not very much for books... Tell me, do you have a library at Longbourn?'

'My father has a substantial number of volumes in his study, and I am allowed to read them as I wish, though I'm sure they are nothing in comparison with your collection here.'

'Well then, Miss Bennet, you must make use of our library freely while you stay at the parsonage. In return you may give me your list of Greek grammars.'

Mary's eyes had sparkled behind the thick glass of her spectacles, as she contemplated not only the feast of knowledge offered her, but the chance to escape the attentions of the Collins children.

'Oh, Miss de Bourgh,' she exclaimed, 'I shall visit the library tomorrow if I am permitted. You cannot know how thankful I am for this privilege.'

*

Turning away from the room where Mr Collins' body lay, Mary wept both for him and for the inevitable loss of her new-found happiness. She had spent two afternoons in the library at Rosings, where, to her delight, Anne de Bourgh had joined her, accompanied, as ever, by Mrs Jenkinson. On both occasions, a warm fire had been lit for them, and they had enjoyed cheerful conversation and even laughter, as they chose the books they wished to study. She had been looking forward greatly to her third visit.

She made her way to Mr Collins' study, where her father was sitting at the desk, staring intently at nothing. He looked up with dull eyes as she entered.

'Papa? Oh, Papa, why has this happened?'

He shook his head. 'Sometimes I feel the ways of this world

are beyond all logic. You have been up to see Charlotte?'

Mary nodded. 'I spoke to her but briefly. She is greatly shocked.'

'Poor Charlotte! She has been like another daughter to me, you know, Mary. Always at Longbourn with Lizzy. Now here she is, widowed, three children fatherless...' He was silent for several minutes, during which Mary shed a few more tears. Then, as if gathering resolution, he stood up and slapped the palms of both his hands on the desk. 'Right. I must go to Rosings.'

8

'We have a strict routine in this house.'

Mr Harries spoke softly but firmly. After more than fifty years in Kent the butler retained only the smallest trace of his original Welsh accent.

'Unless we are entertaining, it is the general rule that house servants retire to bed at nine o'clock. They are, of course, then free to pray, or read if they are able. But they are not encouraged to leave their rooms after that hour, unless required to by her ladyship or Miss Anne.'

This was by now a familiar litany to Bright. He nodded.

'So, it is unlikely that any member of this household will be able to supply me with useful information, unless they are in the habit of being disobedient to the routine you mention.'

'That would not be tolerated, Sir John. We ensure that all our servants come to us with the best of testimonials, apart, of course, from those for whom Rosings is their first position... No, I fear that you must look elsewhere for the information you require.'

Bright frowned. It seemed to him that, whichever way he turned, he was faced with a dead end. There was no way out of the maze. He shook his head regretfully as he sipped the tea which the butler had thoughtfully provided.

'If it were not for that paper knife,' he said, 'we might widen our search with some purpose. But we always come back to the knife.'

'It is perplexing indeed,' agreed Harries. He ran a hand

36

through his thick greying hair. 'As a weapon, it is a most strange choice, and certainly not something which one might expect to find in the gardens. Her ladyship is most disturbed, I may tell you, *most* disturbed. She cannot bear to think of her property – with her crest – being made use of in such a terrible way.'

'According to Lady Catherine, there are several of these knives in the library, and she also keeps at least one in her writing desk. Could you tell me exactly how many there are?'

'I can tell you that there are four knives in the library. They are kept in a wooden box on the main desk, and, yes, I have assured myself this morning that they are all present. As to her ladyship's bureau, however, I fear I can be of no help. Even a great lady has a right to some privacy! I have a feeling, though, that even Lady Catherine is not really certain how many paper knives should be there.'

'So, the knife must have been taken from her ladyship's desk in the morning room?'

'That is how it seems, Sir John, yes, although, I have seen Miss Anne and Mrs Jenkinson with paper knives on occasion, whether borrowed from her ladyship, or the library, or from some source of their own, I know not.'

'Thank you, Harries. That is most helpful. However, the basic conundrum still is unsolved: how and why did our felon obtain one of these knives for his fell purpose?'

'And who, Sir John? Who would do such a thing? I fear that if logic were to prevail, then the finger must point to a member of our staff, myself included. We alone would have the means to lay our hands upon one of the paper knives. And yet, to me, that is unthinkable – as far as the rest are concerned, anyway. As for me, you must come to your own conclusion!'

Bright responded with a grim smile. He had no reason to

doubt the butler's integrity, but he also knew that, in the servants' hall, loyalties ran deep and flowed in two directions, in one way to Master or Mistress, and in the other to fellow servants. To a man like Harries, a good many of the younger servants must seem almost like sons and daughters, having been in his care since they were little more than children.

A tap on the door cut short their interview. The flustered face of a young footman peeped in.

'I beg your pardon, sirs, but Mr Harries is required immediately in the hall. We are visited by Mr Bennet, who insists upon seeing her ladyship, despite her orders not to be disturbed.'

'Thank you, John.' Harries turned back to Bright. 'Mr Bennet is Mr Collins' cousin, sir, from Hertfordshire. He has been staying at the parsonage with the rector. I apologise, but I shall have to speak to him.' He rose a little stiffly and Bright, after a moment's hesitation, followed him upstairs.

*

'I must speak to Lady Catherine… No, please don't prevent me from seeing her. We are quite in the dark at the parsonage. Poor Mrs Collins is beside herself. We need to know the truth about what has occurred.' Mr Bennet was unusually breathless as he addressed the butler.

'I am sorry sir, but I cannot allow anyone into the presence of her ladyship. She is indisposed following the shock she experienced this morning.'

'This news has been a shock to us all. I might remind you that Mr Collins was my cousin.'

'I am sincerely sorry, sir. However, I must obey her ladyship's instructions.'

Harries squared himself up, as if he expected the smaller figure of Mr Bennet to charge past him in his eagerness to see Lady Catherine.

Behind him, Bright cleared his throat. 'Please excuse my interruption,' he said, 'but, if it would be useful, I could answer Mr Bennet's questions, as far as I am able.' He stepped closer to Mr Bennet and held out his hand. 'Sir John Bright, magistrate. I am investigating this appalling crime.'

'Oh, I see. Well, I thank you. I should be glad of any information you can give me.'

'At present, I fear, I cannot furnish you with any suggestion as to the identity of the murderer, but I can relate the progress of my investigation so far.'

'I am most obliged to you.'

Bright turned to the butler. 'If it would be agreeable to your mistress, then, Harries, I shall attempt to provide Mr Bennet with as much information as I can with regard to his cousin's untimely end.'

Harries relaxed visibly. 'I have no doubt that Lady Catherine will be most grateful, sir. You may take Mr Bennet into the library... Will you be requiring more tea, sir?'

Mr Bennet waved the idea away. 'No, I think not. With Sir John's agreement, we shall walk in the gardens. I would have him show me the place where the body of Mr Collins was discovered.'

'As you wish, Mr Bennet.' Bright turned back towards the butler. 'Harries, would you please let Mrs Flowerday and Mrs Penny know that I shall have to postpone our conversations? Now, to the gardens, Mr Bennet.'

*

The coleus bed was a sorry mess of broken leaves and stems, the soil pitted all around by the prints of heavy boots. Some of the mud had spilled over onto the gravel path. Mr Bennet shook his head as he contemplated it.

'If I did not have your assurance, I would find it hard to believe that my cousin should have died in such a place.'

'I saw it with my own eyes, Mr Bennet.'

'And you say the deed was done with a Rosings paper knife? A strange fate, though an apt one, I suppose, considering Mr Collins' disposition.'

Bright shot him a quizzical look.

'His attachment to all things de Bourgh,' explained Mr Bennet.

'Ah, yes, I see.' Bright was silent for a few minutes, unsure how to respond. Finally, he brought his mind back to his inquiry.

'Mr Bennet, I wish to emphasize the fact that it was never my intention to keep you and your family in the dark, as you say. I planned to visit the parsonage tomorrow to express my condolences and to inform you of the progress of the investigation. I merely felt that to do so today would have been to intrude upon your grief.'

'Thank you, Sir John. I appreciate your sensibility in this matter.'

'Are you often at the parsonage, Mr Bennet? I understand that your home is in Hertfordshire.'

'Not often, no. Until he took up his position here, Mr Collins was quite a stranger to us. His wife, on the other hand, has been my daughter Elizabeth's dearest friend, and consequently well loved by all members of my family. This has, as it were, cemented a family bond. At present, though, with my wife and fourth daughter from home, my visit to Hunsford is one of essential business, which I could put off no longer.'

'His death, then, must be doubly painful to you. You have my commiserations.'

'Thank you. I shall devote the rest of my stay here to assisting Mrs Collins as much as I am able, until such time as her father, Sir William Lucas, should arrive from Hertfordshire. She is unwell, you know.'

'Will she be strong enough to receive me? I would still wish to visit the parsonage tomorrow.'

'I feel sure she will be comforted by your presence, Sir John... Now, I will detain you no longer from your investigations. I thank you for giving me your time today.'

As he watched Mr Bennet walking away, Bright pondered for some time on what the nature of his business with Mr Collins might have been, and how it had been affected by the latter's death. He was aware, however, that family relationships could often be complicated. In truth, Mr Bennet did not seem to have been close to the dead man, and his dry comment about the paper knife, although appreciated by Bright, was at odds with the man's obvious distress. Perhaps he would learn more tomorrow, at the parsonage.

9

Archer knew the stable boys well enough. They were brothers, and although the elder was less hot-headed than the younger, both had been involved several times in fights and disagreements at The Three Crowns on their nights off.

'Right,' he said, 'Patrick and Michael Flannery. I've seen rather too much of you two since I became constable, though I've so far not seen fit to arrest you.'

'No, sir,' said Patrick. 'Thank you, sir.'

'And that won't change, as long as you answer my questions honestly. I'm investigating the murder of the rector, Mr Collins.'

'Would you think us inclined to be *dis*honest, then, constable? Because we are Irish, I don't doubt.' Michael's face was dark with anger. 'Perhaps you think we are responsible for the murder.'

Patrick laid a warning hand on his brother's arm. Archer shook his head impatiently.

'I'm not interested in politics, Michael. I want merely to know if either of you saw or heard anything last night – after ten o'clock – which might lead us to the truth – a shout, say, or a light where one shouldn't have been. From your beds in the stable loft you have some sight, I think, of the gardens at the back of the house.'

'We rise at half-past four, Constable', said Patrick. 'Unless we have a night off, or the mistress has guests with horses that need seeing to, we're asleep soon after nine.'

'When are your nights off?'

'Wednesday for me and Sunday for Michael.'

Archer nodded. The previous day had been Thursday.

'Were you acquainted with the rector?'

'We knew him from his visits to Rosings, sir. We are not obliged to attend church with the rest of the servants as we are Catholic. The mistress is lenient on that point.'

'Have you ever heard any ill-will expressed towards the rector when you patronise The Three Crowns on your nights off?'

At this, Michael made a noise in his throat and rolled his eyes in a manner Archer thought insolent. However, he did not speak, and Patrick seemed hesitant.

'If you know anything,' said Archer, 'either of you, it is your duty to tell me.'

'All right, sir,' said Patrick, 'and I mean no disrespect, but sometimes he is regarded – was regarded – as a person to be joked about. Nothing malicious, sir, not at all – just about the manner in which he spoke of her ladyship.'

Archer sighed. He had said as much himself when Sir John had questioned him about Mr Collins.

'Very well. I'll detain you no longer. Please inform me if you hear or remember anything which might shed light on this matter.'

*

From the fragrant heights of the hay loft, the two stable boys looked down to the yard, where the head groom was to be seen deep in conversation with the constable. They watched in silence, serious faced, attempting to make out what was being said.

'I can hear nothing,' said Patrick.

'Nor I,' said Michael, 'and they have their heads too close together for any chance of lip-reading... Ah well, Mr Kirkwood knows nothing. He can't point the finger.'

'You cannot know that.'

'I was careful, I'm always careful. That's what Da taught us, wasn't it? Not to be seen, not to be heard?'

'Even he was caught in the end. That's why he's rotting in Australia and we're over here saving every penny we can for Ma and the girls.'

'And hasn't she been glad of that little bit extra now and then?'

'Sure she has. But we'll have to give it a rest. Just for now.' He looked meaningfully at his brother. 'And that other thing as well.'

'That's *my* business, Pat. I'll do what I please.'

'That's all very fine, but if anyone at all spotted you last night, you'll be straight for the lock-up and the gallows, same goes for tonight or tomorrow and all the nights to come. We're easy meat for them, Mike. They think we're all thieves and cutthroats. Even if you were to tell the truth...'

'Which I cannot.'

'...you'd not be believed.'

'Forget that, I'll not betray a trust.'

'Look – we're well off here. We earn good money, we're well fed and the work is light. Would you spoil all that for some romantic notion that'll come to naught in the end?'

'It's no romantic notion,' said Michael, angry again as he turned his back on his brother and began to descend the ladder.

*

Sir John Bright was staring at the ruined plants on the spot where the rector's body had been found, lost in thought. From behind him there came the click of a latch. Robert Archer emerged from the walled garden.

44

'Ah, Sir John! I did not expect to see you here. I am just come from questioning the garden staff.'

'Did you learn anything new?'

'Unfortunately, sir, most of them live in the village, and are away from Rosings after dark. The head gardener, Mr Dudgeon, is an exception, having a tied cottage at the rear of the glasshouses. His wife was most generous with tea and scones, but assured me that, being in their late seventies, they were both abed well before the hour in question. I was given to believe that the damage to the coleus bed is the old man's major concern at the moment.'

'As it would be to any head gardener worth his salt! But come, Robert. The breeze grows chill and the shadows lengthen. Let's adjourn to the ale-house to compare notes.'

*

Once more at The Three Crowns, but this time seated snugly beside a warm log fire, the two men considered the events of the long day.

'So,' said Bright, 'Dudgeon and his staff had little to tell you. What of the stable staff?'

'Well, it was the same story as elsewhere. The head groom has a cottage near the Rosings boundary. He would have had no view of the rear garden. The two stable boys, on the other hand, are situated sufficiently high up in their hay-loft to be able to see part of the garden. However, they told me that they would have been long asleep by half-past ten.'

'Always the same, Robert, as you say. The early-to-bed establishment at Rosings.'

'There is one thing, Sir John, though it may have no relevance to this matter...'

'Yes?'

'The stable boys are brothers, sir, from Ireland. I have met them on previous occasions, mostly here at The Three Crowns. They can be a little wild at times.'

'So, it is in your official capacity that you've met them?'

'Yes, sir, though I must stress that they have never been in serious trouble. They are high spirited when drinking, that's all.'

'As are many of us, Robert.'

'Indeed, sir. However, I was a little troubled by something the younger brother said. He implied that I was picking them out for questioning merely because they are Irish. He seemed most sensitive on this point, and became quite angry, although the elder brother kept him in check.'

'A good many Irish people are angry – they have yet to forgive us for the bloody execution of Robert Emmet. However, what relation would that have to the murder of a clergyman in Kent?'

'They told me that they are Catholics, sir.'

'So they might have seen the rector as an enemy, you mean?'

'Perhaps in the heat of the moment, sir. Michael, the younger, he could have seen the rector wandering in the garden and lost his head. He is tall and strong and could easily have got the better of Mr Collins.'

'Nothing is impossible. I grant you that, Robert. The cause of Catholic emancipation evokes strong emotions in Ireland. But I still feel that we are a long way from that country. And we always come back to the paper knife. If this crime were the work of a hot-headed Irish stable boy, and committed without any previous plan, a Rosings paper knife would not have been the weapon he grabbed in his frenzy.'

Archer sighed. 'You are right, of course, sir. The business of the paper knife has us all foxed.'

Bright called for more ale. 'This investigation is thirsty work, especially when it appears to lead us nowhere... Tell me, have you ever met Mr Collins' cousin, Mr Bennet?'

Archer shook his head. 'I have heard tell of him. Small villages like this are always sources of gossip.'

'Well, he arrived at Rosings in a great hurry to see Lady Catherine this afternoon. He said he needed to know the truth of what had befallen Mr Collins. He especially asked to be shown the place where the body was discovered.'

'A strange request, sir, if I may say so.'

'You may, Robert. I thought so myself, particularly as it appears that the cousins were not close.'

'Now there I may be able to shed some light, Sir John. I mentioned the gossip which abounds in Hunsford village. Well, it seems that Mr Collins was the heir to Mr Bennet's estate, which is entailed to the male line only. It was said that this was the cause of a rift between the two families.'

'It must have been a matter of much concern to Mr Bennet, certainly, with all his daughters. Thank you, Robert.'

This, then, if it were correct, must be the 'business' which had brought Mr Bennet to Kent. Bright nodded to himself. Mr Bennet's rather ambiguous attitude was more understandable than it had been. He sipped his ale and looked into the fire.

'Of course,' he said slowly, 'if the source of your gossip is not misinformed, we could now find someone with a motive for the murder of Mr Collins.'

'You mean Mr Bennet?'

'Indeed. Think of it, Robert. The rector has a family, but they are all girls. Much like Mr Bennet himself. With a bit of legal wrangling, now that Mr Collins is dead, Mr Bennet may find his family's future restored.'

'But if he were the felon, he would surely not have turned up at Rosings this morning. He would have been on the coach back to Hertfordshire.'

'He could not very well have rushed off and left Mrs Collins to her grief. She is a favourite family friend as well as his cousin's wife. He would need to behave exactly as any onlooker would expect.'

'Yes, I can see that... Yet, what would be the reason for his request to view the coleus bed? Unless...'

'Unless?'

'Unless he left something there during the attack – or feared that he did. It would have looked out-of-place if he had been seen alone there, but in your company, or that of one of her ladyship's household...'

'He would attract no suspicion!'

'Did he seem to be searching the ground, sir – while you stood there?'

'He stared down at the area, certainly, but I saw him pick nothing up. However, as you say, he might simply have been reassuring himself that there was nothing there. Well done, Robert – it is a convincing theory, though we still have no witness or any sort of proof. He would also need to have taken away a paper knife at some time previously.'

'If he has been a visitor at Rosings, that could have been done, sir, though I cannot imagine why.'

'Well, I think I can. It is the paper knife which has confused all our investigations, is it not? If Mr Bennet is our felon, he may have used the Rosings paper knife in order to cast suspicion over members of that household. It would be a crime most cunningly executed.'

'So cunning that it will be difficult indeed to obtain proof.'

'We shall redouble our efforts, Robert. Remember that we have not finished our questioning of the Rosings staff and have yet to visit the parsonage. If Mr Bennet is indeed our murderer, that is surely our best source of evidence, though as to what that might be, I cannot at present think.' Bright turned his eyes back to the flames. 'I shall not send a man to the gallows without indisputable proof of guilt.'

10

'I can think of no man who could even have contemplated such a deed.'

Charlotte Collins sat close to the fire in the small parlour at Hunsford Parsonage, a woollen rug across her knees and plump pillows supporting her back. Her cheeks were flushed from the heat and her eyes dull. 'He was a simple clergyman. He wrote sermons and tended the garden. How could he have made an enemy?'

Bright shook his head. 'I know not, Mrs Collins. I have asked myself that question time and time again since yesterday.'

He looked down with compassion as tears began to dampen Mrs Collins' cheeks. Two of her children had crept into the room and were clinging to her knees, half hidden in the folds of her dress. They were very young but had undoubtedly understood that something bad had happened. Their mother stroked their heads absent-mindedly. On the other side of the fireplace, her cousin, Mary Bennet, looked close to shedding tears of her own, her eyes enormous behind the thick lenses of her spectacles.

'Well,' said Bright, 'I shall disturb you no longer. You must get as much rest as possible, Mrs Collins. With your permission, I shall direct my constable to speak to members of your household staff.'

Charlotte Collins nodded. 'You will find them in the kitchen at this time, though we are not a large establishment, you know.'

It occurred to Bright that the establishment was now smaller than it was, and that it must soon cease to be the Collins family home when a new rector moved in. He made a small bow. 'Thank you, Mrs Collins. I must assure you that we are doing all we can to apprehend the man who attacked your husband.' He turned towards Mary. 'Miss Bennet, might I ask you to take me to your father?'

Mary looked startled but rose immediately. 'He is in the study, I believe, sir. I shall show you the way.'

*

Archer sat at the kitchen table, its wood slightly roughened from frequent scrubbing. He thought of the wood in his own yard and wished for a moment that this confusing case could be swiftly solved so that he could return to the trade he loved. He sighed. Opposite him, the married couple, Mr and Mrs Parkinson, regarded him silently, as did the small general maid, Alice.

'I'd just like to ask you all a few questions,' he began. 'I'm sure you will agree that we need to discover the identity of this felon as quickly as we are able, so that he may be brought to justice.'

All three nodded solemnly.

'Mr and Mrs Parkinson, you have served here at the parsonage for a number of years, I believe.'

'Yes,' said Mrs Parkinson, 'we were originally employed by the previous rector, Mr Vaughan, I as cook-housekeeper, and my husband to do heavy work and gardening. The Reverend Vaughan was not as fond of the garden as is... was Mr Collins.'

'Mind you, though,' put in Mr Parkinson, a melancholy smile on his broad face, 'Mr Collins has needed so many changes made that the garden still fills most of my time.'

'And how long have you been employed here, Alice?'

The little maid blushed. She could not have been more than eleven or twelve years old.

'Just six months, sir.'

'We needed the extra help when baby Martha was born,' said Mrs Parkinson. 'Poor Mrs Collins used to do many of the light household tasks herself – Mr Collins did not believe in luxury – but she became so ill after her confinement that she has more or less been obliged to remain in bed. Now, well, we cannot imagine how she will cope, indeed we can't. She is so frail.' The housekeeper sighed. 'We are dreading the day when a new rector must move in here, as Mrs Collins will then have herself to move... I believe, though, that she will not need to look further than her father and mother, two most pleasant and Christian people.'

As Mrs Parkinson was talking, Alice's face had begun to crumple, and she was now sobbing quietly into a slightly grubby handkerchief. The housekeeper patted her on the back.

'There there, Alice. Don't take on so... Mr Archer, might she be excused? I cannot see how she can contribute to your investigation in this state.'

'Certainly, Mrs Parkinson.'

As the young maid ran from the room, Mrs Parkinson lowered her voice and leaned closer to Archer.

'She is an orphan, you see, sir. Mrs Collins had her taken from the poor-house to work with us here. I believe that this is like a real home for her – the mistress treats her so kindly, and has asked us to do likewise, which is not at all difficult, as she is a willing worker and always most polite. We are all worried that a new rector may not wish to retain her in service here.'

'We're not as young as we were, my dear. He may not wish to retain us, either!'

Mrs Parkinson tutted at her husband's remark. 'I think Lady Catherine might have something to say if that were the case.'

Archer smiled. 'Now,' he said, 'I must continue with my questions, as Sir John wishes. Her ladyship tells us that the rector was in the habit of walking in the gardens at Rosings. Do you know how often he would do this?'

'Oh, daily, Mr Archer, daily. He said often that being in such beautiful surroundings was of the utmost help to him when composing his sermons.'

'And he told me that he learned much from the gardeners there.' Mr Parkinson smiled, a little regretfully. 'I am a simple, practical man, Mr Archer. I am spadework and cabbages. The new scientific methods are beyond my understanding.'

'I am certain you belittle yourself unnecessarily, Mr Parkinson... But as to Mr Collins, did he often do this walking at night? He would have seen no gardeners after dark.'

Mrs Parkinson frowned. 'Of late, yes, he was regularly out during the hours of darkness. Once or twice a week, if not oftener. I am a light sleeper, I know, but the baby, well, once she starts crying, she tends to wake the whole household, notwithstanding the efforts of the nurse. I fear that the disruption was proving difficult for Mr Collins. He liked order, you see, and that is something young Miss Martha has yet to learn. She is a most colicky baby.'

'I see. So, as far as you know, Thursday night was not unusual in any way?'

'Not at all, Mr Archer.'

'And Mr Bennet and his daughter – how long have they been here?'

Mrs Parkinson thought for a moment or two. 'Something more than a fortnight, if I calculate rightly. Mr Bennet has... had business to discuss with the rector.' She frowned. 'I am not one to gossip, Mr Archer, but sometimes the discussions seemed to be somewhat heated, don't you agree, husband? We could hardly help but hear them.'

'I shouldn't be surprised if they could be heard in Canterbury, my dear!'

Archer's eyes widened. 'Were these arguments frequent, would you say?'

Mrs Parkinson nodded. 'The two gentlemen did seem to have some sort of heated discussion nearly every day.'

'They were friendly enough by dinner time, though', said Mr Parkinson cheerfully.

'Very well.' Archer felt for the first time that he had some useful information to report to Sir John Bright. 'Thank you, Mrs Parkinson, and you too, Mr Parkinson. Now, I wonder if I might briefly see the nurse?'

Mrs Parkinson rose. 'Certainly, Mr Archer. She will be up in the nursery at this hour. I will send her down to you.'

*

Mr Bennet stood up as his daughter ushered Sir John Bright into the study.

'Thank you, Mary,' he said, and, as she showed signs of lingering in the doorway, 'I will manage very well on my own now.'

Reluctantly, she turned her back and closed the door. Mr Bennet gestured to a chair on the other side of the desk. 'How may I be of help, Sir John?'

Bright hesitated. 'I must consult you about a delicate matter. I trust you will not be offended – I make my enquiries in my official capacity only.'

Mr Bennet shrugged. 'I cannot take offence until you question me, sir, and by then it will be too late to prevent you.'

'You are correct of course, sir. The matter to which I refer has to do with your estate, which, I believe, was entailed to go to Mr Collins on your demise.'

'It was.'

'And am I right in thinking that the business to which you referred was linked to this fact?'

'Yes. I came to see Mr Collins to put a proposition to him – that an agreement be drawn up which would allow Longbourn to remain the Bennet family home after my death, for as long as my wife should live. By which time I would hope my two unmarried daughters would be safely settled with husbands of their own.'

'Did Mr Collins sympathise with your idea?'

'He did not. I could not persuade him. I think he was set on relinquishing his living and moving to Longbourn as soon as my body is interred.'

'I appreciate the seriousness of your predicament, Mr Bennet, though you have, of course, powerful family connections to call on in times of need.'

'Mr Bingley and Mr Darcy are both generosity itself, but I would not impose my wife and daughters permanently upon either of them. I always think that families are happiest if their branches are allowed to remain unentangled for much of the time.'

Bright was silent for a few moments. He liked Mr Bennet, but had to pursue his line of questioning to its conclusion.

'How would you say Mr Collins' death has affected your prospects, sir?'

Mr Bennet smiled sardonically. 'I have been expecting this

question, Sir John. I can only say that our prospects are much brighter as a result of it, given that Mr Collins has, like myself, been blessed with daughters.'

'So, if I were looking for someone with a motive for this murder...'

'I should be your principal suspect, Sir John.'

*

Outside the study door, Mary Bennet gasped. She made her way to the stairs and sat down on the lowest step, her head in her hands. It was too late to remember the admonishment she had received as a child – that listening at closed doors seldom benefits the listener.

11

'Oh, that poor family! Those dear little girls! What is to become of them?'

Mrs Penny sat in one of a pair of chintz armchairs in the housekeeper's parlour at Rosings, wringing her plump, pink hands. Mrs Flowerday, in the second chair, regarded the cook with a slight look of irritation.

'We are all most concerned about Mrs Collins and her children, Mrs Penny, but I do believe that they will be well taken care of by Mrs Collins' father, Sir William Lucas.'

Sir John Bright nodded in agreement. 'My constable and I were at the parsonage this morning. We were assured of the same thing.'

'But Mrs Collins is so unwell, Sir John. How can she contemplate the journey to Hertfordshire? I have been told that she is scarcely able to leave her bed. And after this terrible shock... Well, I should not be surprised if the poor lady were unable to rise ever again.'

Bright sipped his tea and took a bite of the sweet griddle cake which Mrs Penny had pressed on him. It tasted good, especially when compared with the miserable repast he had again endured earlier at The Three Crowns. The small bright fire crackled gently in the hearth, and there was a comforting aroma of wax polish. He was reminded of the gentler days of his childhood, when their own housekeeper had sometimes given him illicit treats of sweetmeats in a room very like this one.

'Mrs Collins is in good hands,' he assured the cook. 'She has excellent servants, and also, at the moment, the company of Mr Bennet and his daughter.'

Mrs Flowerday sniffed. 'With respect, sir, that young lady has some strange ideas, encouraging Miss Anne to learn Greek, if you will. Though,' and her voice softened, 'dear Miss Anne does seem to enjoy her company, and has been quite animated when they are together. We do love to see Miss Anne happy!'

'Indeed we do,' agreed Mrs Penny, 'and she so rarely has company of her own age. Mrs Jenkinson has been a faithful friend for many years, I know, but she is old enough to be her grandmother... We were all so sad when poor Miss Anne was disappointed in her expectation of Mr Darcy. It shows you what a fine Christian young lady she is, that she is forgiving enough to welcome Miss Mary Bennet into her home.'

'I can't disagree,' said Bright.

'Lady Catherine, too,' put in Mrs Flowerday. 'She did not hesitate to invite the Bennets to dine at Rosings when she knew that they stayed with Mr Collins, though it is with the utmost reluctance that she receives Mrs Darcy here, not more than twice since her nephew's marriage.'

'So Mr Bennet has dined here recently?'

'It was but Tuesday evening of last week, sir. Mr Bennet, Mr Collins and Miss Mary Bennet. It was after that occasion that Miss Anne and Miss Bennet became friendly and began to spend afternoons together in the library here.'

'I see.'

Mrs Penny proffered the plate of griddle cakes again, and Bright was happy to accept a second serving.

'You are an excellent cook, Mrs Penny.'

'You are very welcome, Sir John.' I am happy to bake

something for you every day if it might help you to discover the person who did this terrible act!'

'Tempting, indeed, Mrs Penny.'

'Are you near to discovering the felon?' asked Mrs Flowerday.

'We have some ideas as to his identity, but no real proof as yet.'

The housekeeper nodded. 'I hope your investigations will bear fruit very soon, Sir John. This business has unsettled the household here most severely. Several of the female servants are quite unwilling to venture out alone even in broad daylight, and your young constable has quite turned the heads of the kitchen maids.'

Bright suppressed a smile. 'You have my apologies, Mrs Flowerday. But please be assured that my constable and I will do our utmost to resolve this awful crime as quickly as we can.' He paused, clearing his throat. He was more a man of the world than the constable but was still reluctant to bring up, with the housekeeper and cook, the thorny subject of Lady Catherine's nocturnal wanderings, and yet he manifestly could not do so with any of the male servants.

'You speak of venturing outside, Mrs Flowerday... I have been given to understand that her ladyship is inclined to walk abroad alone, even after dark.'

The two women glanced at each other, and Mrs Penny's pink face became a tone or two pinker. Mrs Flowerday pursed her lips and sighed.

'You are right, Sir John. My mistress has complained, of late, of being over-heated. Pearson, her personal maid, has been extremely concerned, and rightly so, in the light of Thursday's most terrible mischief. However, her ladyship will not be dissuaded, and has refused to allow Pearson to accompany her, even late at night. She has ever been a supremely independent woman, you see.'

Bright nodded. He thought, for independence, assume stubbornness. He took another griddle cake from Mrs Penny, who had grabbed up the plate in an effort to hasten away the embarrassing moment. She paused on setting it down, and then looked at Bright in some consternation.

'Sir John, you don't think... Surely you can't think that my mistress has anything to do with the death of Mr Collins!'

She had every opportunity, he thought, and no shortage of paper knives. Nonetheless, he shook his head emphatically.

'I cannot believe her capable of a felony of any description, Mrs Penny. Please set your mind at rest. I am merely concerned with her safety. However, can either of you think of anyone who might have borne the rector ill-will? What, if I may ask, was your own opinion of the man?'

Mrs Penny wiped her cheek with a starched white handkerchief, releasing a scent of lavender into the room.

'He was a good man, Sir John. I can think of none who would disagree.'

Mrs Flowerday frowned at her. 'Mrs Penny is too little above stairs', she said, 'though she has sat beside me through all of the rector's two-hour sermons. You will pardon me for speaking plainly, Sir John. The man was tedious and pompous.'

'Oh, Mrs Flowerday!' The cook's face had become almost magenta. 'It is a sinful thing to speak ill of the dead.'

The housekeeper remained firm. 'This is an occasion when opinions must be given plainly, Mrs Penny, if Sir John is to make any headway at all. It would be a greater sin to mislead him because of some petty adherence to polite form.'

Bright regarded the housekeeper, with her straight back and stern face, and smiled inwardly. He bowed his head.

'I thank you for your honesty,' he said.

Mrs Flowerday gave him the ghost of a smile in acknowledgement. 'Honest as the opinion is,' she said, 'I doubt that the rector was attacked because of his sermons!'

'I doubt that, too. However, you may be interested to know that you are not the first person to mention those aspects of Mr Collins' character.'

'Well, I don't know what we're all coming to, indeed I don't.' Mrs Penny sighed and proffered the griddle cakes yet again.

12

The midday meal at the parsonage had been a miserable affair indeed. Charlotte had retreated to her bed as soon as Sir John had finished his interview with her, which had left Mr Bennet and Mary alone in the dining room. Good as it was, the game pie had remained largely uneaten and Mr Bennet had returned to the study with scarcely a word.

Mary had lasted until around three o'clock, pacing about the house and garden, by which time she could wait no longer. She rapped on the study door and burst in before her father could prevent her. She found him standing before the window, seemingly absorbed by the sight of a tall privet hedge. He did not turn around.

'Papa! Papa! I must know!'

For some moments, she thought that he would not answer her and was about to call to him again when he finally turned and sat down wearily at Mr Collins' desk. His face was grey, and he seemed somehow smaller. Mary was seized by a sudden urge to put her arms around him but did not, as their relationship was not a demonstrative one.

'Papa, you must tell me! What's happening? Is Sir John going to arrest you? I... I overheard some of your conversation this morning.'

Mr Bennet regarded her sadly.

'It was wrong of you to listen, my child. I should have guessed what you were about when you persisted in lingering in the doorway. However, you may as well know. I am the obvious choice. Who else has a motive like mine? Mr Collins and I have been arguing over the matter of the entail ever since we arrived here. I had hoped to get the thing settled while your mother was safely away – she upsets so easily – but we ended each day at daggers drawn...' He sighed. 'That was an unfortunate turn of phrase, my dear.'

'But they must know you would do nothing to hurt anyone, let alone Mr Collins! You're the kindest man I know, Papa.'

'You may say that, but others may well not see me in the same light. You are my daughter, after all, and are scarcely impartial.' He sighed again. 'I fear we may be ruined, Mary. I know not what your mother will say, or, rather, I know only too well. How could she ever even contemplate a future as the wife of a... a... convicted murderer?' Closing his eyes, he rested his forehead in his hands.

'But there is no proof, Papa. They cannot arrest you without proof, just because you disagreed with Mr Collins. They might as well arrest Lizzy for refusing his marriage proposal.'

'That may be so, child, but the difference is that I am here, and Lizzy is not. And as I said before, there is none other, as far as I am aware, who stands to benefit at all from the death of my cousin. No doubt there are several people in this house who will testify to our prolonged arguments. However, Sir John Bright is an intelligent man, and, I believe, a fair one. We must trust him to serve the interests of justice and hope that the true murderer is uncovered before I am detained in the absence of a better suspect... Oh, no, my dear, no tears, I beg you!'

Clutching her handkerchief, Mary perched on the very edge of one of the hard straight-backed chairs which Mr Collins had kept for the comfort of his parishioners. She took off her spectacles and mopped her eyes. Without the thick glass, her face was still childlike.

Coming out from behind the desk, Mr Bennet sat down beside her and put his arm around her shoulders, an act sufficiently unusual as to make her tears flow afresh.

'Now my dear,' he said, 'I fear you have sometimes been overlooked, with your sisters and mother being as they are... a little larger than life, I mean, at times.'

At this Mary managed to produce a weak smile.

'But lately, you know,' he continued, 'since you and I have had the household to ourselves, we've been very comfortable together, haven't we, sharing our books, and you with your Greek. I regret that I decided to bring you away, most sincerely, as it now transpires... But I think that you at least have benefitted from our visit. I've scarcely recognised the lovely young lady who visits the library at Rosings and keeps company with daughters of the aristocracy. Indeed, I've found myself looking around and wondering where Mary might be!'

'You make fun of me, Papa.'

'As long as I make you smile, child. But, seriously, you cannot know how pleased I am to see you making friends – even if it is only Miss Anne de Bourgh!'

'I like her very much, Papa. She is not at all disagreeable, as Lizzy used to believe, but just shy, I think. She is seldom away from Rosings, just as I am rarely from Longbourn. We have had such happy times in the library, and Lady Catherine has been kind enough to order a fire lit for our benefit. Miss de Bourgh was starting on her Greek and I was able to help her. Just imagine, Papa! Oh, why did this awful thing have to happen, and what can we do?'

'Only God can tell you that, Mary, and so the only action we can take is to pray.'

'I pray all the time, Papa. There must be some way to prove your innocence.'

Mr Bennet shrugged. 'Take heart, my dear. I am not arrested yet. Sir John and the constable may yet turn up some vital piece of evidence. They are very thorough. Now, it would comfort me greatly if you could just go up to see how poor Charlotte does. She ate nothing earlier and looked almost beside herself.'

'Of course, Papa.'

'Oh, and Mary...'

'Yes?'

'I would not have you writing to your mother and sisters, at least not until something is resolved here. I cannot stomach more fuss, not after Lydia. If the worst happens, and I am arrested, send word to your uncle Gardiner. He will know what to do.'

Mary stared at him for several seconds before rushing from the room, tears flowing afresh.

13

'So, Mr Bennet and the rector had prolonged arguments about the entail. He did give me to understand that they disagreed, certainly, but not that their discussions extended to the raising of voices.' Bright raised his tankard to his lips.

'Mr and Mrs Parkinson were quite adamant, sir. I also asked the nursemaid if she had heard anything, and she said she had.'

'So, you feel that Mr Bennet may be our man after all.'

'Yes, sir, given the passionate nature of these arguments.'

'And yet, this passion, as you say, it seems quite out of character for either man. Come, Robert – does Mr Bennet fit your notion of a murderer?'

'I know little of murderers, sir, but I do know that felons appear in the unlikeliest of guises. Last year I had to arrest an elderly woman who had been stealing eggs from her neighbour.'

'Oh? I have no memory of that case at the assizes, Robert.'

Archer blushed. 'Well, no, sir. I let the person go, the following day. She was more than eighty years old, you see, and the fox had had all of her hens. I felt that she had already been punished, in a way and...'

Bright raised a hand. 'Enough, Robert. I agree with you completely. If I had been trying this woman's case, I should have found some means of dismissing it. The poor creature would never have made it as far as Tilbury, let alone Australia.' He smiled at Archer. 'That's the kind of peace-keeping I approve of.

A constable who knows what is trivial and what is not. You're a good man, Robert.'

'Thank you, sir.'

Bright sighed, and sat silently for some minutes, looking into the flames. There were worse places to be, he reflected, than the cosy fireside seat at The Three Crowns. If only they were closer to finding the murderer of Mr Collins, and that their only suspect were not a man whom he had come to respect. However, if all the signs continued to point that way, then so be it. The law must be impartial where serious crime was concerned.

He drained his tankard and declined Archer's offer of another.

'Westerham beckons,' he said. My wife is set on entertaining our neighbours tonight and will look upon me very ill if I am late!' He stood up, stretching stiff limbs. 'But keep thinking, Robert. Have we slotted all our pieces of information into the puzzle? This case is proving to be the most devilish of conundrums... Now, tomorrow is the Sabbath. Pray as hard as you can, and perhaps the Lord will show us the way. We shall tackle the case anew on Monday. Good night, Robert.'

'Good night, sir.'

*

Archer sat alone while he drank another two tankards of ale, preferring the warmth and bustle of the inn to the quiet chill of his cottage. He knew that by that hour his two apprentices would be long gone to their homes in a nearby hamlet. He had agreed when taking them on that they should be allowed to spend Saturday evenings and Sundays with their parents, though they lodged with him for the rest of the time. In his own case, he had been permitted to go home only rarely once apprenticed and could well remember the sadness he had experienced. His daily woman, too, was given Sundays off, provided she prepared sufficient cold food to last him until she came again on Monday morning. Sunday was the day of rest, after all.

His mind wandered to the previous day's encounter with Mrs Smith, the draper's wife, and her niece, and to Sir John's remark about finding a wife. How pleasing it would be to find warmth and adult companionship awaiting him at the end of every day! If only he were not so tongue-tied where young ladies were concerned, and Miss Smith in particular. He poked at a log with the toe of his boot and watched the bright scatter of sparks as they rose up the chimney. Practise, that was what Sir John had said, but how could he do that in the very masculine environment of his wheelwright's shop, and especially now that there would be no church services until a new rector were appointed? It was most frustrating.

'Mr Archer?'

The voice interrupted his reverie. He turned to see a young man standing awkwardly beside him.

'Oh, it's Philip, isn't it?' Archer recognised the newcomer as one of the under-footmen from Rosings; he had been on duty on the last occasion when a carriage from the estate had cast its wheel.

'Yes, sir. I wondered if I might speak to you.'

'Of course you may. Come and sit down. This is the best seat in the inn!'

The young man sat hesitantly on the very edge of the wooden settle.

'Now', said Archer, 'what can I do for you? I trust it's not another carriage in trouble?'

'No. I... I wanted to see you as constable, sir. There's been something bothering me, and I don't know what to do.'

'Yes?'

Philip was silent for a few moments, looking away and biting his lip.

'Is it to do with the death of Mr Collins?'

'Yes, well... it could be. I don't want to tell tales, Mr Archer. I was brought up to know that that's a bad thing... but it's my night off, like, and I saw you here, and... oh, I don't know...'

'Just tell me what you know, Philip. No-one will overhear you. Sir John and myself were going to interview all you footmen on Monday anyway, so you'd have spoken to me then.'

'All right. It's Michael, sir, Michael Flannery. I... I saw him, you see, sir, on Thursday night. Miss Anne was restless, and Mrs Jenkinson had requested a posset to calm her. I'd just taken it up to the antechamber by Miss Anne's room – Mrs Jenkinson said to leave it there – and I happened to look out of the window. It overlooks the lawns at the back of the house, and that was where I saw him, sir, running.'

'Running where, Philip?'

'He was going in the direction of the small gate, sir. It leads out onto the path on the west side.'

'The one that goes to the village?'

'Yes, sir.'

'You're sure it was Michael Flannery?'

'Oh yes, sir. The moon was quite bright just then, and he's a big man, isn't he? Not easy to mistake.'

'No.' Archer thought for a few moments. 'What time was this, Philip?'

'About half-past nine, sir.'

Archer felt his pulse quickening. This would put Michael Flannery in exactly the right place and near the right time to have accosted Mr Collins, argued with him, perhaps, and ultimately killed him. He thought quickly.

'Have you mentioned this to anyone else, Philip? Anyone at all?'

'No, sir.'

'Well, I think it would be best if you kept it between ourselves just for now. If Flannery is guilty of anything, we don't want him alarmed and running off. Do you see what I mean?'

'I think so.'

'Good.' Archer picked up his tankard, feeling almost light-headed with the sudden certainty that at last their enquiry was yielding fruit. 'Let me buy you ale, Philip.'

*

Sleep did not come easily that night. Archer's spirits had at first been raised by the footman's evidence, but after climbing into his cold bed and extinguishing the candle, his mind constructed unlooked-for concerns. He remembered that Michael's night off was Sunday. If the young man were guilty, surely that would provide him with an ideal opportunity to make good an escape. The only way to prevent this would be to arrest him before it could happen. However, unless he was willing to make a confession, Archer had no real proof of misdemeanour, only the footman's assertion that Michael had not been asleep at the time his brother had stated. Otherwise, there was no particular reason why a stable lad should not be out and about within the confines of the estate.

Archer wondered what course of action Sir John would recommend. It was vexing that this important information should have come his way just after the magistrate had retired to his home for the Sabbath. Archer was loath to disturb him. Certainly, the stable lad would have to be interviewed again, and preferably without the brother to speak for him, but when? Lady Catherine had been made aware that the investigation had been suspended until Monday morning; she would without doubt regard any other course of action as an affront to the smooth running of her household.

The hours of darkness passed all too slowly. Archer rose early to attend to his horses, and by the time the sky began to lighten he had come to a decision.

14

At the parsonage, Mary too had found sleep elusive. She had left her candle burning, in a bid to find some comfort on this most dreadful of days, but it just made the shadows more visible and threatening. She pulled the counterpane up to her chin and lay in misery as she relived over and over the conversation she had heard between her father and Sir John Bright, and the subsequent one between her father and herself.

Eventually she rose, and, taking up the candle, made her way downstairs to the back parlour, where the ashes still glowed red in the fireplace. It was the custom of the house to keep a brass bucket of coals near the hearth, and Mary soon had the fire brightened. She huddled gratefully in front of it, gazing into the flames. She thought of her childhood, when it had been a favourite pastime of hers to look for pictures in the fire. Sometimes her mother had brought her some bread to toast on the end of a long fork. How happy she had been then, so long ago. Now all she saw was the black outline of Mr Collins, laid out in death. She shivered as she remembered that his body was still nearby; it would not be buried until the following week. She pulled her shawl more closely around herself and closed her eyes.

She must have fallen into a doze, because, when she next opened her eyes, the fire was a heap of mere ashes again. A voice was calling her name.

'Miss Bennet!'

Mary looked around, confused, her spectacles slipping down her nose.

'Miss Bennet, are you all right?'

The children's nurse, Ellen, was there, holding a feeding bottle wrapped in a table napkin.

'I don't want to disturb you, Miss Bennet. I needed to warm some milk for Miss Martha's next feed, and I wondered why there was a light in the parlour.'

'I couldn't sleep. I... I kept thinking of Mr Collins.'

'I am the same, Miss Bennet. I can think of little else. I just thank God that all the children are well and are too young to grieve. It is not possible to stray too far from normal routine with young children in your charge, and I am very grateful for it. Now, let me make up the fire for you.'

Kneeling down, the nurse picked up the fire tongs and piled on some more nuts of coal. She turned towards Mary with a kind smile. 'There! Now, is there anything I can get for you, miss? Might you take a cup of warm milk? I have found it soothing for all ages of person, not just infants.'

Mary opened her mouth to reply but could manage only a sob. Her misery and exhaustion had at last overcome her, and she found herself crying openly like a child. The nurse patted her hand, much as she would one of her charges.

'Oh, Miss Bennet, this has been a terrible ordeal for you, I know. Losing your dear cousin in such circumstances.' She pressed a clean, starched handkerchief into Mary's hand.

Mary shook her head. She dabbed her eyes and blew her nose. 'No, it's not Mr Collins. I mean, it is, of course, but he... he wasn't very close to us, not really, except for wanting to marry Lizzy before he married Charlotte, and helping me with the Bible, sometimes.' She was aware that she was babbling, but, somehow,

73

she could not restrain her tongue. 'No, it's my dear father. I'm so afraid that Sir John means to arrest him, and he has done no wrong... I mean, how could he have? He's the kindest and best man I know.'

She gazed at the nurse, who, she realised, was probably not much older than she was, though the responsibility of her work had given her a confidence which Mary lacked.

'I am sure your father is completely blameless, Miss Bennet. He does seem a most pleasant man, indeed. Sir John and the constable have been questioning everyone. Poor little Alice was most affected by it. I came across her in tears in the scullery and it took me a good while to reassure her. You may be sure that they will discover the person who attacked the rector, and that it will not be an innocent man like your father. I have little doubt that it will turn out to be some local thief or poacher who was surprised by Mr Collins.'

Mary was little convinced by this, though she found the warm fire and the closeness of the young nurse oddly comforting. 'My father fears the worst, Ellen – I tell you this in confidence – and, to make it yet more painful, he will not permit me even to write to my sisters.'

'With respect, Miss Bennet, I feel sure that he is simply trying to spare their feelings for as long as possible. Mrs Collins speaks frequently of your two older sisters – they both write often, you know – and I am aware that they are nearing their confinements. It is most important that young ladies in their state are not unduly upset, as I am sure you know.'

Mary looked at her bleakly. 'There will be no saving them, then, if my father is arrested.' She wiped at her eyes again. 'Oh, why must all my married sisters insist upon producing infants at this time? If my mother had not gone to be with Lydia, my father might never have decided to come here at all, and he and I would have been safe at home with our books. And why was Mr Collins not attending Mrs Collins instead of wandering about the grounds of Rosings at all hours of the night?'

Ellen patted her hand again.

'You must not blame your father for the rector's habit of walking out at night, miss. He has not been himself since Baby Martha was born. His routines have been sorely interrupted, you see. Why, some weeks ago he...' She stopped in obvious confusion, turning away from Mary. 'I must go, Miss Bennet. Little Martha will wake any minute, I am certain, and will rouse the whole household if I am not in attendance.'

She started to rise, picking up the child's bottle, which she had placed in the warmth before the fire, but Mary plucked at her sleeve.

'What, Ellen? What did my cousin do? Oh, please don't go! I must know everything if my father is to be saved.'

'I almost forgot myself, Miss Bennet. I am sorry. It is not something I should speak readily about. We are all taught not to speak ill of the dead, and doubly so when that person is a clergyman, and your relation as well.'

'I care not that he was my cousin, Ellen. Please tell me!'

The desperation in Mary's voice caused the nurse to pause.

'It is not important, miss, I am sure. It's just that I have been dwelling on it, especially since Mr Collins' death. I have told no-one of it before this, and I wish no-one else to know. I would not have word come back to poor Mrs Collins.'

Mary gazed at her expectantly, her eyes huge behind the spectacle lenses. 'The very last thing I would wish in the world would be to cause added grief to Mrs Collins,' she said earnestly.

'Very well, Miss Bennet, though I know not how I can tell you this. It makes me most uncomfortable, as a person from a respectable home.' She glanced at Mary, whose eyes were growing rounder by the minute, then turned her head away. 'It took place, as I said, a few weeks ago. I was... I was coming down the back stairs and I was rounding the corner when I came upon Mr Collins coming up. He... We almost collided, and he put out his hand to steady me and he... he did not let go but came closer. He tried to kiss me, Miss Bennet! I could not think how to escape his grasp, but at that moment, Miss Martha began to wail in the nursery, and I believe it brought him to his senses. He did not speak but hurried back downstairs. After that day, I contrived to be as little in his presence as I could arrange... You will doubtless find my story difficult to believe, miss, but I tell no word of a lie. I would swear it upon the rector's own Bible if you so wished it.'

Mary thought of Mr Collins as he had been in those days when he had come to court Elizabeth, and that way he had of sidling up to her sister, of putting his hand on her arm, of leaning a little too close to her. She shuddered slightly. Perhaps, on reflection, she was fortunate that she herself had never been considered as a possible match for him.

'Please don't distress yourself further, Ellen,' she said. 'I have no trouble believing your story, though what could have prompted such an act, I cannot imagine. My cousin indeed was not in his right mind to attempt such a thing.'

The young nurse nodded. 'That is my belief. The rector was much put out after the birth of Miss Martha, as I told you. Her cries carry far in a house such as this.' She paused, frowning. 'Mrs Collins, too. She has been unwell since the birth. They – Mr and Mrs Collins, that is – they have not shared a bed since that time. You will pardon me, Miss Bennet. I would not wish to offend you, as a young unmarried lady, by speaking of such matters.'

'We are both young and unmarried, Ellen. However, I am most grateful to you for recounting your story. It may yet have some bearing on Mr Collins' murder, though I do promise you that it shall not come back to poor Mrs Collins.'

'I feel better for the telling of it, miss. Now, I really must go to Miss Martha.'

'And I shall go to bed. Thank you, Ellen.'

'Bless you, miss.'

*

Warm after her sit by the parlour fire, Mary at last fell into a deep sleep, waking only when broad daylight entered her room. She lay in bed for a few moments, musing on her encounter of the night before, uncertain whether it had occurred in reality, or had been merely a dream. However, she assured herself that such was the nature of the nurse's tale that she could not have imagined it, even when sleeping. The fact that her cousin could have behaved in such a fashion toward a servant cast him in a most unwelcome and distasteful mould. She thought of Charlotte with the utmost pity, and now felt entirely thankful that her father had rejected him as a suitor for any of his daughters, and particularly herself.

Mary had ever been the least worldly of the five Bennet sisters, preferring her books and her music to the social intercourse favoured by the others. The notion of marriage was, in her mind, largely a matter of escaping to a quiet home of her own where she would be able to pursue whatever studies she fancied, without disturbance by her family. She had given little consideration to the role of a husband in such an arrangement. This morning, however, with her thoughts in turmoil, she felt disinclined to seek out the future attentions of any man at all, even if such were forthcoming, which she somehow doubted. She resolved to devote her life to her studies and to caring for her dear father, if only he were spared.

15

Making his third circuit around the village, Archer found his spirits sinking. Although he had met, and passed the time of day with, upwards of ten or a dozen others, he had started to despair of ever encountering Miss Smith. He consulted his timepiece; it was nearly half-past three. He sighed and turned in the direction of his own stable yard, where his horse was saddled and ready to go. He silently cursed Mr Collins' unknown murderer, who had made sure that the church bells would be silent that day.

Archer's plan was both simple and necessary. He knew that Michael Flannery would be off duty from four o'clock onwards. Therefore, it was essential that he should be watched, and followed, if he left the grounds of Rosings. Archer's horse was young and fast; he was confident that he could apprehend the young man should a chase ensue. If Michael were to attempt an escape, he would surely need to take one of the Rosings horses.

Archer rode quietly by back paths, keeping under the trees as far as was possible. At one point, where the branches bent low, he was obliged to dismount and lead the horse on foot, crossing a stream as he did so, and cursing loudly as the cold water entered his boots. It was at that moment that he caught sight of her, sitting prettily on a fallen tree-trunk, a posy of wild-flowers in her hands.

'Why, Miss Smith! I... I must apologise for my language! It was most ungentlemanly! You are far from home.'

Miss Smith, who had jumped up as he spoke to her, regarded

him with a shocked expression. 'Not so far, Mr Archer. It is a fine afternoon for a walk, is it not? I was resting before my return to the village.'

'I would not disturb you.' He searched for something to say, all the time remembering the reason for his being there himself, and the steady march of time. He felt increasingly warm and uncomfortable.

The young lady quickly recovered her composure and smiled at Archer. 'Do not trouble yourself, Mr Archer. Your company is most welcome.' She glanced into the nearby thicket, where there was a burst of birdsong. 'I like to study nature, when time permits. This is a lovely place to visit, especially at the turning of the seasons, don't you think?'

'Indeed I do!'

'I have plucked these pretty flowers with a view to pressing them when I return home. I shall also attempt to make drawings of them, in my own poor way.'

'I am most certain that you draw beautifully.'

She blushed at his words and cast her eyes downwards modestly.

'You are very kind, sir. I am a simple seamstress, as you know, but I am nevertheless anxious to better myself in every way possible.'

'You are... most virtuous.'

There followed a brief silence, during which Archer felt a trickle of perspiration at the back of his neck.

'I trust you will make your way home shortly', he said, eventually, pulling at his collar to loosen it a little. 'I am most anxious that you do not put yourself in the way of danger, Miss Smith. There is still a most villainous felon abroad.'

She looked away for a few moments, then smiled at him, gathering her flowers a little more closely.

'Well, then, Mr Archer, it would be of great comfort if you could accompany me, at least to the outskirts of the village. Your warning makes me nervous!'

Archer could have wept at her words. Was this not the very opportunity he had been praying for? It was all too easy for him to picture the leisurely stroll back to the village in her company, with perhaps some discussion of nature, a subject of which he had a little knowledge, at least. There were places along the paths where he might have offered her his arm... He felt his throat tightening as he forced himself to reply to her request.

'I am so sorry, Miss Smith!' He spoke louder than he had intended and knew that his face was rapidly turning scarlet. 'I am truly sorry. I have... I am on official business and must make my way quickly to Rosings. My journey through these woods was made necessary by circumstance.' He gazed in misery at her wide blue eyes. 'I fear I am most ungallant.'

Miss Smith regarded him sympathetically. 'Don't worry, Mr Archer. I am certain that I shall come to no harm on my way home. It was merely a passing fancy of mine.'

She fastened her shawl more securely and nodded to him. 'I shall make my way back swiftly, as advised. Good afternoon, Mr Archer.'

'Good... afternoon, Miss Smith.'

He watched until she disappeared into the trees, noticing how a shaft of sunlight had turned her hair into shining gold. Then, bending down, he removed his wet boots and pounded them unnecessarily hard against a tree trunk.

*

Michael Flannery grinned at his brother Patrick, who was cleaning brasses in the small tack-room. The latter scowled at him.

'Back already, brother? I thought you had grand plans. You even persuaded Mr Kirkwood to let you go early.'

'A bit of a hitch, Pat. That fine young constable was lurking in the woods. I had to do a quick turnaround. But,' here he produced a small sack from behind his back, 'not before I grabbed me these.'

Patrick looked down and saw slightly bloodied fur.

'Two rabbits and a hare! I'll take them down to The Three Crowns in a bit. That'll be a few more pennies to send home to Ma and the sisters. I tell you, those new snares I made are doing the business all right.'

Patrick's expression darkened as he stood up, grasping his brother roughly by the arm. 'You idiot! In broad daylight and with the constable right there! You're lucky you're not on the way to the gallows even now. Or set to join Da in that God-forsaken wilderness. Or shot! It would kill Ma to lose you as well.'

'Look, I'll be careful, all right? I'm quiet and fast. I'll not be caught.'

'Don't you think every single poacher in history has said the same? And isn't the ground red with their blood? And that constable will name you as the murderer the first chance he gets. I keep telling you. Lie low for a while, or, by God, I'll break one of your legs and make you. Better crippled than dead.'

Michael shrugged and shook himself free. 'Whatever you say, brother. Now, I'll just wash this bit of blood off my hands and I'll be ready for some ale!'

A short time later he left the stable block as he had entered it, by a small window at the back, making a wide circuit of the park before climbing its boundary wall and running along a little-used track to the far edge of the village. From there he proceeded with caution until he reached the back door of The Three Crowns, where the landlord's wife took charge of the sack, passing Michael some coins from the purse at her waist.

'There's a pint in the taproom for you, Michael. You're a good lad!'

'Thank you, Grace. I have a powerful thirst after running half-way round the county to escape the attentions of that constable of yours!'

'Just make sure he doesn't hear you say that, that's all. Now, off with you out of harm's way, and I'll get this lot down the cellar.'

Grinning, Michael leaned over and kissed her cheek, before dodging a slap and running lightly into the warmth of the taproom.

*

After four hours in his concealed position near the Rosings stable yard, Archer was feeling stiff and cold. To his relief, he had arrived there just before four o'clock but had so far not sighted Michael Flannery. A light rain had begun to fall, soaking his coat, and this, together with his wet feet, had put him in the worst of moods. He had left his horse in a nearby meadow, tethered to the gatepost by means of a long rope, and, as the rain became heavier, he started to worry about the welfare of the animal. He was not so prosperous that he could risk its health.

He sighed and shuffled his feet in a vain attempt to keep warm. He had started to regret the entire enterprise, and especially the way in which it had so cruelly prevented his further acquaintance with Miss Smith. He had relived their encounter many times in his head and was increasingly aware that he had emerged from it seeming extremely ill mannered. He was unable to imagine any situation now in which he might feel at ease in the young lady's company. Why must she have chosen today, of all days, to walk in the woods?

After another half hour or so, he felt inclined to abandon his post and make his way home, where he could take care of his horse with time to spare for a pint or two by the fire in The Three Crowns. He was just about to set off when the rain stopped. After that his sense of duty prevailed.

It was fully two hours later when he became aware of footsteps nearby. He peered into the gloom and finally saw his prey, coming not from the stable yard but from the direction of the village. As the young man drew level with Archer's hiding place, he called out. 'Constable! You've missed a fine evening down at the inn!'

Archer, confused and increasingly angry, was unwilling to humiliate himself further, so kept his position and did not reply.

'You'd best look to that mare of yours. She's looking pretty sorry for herself... I give you good night!'

Archer watched in fury as the dark shape of Michael Flannery made its way into the stable block. He could hear the whistled strains of a tune he recognised as 'The Wearing of the Green', one which Flannery was wont to sing when in his cups. If he could have found an excuse to arrest the insolent young man that night, he would have done so. However, there was none, so he stretched his stiff limbs, collected his unhappy horse, and rode home as quickly as he could, wondering all the way how Flannery had managed not only to pass him by that afternoon, but also to discover the place where he had hidden himself.

16

Archer had spent a cold and restless night. It had taken him an hour or more to dry off, groom and bed down his horse, after which his anger had kept him awake almost until dawn. What had started out as a promising venture had turned into utter humiliation for him. He feared he would be a laughing-stock.

At length, he had composed in his mind an account of his day which would not cast him as too much of a fool. He'd resolved to say very little to Sir John of the young Irishman's taunts at the end of the evening, and nothing at all of his encounter with Miss Smith. In this way, he had settled his mind sufficiently to sleep for two or three hours.

Now, still stiff from his long wait in the rain, he was in a poor mood, although Sir John, far from ridiculing him, had commended him on his dedication. They were in the housekeeper's parlour at Rosings, to which Philip the footman had been summoned. The young man was looking nervously from one to the other.

'Thank you for the information you gave my constable, Philip. We have found it most useful. Is that not the case, Constable?'

Archer nodded glumly.

'How well do you know this young man, Michael Flannery?'

'Not what I would call well, Sir John,' Philip replied. 'The stable lads don't live in the house like the rest of us, and they generally have their meals up in the hay loft. One of the kitchen maids takes them over in a basket. Mr Harries explained it to me when I started here. He said it wouldn't really do to have the servants' hall smelling of horses. Of course, they come over for special days, Christmas and the like, but mostly they keep to the stables.'

'As is right and proper! Now, Philip, there's just one more thing. Have you ever seen Michael Flannery out and about on any other occasions when, say, he would be expected to be in bed, or was it just last Thursday night?'

'Well, sir, I think I may have seen him once before, though not clearly like Thursday. Mrs Jenkinson often calls down for something or other for Miss Anne at bedtime, and I did see someone out there a few weeks ago, though it was raining, and the windows were running with water. I couldn't say if it were him or not.'

'Thank you very much, Philip. Do you have any questions, Constable?'

'Er... no. Thank you, Philip.'

'Very well, that's all for the present. Would you mind sending in your head footman now?'

'Certainly, sir.'

As the young man closed the door behind him, Bright turned to Archer with a questioning look.

'You are still out of sorts after your ordeal yesterday, I think, Robert. Shall I request some refreshments from the kitchen?'

Archer shook his head. 'No, I'm quite well, sir. I did not sleep very soundly last night, that's all.'

'You must get your head down earlier tonight. I cannot afford to lose my constable to illness! Now, how may we account for the nocturnal wanderings of Michael Flannery? He is up to something, for sure, provided Philip is not mistaken.'

Archer sighed. 'There is one obvious answer, sir. If he is not our murderer, then he may well be a poacher.'

'My thoughts exactly, Robert, and a problem I shall leave to yourself and the keepers. Though we must, of course, interview the young man again once we have finished here.'

'I have already informed Mr Kirkwood, sir.'

'Thank you, Robert... Now, here comes our head footman.'

Richard Barker was tall, well muscled, and carried a superior air which befitted his senior position at Rosings. No doubt, thought Bright, he had his sights set upon that time when Harries would retire and the butler's post become vacant. Though, as he looked into the man's hard grey eyes, the magistrate could see none of the warmth and humanity which characterised the current incumbent of the job. He felt that the rest of the staff would be greatly to be pitied if this man indeed were the recipient of future promotion. However, that was by the way.

Bright gestured to a vacant chair. 'Sit down, Barker. You know the constable, of course?'

The footman glanced at Archer in a way which displayed little respect for his position. 'Certainly, sir. We have reason to call upon him to assist in the carriage yard.'

'Of course. Now, as you must know, we are questioning all members of the household staff here regarding the murder of Mr Collins. We understand that the rector was given to walking the grounds here quite late at night, and that he met his death at around half-past ten. Is it possible that any of the Rosings staff are ever abroad at that sort of hour?'

There was a moment of fleeting hesitation before Barker replied.

'No, sir, not unless we are entertaining guests. Her ladyship likes all members of staff to retire soon after nine o'clock unless we are needed to attend upon her or Miss Anne.'

'What if a servant has an evening off?'

'We must return to Rosings before ten, when the doors are locked and barred.'

Bright consulted his notebook.

'I understand that Thursday was the evening off of your footman, John.'

'That's right.'

'We shall be talking to him in due course. I believe he is currently on an errand to the village.'

Barker nodded.

'Now,' continued Bright, 'as regards Thursday night, have you any knowledge of anything out of place, anything at all which you might regard as suspicious?'

'Nothing at all, sir. It was a routine evening. The first I heard of any trouble was the next morning.'

'And you know of no-one with any grudge to bear against Mr Collins?'

'None at all. We saw the rector at church each Sunday, of course, and served him when he dined at Rosings. That was all. I cannot think that any member of the Rosings staff came close enough to him to bear any grudge.'

'Can you tell us what you know of the Rosings paper knives?'

'They are kept in the library, sir, in a box used for that purpose.'

'Are they sometimes taken to other rooms?'

'I have occasionally seen one in the drawing-room, in which case it is returned to the library.'

'Have you any opinion as to how our murderer might have obtained one?'

'We do show callers to the library, sir, to await our mistress. I suppose someone could have taken a knife on such an occasion. But to my knowledge no knife is missing from the box.'

Bright thought of the unknown number of paper knives which Lady Catherine seemed to have in her personal possession. Knives which were identical could be exchanged.

'Would you say all your fellow servants are trustworthy?' he asked. 'There is no-one you would regard as dishonest?'

Another almost imperceptible moment of hesitation. 'No, certainly not, sir. I would trust them all with my life!'

Bright frowned. 'Very well. We will not detain you further, unless Mr Archer has a question for you.'

Archer shook his head.

'Thank you, then, Barker. When John returns, would you be so good as to inform us? We shall be in the stables meanwhile.'

*

'The point, Flannery, is that we have a witness who saw you out on the lawns on Thursday night, at half-past nine.'

'The grounds are not barred to us, Sir John.'

The young groom did not look at them as he spoke but continued in his task of brushing down the chestnut gelding before them. Its coat gleamed, and it snickered softly from time to time. The stables were warm with sunlight and smelt sweetly of hay.

Bright persisted. 'Could you tell us why you were out that particular night? Where were you going? It was not your evening off.'

'It was a pleasant night, sir. I was out for a constitutional. My Da always told us to make the most of God's good blessings when we could. We were a poor family, sir, and the joys of nature are free. As it was, my night off turned out to be wet like the very devil, as Mr Archer here will tell you.'

'All that's as may be, Michael,' said Archer grimly, 'but you told me when I saw you last that you were abed early on Thursday.'

'You asked us if we'd seen or heard anything, sir. I hadn't, and that was the truth. If I'd told you I was out for a walk, you'd surely have arrested me on the spot, and me innocent!'

'God give me strength!' Archer's gloomy face had darkened considerably, and Bright put a hand lightly on his arm, as if to restrain him.

'Just to clarify what you've told us', he said. 'Am I right in thinking you wouldn't go out for a constitutional, as you put it, if it were raining?'

'No sir, I'd prefer the comfort of my bed.'

'The reason I ask is that our witness believed he may have seen you out at night on a previous occasion, when it was indeed raining.'

'Not me, sir. Whoever it is must have been mistaken. I'd have no wish to get wet for no reason. My evening off, now, that's another matter. A pint of good ale in congenial company, that's something worth walking in the rain for.'

Archer could contain himself no longer, although it galled him to admit that he had, indeed, witnessed Flannery's return from the inn, and heard the taunts thrown at him.

'You were out very late when I saw you yesterday evening, Michael. It was gone half-past ten. I was told that Lady Catherine prefers her staff to be in by ten at the latest.'

'She is not so particular with regards to the stables, Mr Archer. We have a bit more freedom, if you like, so long as we're up bright and early to get our jobs done. It was a good evening at The Three Crowns last night, as I told you.'

'And when it's a fine evening, how far do these nocturnal wanderings take you, Michael?' Archer's voice was raised now, his frown deeper still. 'As far as the woodlands?'

'Sometimes, yes, sir. I'm very partial to the song of the nightingale.'

'And to the sight of a fat rabbit, I don't doubt.'

'There you go again, Mr Archer. I'm Irish, so I must be a thief! So long as her ladyship is happy for me to work here, then I am free to walk the estate.'

Bright intervened. 'No-one is calling you a thief, Flannery. The constable is merely doing his job, as you are. I just want to return to Thursday evening, if I may. You have admitted that you were out in the gardens. Did you see the rector at any time at all?'

'No sir, not on Thursday. Though sometimes I have seen him. I think he liked a walk just as much as I do.'

'Did you see anyone else at that time? Someone from the village? Another member of the household?'

'I saw no man, Sir John.'

'All right, Flannery. I think we're just about done here for now.' Bright glanced at Archer, who shrugged. 'Of course, if the head keeper has reason to speak to the constable in future, he may need to see you again then.'

The young man said nothing.

*

At the near end of the main corridor below stairs, where a long row of bells hung ready to summon the servants to their mistresses' will, Richard Barker, the head footman, was in conversation with John, the under footman, who was newly returned from the village. He kept his voice low.

'I am to send you into the presence of Sir John Bright. He'll be asking you about Thursday, especially with it being your evening off.'

91

'I understand, Mr Barker. I have heard that all are being questioned in turn. Though I've precious little to tell him, you know that. We did what we planned, didn't we? You and I were at cards for much of the evening. I didn't set foot outside.'

'Yes, of course I know, but there's no reason to tell him that, is there? About the cards? Say something else to them. Say you were unwell or something, puked up your supper and went to bed early. You know her ladyship's opinion on gambling, John. And I was supposed to be on duty. I'm not having my name blackened for no reason, and you wouldn't want to be in trouble, would you?'

'All right. I'll say I was sick, then. No skin off my nose. Nobody saw me going to my room.'

'And they'll ask you about other nights, whether you're ever in the grounds late. I've told them we're all tucked up in bed by nine or ten. You say the same.'

Barker leaned in a little closer, but the young under footman was unaffected by his attitude.

'All right, Mr Barker. Keep your hair on! Why'd I tell them any different?'

17

Mary Bennet arose to find her father missing from the parsonage. At first, she was ready to fall into the blackest despair, fearing that he had indeed been arrested while she slept. However, on learning from Mrs Parkinson that he was merely out walking to clear his head, she felt a little better, though still not well enough to do more than pick at the breakfast dishes left out for her in the dining room.

She was still very shaken by the nurse's revelation of Saturday night, and wished more than anything that she could share her knowledge with her sisters. Of course, she could not mention it to her father, useful though it might have been to him. And there was certainly no question of her giving it as evidence to Sir John Bright or the constable. Her cheeks burned at the very thought.

Sometimes, when they were children, the Bennet sisters had played the card game known as Old Maid. For some reason, Lizzy, Kitty and Lydia had all been particularly adept at passing the unwanted card on, and Mary or Jane had usually ended up with it in their possession. Mary could still remember the sinking feeling when she looked at the depiction of the old hag, and her frustration when she could not get one of her sisters to take it. For her part, Jane had accepted her fate philosophically if she had lost, but Mary had always hated it, a fact which did not escape her younger sisters, who had teased her mercilessly. Now, Ellen's story gave her the same feeling inside. It was something she needed desperately to pass on; indeed, she had a notion that, for some reason she couldn't quite work out, it might be crucially important in clearing her father's name. But she could not tell anyone, so the knowledge would go to waste.

Telling Mrs Parkinson that she was going out in the hope of meeting her father, Mary put on her bonnet and cape and left the parsonage, though she had no clear idea of where she was going. Thinking it was likely that her father might have gone to Rosings, she took the path in that direction. Contrary to her mood, the morning was bright and warm, filled with the earthy scents of soil and leaves after the heavy rain of the night before.

Eyes downcast, lost in her own black thoughts, she did not become aware of the pair approaching her until she was almost upon them.

'Oh, Miss de Bourgh, Mrs Jenkinson! I did not see you!'

'Good morning, Miss Bennet.' Anne's voice, as usual, was a little hesitant. 'We are on our way to visit Mrs Collins, and you and your father, of course. It is a lovely day, is it not?'

'Yes... Yes, indeed it is. But I fear that Mrs Collins is unwell today and my father is out walking, I am not sure where.'

'Well then, might we walk with you? We are not far from the gate into the gardens. It might please you to see the rose-walk. We have some wonderful autumn roses.'

Mary felt her spirits lifting. She smiled gratefully at Anne. 'I can think of nothing I should like more,' she said.

Turning, Anne and Mrs Jenkinson made their way back towards Rosings with Mary beside them, occasionally stopping so that Mary could be shown some special view, or place of interest. On reaching the rose-walk, Anne was able to name each rose in turn and to point out those which had the sweetest scents. Her face – flushed from the sun and exercise – looked almost pretty.

Having seen all the roses, they took a seat on a rustic bench set against the wall. The hum of bees was everywhere around them, and very soon the elderly lady, Mrs Jenkinson, was nodding in sleep. Anne glanced at her, and then back at Mary.

'I see that my companion needs to rest,' she said. 'Would it trouble you to move to another of these seats? There is one beyond the next line of bushes. I should like to speak to you and am loath to wake her.'

Mary nodded, and soon they were re-seated in an attractively decorated alcove in the garden wall. In her usual shy way, Anne took a little time before she spoke.

'Miss Bennet, I... I wanted to tell you how sorry I am about your dear cousin. My mother has been intending to call upon poor Mrs Collins, but we have heard that she is still very unwell, and with this shock, she felt it discreet to wait a little. I thought that, if I called this morning, I might at least see you and your father, and then you might pass on our deepest condolences.'

'I shall certainly do so, Miss de Bourgh. Poor Mrs Collins is in bed much of the time, or by the fire wrapped up as for a fever. I cannot tell when she will recover.'

Anne was silent for a few more minutes, then spoke in rather a rushed way. 'This whole business has been most unsettling, Miss Bennet. The magistrate and the constable are at Rosings at all hours of the day, and all our staff seem affected by it. I... I've heard some whispering – servants do like to gossip – and there have been things said, terrible things... I cannot bring myself to repeat them to you, but...'

'But they refer to my dear father, Miss de Bourgh. I know what they say, that he had reason to murder Mr Collins.'

Anne reached over and touched Mary's arm.

'I cannot think why they would say such things, Miss Bennet,' she said earnestly. 'I am perfectly sure that your father is completely blameless. I like him very much. I thought you might have heard of these vile rumours and I could not rest until I told you that I believe no part of them, and I am sure my mother is of the same mind. I have been so worried, Miss Bennet. I cannot bear to think of it.'

Mary felt her eyes filling with tears. 'You are so kind, Miss de Bourgh.' She fumbled for a handkerchief, discovering the one which Ellen had given her two nights previously. If only she could share her knowledge with Anne!

'I can think of nothing else,' she said. 'I know my father is innocent of this felony, but there is no way of proving it. No-one has seen or heard anything of what truly happened. I am without help, Miss de Bourgh, and know not where to turn.'

'What of your mother and sisters? You must surely send for them without delay.'

'My father has forbidden me to write to any of them. Three of my sisters are soon to be confined, and my mother is of a delicate disposition. She takes ill easily, and such knowledge as this would affect her gravely.'

Anne was silent for some minutes, a frown contorting her previously animated features.

'There must be a relative somewhere who can come to your assistance, Miss Bennet. Can you really think of no-one?'

'My uncle Gardiner... My father has instructed me to write to my uncle Gardiner if... if he is arrested. But Papa would be unhappy if I did so now, I think. I would not make him unhappier than he is, Miss de Bourgh.'

'No, I can understand that. But I would not have you so wretched, dear Miss Bennet. Can I do nothing to help you? I have been hoping that we might renew our study of Greek. Do you think that might be of use to you?'

Mary looked into her friend's earnest face, and thought of the peaceful library at Rosings, so different in atmosphere from the parsonage, where the children cried constantly, the housekeeper regarded her father with ill-concealed suspicion, and there was always the presence of her cousin's body behind the closed door to the room where he was laid out. She sighed and smiled gratefully.

'I would like that so much, Miss de Bourgh.'

'Then shall we settle upon tomorrow afternoon? I shall look forward to it most eagerly!'

*

Although Mary had returned to the parsonage in better spirits than when she had left it, her mood was quickly dampened by her father's despondency at the lunch table. He had come back from his walk shortly after her own return, but, after discarding his muddy boots in an uncharacteristically thoughtless fashion, had made straight towards the study and shut the door with a slam. He had scarcely acknowledged her tentative greeting from the doorway of the small parlour.

Now, bent over his dish of steamed trout, he made a show of concentrating on his meal, but was actually eating very little. Mary watched him, her distress increasing moment by moment. As usual, they were alone. Charlotte Collins had felt too unwell to venture downstairs at all so far that day.

'Papa...'

Mr Bennet's head stayed resolutely downcast.

'Papa... I have a message from Miss de Bourgh.'

Her father sighed and finally raised bloodshot eyes to meet his daughter's.

'She sends her condolences – and those of her mother. They are most upset to know of the tragic death of our cousin.'

'You have told this to Charlotte?'

'As soon as I returned from my walk, yes, Papa.'

'Well then. It is good of them to think about us.'

Emboldened, Mary pressed on.

'They said... well, Miss de Bourgh said... that she did not believe a word of the rumours which are abroad regarding your... your involvement.'

'So there are rumours already? Well, I knew it couldn't be long. I imagine that they have me already convicted and hanged.'

'Papa! You cannot talk of such things! I cannot bear it.' Mary felt the tears begin to gather behind her spectacles and hurriedly wiped her eyes on the now much-used handkerchief, which showed signs of becoming almost as grubby as that belonging to poor little Alice. 'I just wanted you to know that Miss de Bourgh believes in you, just as I do.'

'That will comfort me greatly in the condemned cell... But there, my dear, I'm sorry. I would not have you upset like this. Of course, I am most affected by Miss Anne de Bourgh's kind words. I can see now that she is a sweet and generous young lady, though it surprises me to say so. She will be a good friend to you, Mary. Don't forget that.'

'Indeed I won't, Papa. I am so fortunate in her attentions. She has invited me to Rosings tomorrow afternoon, to resume our Greek studies... if you can spare me, of course.'

'It would cheer me greatly to think of you there.'

'And Lady Catherine de Bourgh intends to call upon us as soon as she receives word that Charlotte is well enough to receive her.'

Mr Bennet smiled grimly.

'A slightly less cheering prospect, perhaps, though goodness knows that I should be delighted to see Charlotte up and about again. Perhaps once Mr Collins is buried...'

'We should all feel better then, I think,' said Mary.

18

Sir John Bright wiped the last of the gravy from his platter with a chunk of bread and took a deep draught from his tankard of ale.

'Now, that's what I call a midday repast! It is a long time since I tasted a better rabbit stew, wouldn't you agree, Robert?'

'I would, Sir John.'

'My compliments, Mrs Dawson! May we have more ale, please?'

'Certainly, sir.'

Grace Dawson smiled coyly as she removed the men's dishes and proffered the ale jug, though she turned her head from Archer's gaze. There was a small suggestion of pink in her round cheeks, and this stirred a little uneasiness in him. He watched the landlady as she waddled towards the scullery.

'Now, Archer, we must discuss this morning's interviews with the footmen.'

Bright's words cut across Archer's musings. He sighed. The meal had indeed been good and had gone a long way towards reviving him after his ordeal of the evening before. He nodded.

'I have no problem with the accounts given by Philip, sir, or Stephen, but have some misgivings regarding Barker and John. For some reason, I could not be certain that they spoke with absolute truth.'

'I was of the same opinion, Archer, exactly. John seemed very uncertain about the nature of the sickness which kept him home on his night off, and I am rather surprised that neither Mr Harries nor Mrs Flowerday knew of it at all. He appears to be rather a flippant young man and little affected by the tragic event which has befallen the estate... I suppose you could say the same for Michael Flannery, though perhaps *angry* is a better way to describe his demeanour.'

'You know my thoughts about that man, Sir John. I still believe that he has something he wishes to hide, if only I could get the better of him.'

'It's possible, as all things and any are possible in this most confusing of cases. However, we always come up against the paper knife, don't we? What do you say to his story regarding his wanderings in the gardens on Thursday evening?'

Archer shrugged. 'He has an answer to that, as to every other inconvenient detail in his testimony. I find it strange that he claimed not to have seen Mr Collins at all that night, if he were walking in the garden as he stated, for that is one fact that we can be certain of, that Mr Collins was there at that time.'

'Yes, poor man, there and then not there. Young Philip mentioned that Miss Anne was restless, and that Mrs Jenkinson had requested a posset. I am right in thinking, am I not, that their rooms overlook the gardens?'

'That must be so, Sir John, or the footman would not have been in a position to see Flannery.'

'That being the case, it seems that we must try to interview those two ladies again. When I saw them on the morning after the crime, they were too affected to think much on the matter. Though arranging such interviews would be awkward, to say the least. Ladies of their breeding are not generally called upon to answer to officers of the law. And I should much prefer it if Lady Catherine might be absent at the time of interview. She is such a strong presence that I believe neither of the other ladies would feel able to express an independent opinion in her company. However, how that might be achieved is a puzzle requiring a more agile brain than mine at present!'

Archer shook his head. 'Don't look to me, sir. I would prefer to separate John Pearce's prize bull from the rest of the herd than to even attempt to draw Lady Catherine's attention from her daughter.'

'Exactly so, Archer. I fear I must agree with you! Now, what of Barker? What say you to his answers to our questions?'

'He did not tell us all he knows, Sir John. When you asked him about timekeeping, and whether the servants might ever be abroad after ten o'clock at night.'

'You are thinking of the door to the orangery, Robert. Yes, I am quite sure that our Mr Barker is very familiar with comings and goings that way, and is, or was, probably a willing participant.' He shrugged. 'Servants are only human, after all, and young blood will run hot. Because someone is guilty of an illicit liaison does not mean that they are guilty of murder. It just means that our jigsaw puzzle is a very untidy one.'

Archer shook his head again. 'Untidier yet, when you consider that Lady Catherine uses that same door herself during the hours of darkness. All I can say is that those servants have been very lucky so far not to have met her coming out as they're going in!'

'Barker was also rather indecisive when I questioned him on the honesty of members of staff. Mr Harries was quite adamant that every servant is reliable and truthful, but he is an old man. He keeps to the daily routines he has set in place, and because he himself would not deviate from them, he cannot envisage such deviation in others. That said, loyalty is a fine thing, and not absent among servants. We should be hard put to it to find someone willing to "tell tales" on the others, I think. Who was it who mentioned the orangery door, by the way?'

'That was young George, sir, the boot-boy. I think he's probably too young to know that it should have been kept secret – or the reason some of his fellow-servants may want to make use of it. I cannot question him further. It would not be fair on the young fellow and would probably be pointless anyway.'

'And the informant regarding Lady Catherine's nocturnal adventures?'

Archer briefly consulted his notes.

'The house maid, Jane. She is, I think, someone who likes to gossip.'

'A poor quality in a servant but a good one in a potential witness. Try and see her again, Robert, though informally, if you can. I fear that Mrs Flowerday is fast losing patience with this whole enterprise, and, besides that, will know very well what sort of woman Jane is and will try to protect her household at all costs from any unwelcome gossip. The appearance of order and respectability will be paramount, I'm afraid.'

'I will do my best, Sir John.'

'I know you will, Robert. But first we have the lady's maids to see.'

*

The Upper Gallery at Rosings was a place of stern beauty. The panelling was dark and adorned every few paces by a de Bourgh family portrait, all the faces stiff and unsmiling, and all long dead. Here and there, under the windows, were bench seats, hard and uninviting. A long carpet ran along its centre, and the place smelt of wood and beeswax.

Archer looked around him in some wonder, never having suspected the existence of such a room. Something about its sheer length made him want to run down it, or, better still, engage in a wheelbarrow race as he had done as a child. He smiled to himself at the thought, his mood lightening a little as he ceased for a few moments to dwell upon his humiliation of the day before.

Sir John Bright had obtained Mrs Flowerday's permission to speak to the two lady's maids in the sewing room, which opened off a small passageway at the far end of the gallery. As they'd climbed the grand curving staircase, he'd explained to Archer that in being allowed access to the upper storey he hoped, perhaps, to visit the anteroom of which Philip had spoken, and to see for himself what view could be had of the gardens at that side of the house. Of course, they could not presume to set foot in any of the main bedchambers. Archer meanwhile was attempting to tread as lightly as he could upon the dark polished oak, conscious all the time of his clumsy and not too clean boots.

Upon entering the passageway, which connected the gallery with the back stairs, they found Lady Catherine's maid, Pearson, awaiting them at the door to the sewing room. She was tall and slender with a very upright posture and a serious demeanour. She glanced a little suspiciously at Archer before standing aside to let them in. A younger woman was introduced to them as Miss Anne de Bourgh's maid, Cavanagh. Shorter and more rounded than her colleague, she smiled nervously.

They all seated themselves on the small ladderback chairs which were arranged before a guarded coal fire. The room was light and airy, and smelt of fresh linen and lavender. There was a wire stand in one corner where some clothes were hanging, and a large table accommodating fabric, scissors and a selection of threads. The fire-guard itself was draped here and there with items which, on inspection, turned out to be ladies' underclothing, obviously washed and left to dry. Archer – after one quick look, his face a little flushed – turned his eyes resolutely towards the floor.

Bright began, 'You will know, of course, of the terrible event which occurred in the gardens on Thursday night?'

Both women nodded.

'It has left Lady Catherine and Miss de Bourgh most upset,' said Pearson.

'We are questioning everyone in this household regarding the events of that night. I understand from Lady Catherine that she and her daughter retired at around nine o'clock. May I ask if you were both in attendance at that time?'

'Certainly. We do not leave our mistresses' sides until they are comfortably in bed.'

'And then?'

'We attend to any remaining duties and then retire ourselves. Lady Catherine is of a mind that domestic servants fare best if they are early to bed and early to rise.'

'So you would not have been awake at, say, ten o'clock?'

The women shook their heads.

'And were you aware of anything unusual at all last Thursday evening? That could be a noise outside, or perhaps you saw something from one of the back windows?'

'There was nothing out of the ordinary. It was a night like any other, and it came as a great shock to us when we were made aware on Friday morning of Mr Collins' fate.'

Bright was silent for a few moments, pondering upon whether he could dare to introduce the delicate question of Lady Catherine's nocturnal wanderings. On careful consideration, he decided that they would learn very little from repeating the question. Archer's gossipy house maid had already given them as much information as they were likely to get on that subject. He turned towards Miss Anne's maid, Cavanagh, who had so far not spoken.

'Miss Cavanagh, I understand that Miss de Bourgh was restless on Thursday night and that Mrs Jenkinson requested that a posset be brought to her. Were you still in attendance at that time?'

Cavanagh flushed slightly. She was obviously a good deal less confident than Pearson. Bright surmised that she was probably fairly new to the position of lady's maid. 'I had retired by then, sir. Miss Anne was safely abed and Mrs Jenkinson is always nearby should my mistress need her.'

'Does Mrs Jenkinson's room adjoin that of Miss Anne?'

'There is an anteroom between their chambers. It is a suite of rooms which share a common door onto the gallery.'

'I see...'

Bright was interrupted by a jangling bell which sounded in the passageway outside. Pearson rose immediately.

'You will excuse me, Sir John. That is my mistress's bell.'

'We have more or less finished, anyway. Thank you, Miss Pearson.' Pearson nodded solemnly and made her way out. Cavanagh looked to be on the verge of following suit, but Bright stopped her. 'Miss Cavanagh, as we have been speaking of this anteroom, do you think it would be possible for you to show it to me? I should not expect to enter either of the bedchambers.'

Cavanagh hesitated before replying. 'Perhaps we should await Miss Pearson's return, sir. I generally look to her for advice about household matters.'

'All I ask is that I should be able to look out of the window of that room. I do have a reason for requesting this, in that another member of staff here believes that he saw someone through that window on Thursday night.'

Cavanagh's face drained of all colour and she clasped her hands at her throat. 'Oh, sir! Not the murderer, I trust? We shall all be in danger!'

'No... no, we don't think so. Please don't upset yourself. But if I just might have one glimpse of that window...?'

'Very well. We must do all we can to discover and bring to justice this foul man. It is this way, sirs.'

The anteroom was oak-panelled and contained two chests and a bookcase full of what seemed to be religious tracts. Heavy doors on either side led to what were presumably Miss Anne's and Mrs Jenkinson's bedchambers. As promised, there was a large window overlooking the gardens at the back of the house and it was possible to see the very coleus bed where the rector had met his demise. Bright cursed inwardly. If only the household at Rosings were not quite so early to bed and Philip had been summoned a little later...

He sighed. 'Thank you, Miss Cavanagh. You have been helpful indeed... Does your mistress ever summon you later in the night, after you have retired?'

'Oh no, sir. She is a most thoughtful and considerate young lady. And Mrs Jenkinson has the two doors open, you see, so that she can go in if she is needed. She has done so ever since Miss Anne was a small child.'

'Very well. I think we have finished here. Constable?'

Archer hastened towards the door, anxious to be back in the familiar surroundings of the servants' hall. However, at that moment the inner door to one of the bedchambers opened, and the elderly lady, Mrs Jenkinson, emerged. She stopped in some consternation at the sight of Bright and Archer and seemed about to return to her room immediately.

Bright seized his moment. 'Mrs Jenkinson! You must please excuse our presence in your sanctum. I requested that Miss Cavanagh here show me the view from this window. It may have a bearing upon our investigation.'

Mrs Jenkinson looked fearfully at the window in question.

'It overlooks the gardens, Sir John.'

'Of course, but what concerns us, you see, is whether it would have provided some view of... of the deed of Thursday night.'

'The deed?' The old lady looked aghast.

'I am so pleased that I have had this chance to talk to you, Mrs Jenkinson. Our meeting on Friday morning was not fortuitous, I fear. What I am wondering is... did you chance to look out of this – or your own – window on Thursday night?'

'I cannot recall...'

'Might you have seen someone – anyone – abroad in the gardens after retiring to bed?'

'It would have been dark. I cannot see how...'

'Ah, but there was moonlight, Mrs Jenkinson. We have that on best authority.'

'I cannot recall. I... I don't...' Mrs Jenkinson's distress seemed to deepen. She turned her head from side to side as if seeking assistance from somewhere, and her hands were tightly clasped. Archer began to feel uncomfortably sorry for the old lady. 'What could I have seen from such a distance?'

Bright pointed through the leaded pane.

'If you look there, you can see the flowerbed where... the deed was done.'

Mrs Jenkinson screwed up her eyes, then shook her head vehemently.

'I see no flowerbed, Sir John.'

'There, look. Just to the right of the green door.'

'It is no good, Sir John. You will not make me see.' Bright regarded her quizzically while she fumbled in her reticule, eventually drawing out a small pair of wire-framed spectacles, which she held out to the magistrate with a shaking hand. 'I have these to read, Sir John, and they are some use, but it is some years now since I have been able to see far. Miss Anne makes such sport when we are out together, always saying that if it weren't for the noise of the wheels I should be knocked down by the carriage.'

'Oh.' Bright was, for once, a little discomfited, and Archer could not help but feel slightly gratified. After all, the poor lady had seemed to be on the verge of tears at all the questions, and he could not imagine her giving any answer which would be at all useful to them.

'Oh, well... Thank you, Mrs Jenkinson. We value your help very highly.'

The old lady nodded uncertainly and retreated into her room.

19

Lady Catherine de Bourgh and her daughter Anne were sitting in the drawing room. Dinner was over, and, for once, Mrs Jenkinson had retired to bed early, pleading a headache. The only sounds in the room were the ticking of the mantel clock and an occasional hiss from the coal fire. For some time, indeed all throughout dinner, Lady Catherine had been largely silent. Now, with the footmen dismissed, she turned towards her daughter with a sour expression.

'It is not often since your early childhood that you have given me reason for displeasure,' she said, 'but I must tell you in no uncertain terms that I am now most displeased, most displeased indeed.'

Anne de Bourgh shrank into the soft velvet of the couch as if she wished to disappear completely from her mother's company.

'Do you have nothing to say to me?'

'I am uncertain as to what you refer, Mamma,' attempted Anne in the smallest of voices.

'I think you know very well to what I refer! You *will* answer me truthfully, my girl. This is quite unlike you, Anne, quite unlike. I cannot abide disobedience and stubbornness of spirit in a young lady... I see how it is, don't assume that I don't. You have been altogether in the wrong company these past days. I have seen for myself that stubbornness of spirit in the one sister and it no doubt persists in the others.'

Anne stuttered a little without producing words, and her mother's thunderous tone became yet louder.

'I understand that you are to resume your acquaintance with the Bennet girl, and quite without consulting me.'

Anne flinched at her mother's tone of voice, and spoke almost inaudibly. 'I met Miss Bennet while out walking, Mamma. I had intended to call upon the family to express our condolences, just as you had asked...'

'Condolences, just that. And I was thinking chiefly of poor Mrs Collins.'

'...and I met Miss Bennet, who said her father was not at home and that Mrs Collins was unlikely to rise. I asked Miss Bennet to walk with us, Mrs Jenkinson and myself, and I felt so sorry for her. Mamma, she is so sad! I believe that resuming our study of Greek may go some way toward helping her to feel a little better.'

Lady Catherine shook her head in exasperation.

'You did not mention this at luncheon, nor indeed at the dinner table. If it were not for Mrs Jenkinson, I should have no knowledge of it.'

'I was afraid you might disapprove, Mamma. I have heard the rumours about poor Mr Bennet but, oh, they are not true!'

'And you know this, despite the fact that the man is probably the magistrate's chief suspect and is only free at this moment because Sir John is a scrupulous officer who is searching for irrefutable evidence.'

'I know nothing of this, Mamma. I heard some of the servants talking and I cannot believe what was said.'

'That young woman's family stood to lose their entire estate to Mr Collins. With him dead, that may very well not happen. There is no man with better reason to plot against our rector than Mr Bennet, none at all. Now, tell me, is that an association you wish to preserve?'

'I know Miss Bennet, Mamma. I cannot but believe her when

111

she says that such accusations are quite impossible...' Anne paused to wipe away a tear. 'We have had such good times, Mamma, studying together...' Her tone saddened. 'It is rare for me to find a friend of my own age whose life is not centred around balls and new dresses and receptions. Those have never been my interests, as you know, even were I sufficiently well to enjoy them all.'

At Anne's mention of her illness, Lady Catherine's expression softened. She turned away from her daughter and was silent for some minutes, eventually addressing her again with a sigh.

'I understand that your life has not been quite like that of other young ladies, my dear, though I have always hoped that the peace and tranquillity of Rosings might go some way toward raising your spirits...'

'Of course, it does, Mamma!'

'...and I admit that it has not been an easy task to find suitable companions for you. I fully acknowledge that Mrs Jenkinson is over-old for that position, though a truer and more attentive friend would be hard to discover...'

'She has been my most faithful and loving companion, yes!'

'...but it *has* been my wish that you might one day meet a friend who is closer to your own age, and, though it galls me to say this, it seems that you now may have found that person, albeit a sister of that very young woman whose grasping and sly ways deprived you of the husband you were intended for!'

Anne shrugged sadly. She hesitated for some time before replying, in a very small voice.

'I do not believe I could ever have fulfilled that role, Mamma, not if I am honest. I would have been required to take up a place in society, not to mention the supervision of a great house and... and the production of an heir. All those things for which I am not sufficiently strong… I believe that my place is here at Rosings, where I am happy.' Her voice was trembling; she had scarcely ever spoken to her mother so boldly and greatly feared the response.

Lady Catherine gazed at her daughter for a long time, then turned away, frowning. She was silent for many minutes, so that Anne began to believe that their conversation was over, and gathered up her reticule in preparation for departure to her bedroom. However, as she was about to rise, her mother finally spoke again.

'The understanding as to your future marriage was come to those many years ago, when you were just a babe and your father still hale and hearty. Time passes swiftly, and things change without our noticing…' She regarded Anne a little sadly. 'We could not, at that time, have foreseen your present delicate constitution… It is possible that, as you have said, such responsibility would have been a step too far for you. We shall never know. However, I am thankful that you value your life here at Rosings, and I would be failing in my duty if I did not permit you to live that life as fully as you wish… I fear that the untimely death of Mr Collins has made me reflect on mortality, and the brevity of our span here on earth.' She paused, frowning into the distance. 'So, if it makes you happy to keep company with Miss Bennet, while she stays at the parsonage, then so be it. You are my only daughter, and I cannot deny you. It was not your fault that Fitzwilliam Darcy fell under the spell of that scheming witch – I will not mince my words, Anne – but neither, I suppose, was it the fault of a younger sister. I cannot feel that I could entertain the father here again, not while this shadow is over him, but you may keep your word to the daughter. She will be despatched back to Hertfordshire before very long, one way or another. Meanwhile, you may have her here if that is what you wish – so long as her father is not accused, of course.'

Anne's smile was so radiant as to transform her face. 'Thank you, Mamma... You are so generous to me!'

Her mother looked at her archly. 'One thing's for the good, anyway, my dear. She is such a plain young woman that you will never fail to show yourself to best advantage when you are with her!'

*

In the servants' quarters too, the evening meal was over. The two young kitchen maids, Sally and Ruth, had finished carrying the dishes to the scullery and were scrubbing the kitchen table, one at each end. It was their last task of that day.

Sally paused for a moment, rubbing her hands together. 'Lord, how this soap stings! It has been made with too much lye. Look how red my hands are! I'm done with scrubbing tonight, Ruth. I shall rinse the table directly.'

'If you say so, Sal. My hands are sore, too.'

Sally fetched one of the buckets of water which they had earlier drawn from the pump in the scullery. She looked coyly at her friend.

'Have you thought of anything yet... to tell Mr Archer?'

Ruth shook her head. 'I can think of nothing at all.'

It had become their favourite topic of conversation – when out of the presence of Mrs Penny, of course – and had taxed their imaginations to the limit. They had been through the events of the last Thursday, and, indeed, the events of days both before and after, in minute detail, but had found no juicy piece of information which they could pass on to the constable.

'The murderer will be discovered, and we'll have had no hand in it!' said Sally glumly. 'Mr Archer will never notice us then.'

'I should be glad to see the murderer caught even so,' said

Ruth, looking around nervously. 'You never know what he's going to do next, do you? It's giving me nightmares.'

'Don't I know it! You were kicking something dreadful last night. I've got bruises all down my leg. We're all scared, you know we are. But we don't want someone else getting all the glory, do we? They was upstairs today, talking to the lady's maids. We don't want that snooty Miss Pearson getting all the praise.'

'What do we do then, Sal? We can't really make things up, can we?'

At this, Sally looked contemplative. 'Well,' she said slowly, 'we might be able to think of some little detail that we've sort of forgotten before. We'd just have to decide on the right one. It needn't be something about anyone in particular.'

'Like Mr Barker or somebody?'

'No, better not. Pity, though!'

The two girls giggled as they mopped the fresh water over the well-scoured wood.

'What are you two laughing about?' Jane, the house maid, was struggling through the door with the buckets of coal which the kitchen maids would use in the early morning to re-light the kitchen range. She was breathing heavily, and her face was ruddier than ever.

'I swear these buckets get heavier every day!'

She deposited her load near to the fire-box and drew a rather sooty hand over her sweating brow.

'I can't find young Maggie tonight. Either of you two seen her? She should have been helping with the coal.'

'I haven't seen her since supper,' said Sally. 'You, Ruth?'

'Not hide nor hair of her. I hope she's all right. She's been in a proper state since Mr Archer asked us those questions on Friday. Don't know what she thinks is going to happen to her.'

'Yes, she has, bless her,' said Jane, 'though she doesn't say much to me and Margaret, us being that much older. Poor little thing's usually asleep anyway, by the time we're ready for bed.'

'Do you think that's where she is? Gone to bed early?'

Jane shook her head.

'No, not Maggie. She'd never dare to go to bed without being told, or shirk her duties. I'm feeling a bit worried about her, truth to tell. I only wish I hadn't so much to do yet, tonight. I'm a bit behind, or I'd be off looking for her straight off.'

'We can look, Jane, can't we, Ruth?' Sally was already drying her hands and starting to tidy away the buckets. 'We don't want her in trouble with Mrs Flowerday.'

Ruth was beginning to look alarmed as she gazed at Jane. 'It's not... You don't think *he*'s got her? The murderer, I mean? We'll be safe looking for her, won't we?'

Jane smiled broadly. 'Of course you will, you silly! What would a wicked felon like that want with a little girl? Likely as not she's had a bit of an accident, got nervous and wet herself like last week, and too scared to tell anyone. That'll be it... When you do find her, send her up to bed, tell her I said so, and then find me to let me know. It'll take a bit of weight off my mind.'

As it happened, the two kitchen maids found the little maid-of-all-work after only a few minutes' searching. She was sitting on a closed wicker hamper in the small storeroom where necessities for the now-rare shooting parties were kept. Her face was already stained with tears and she started weeping afresh when the girls burst in on her. Ruth was quick to enclose her in an embrace.

'Why, Mags,' said Sally, 'what you doing here all on your own? What you done that's so bad?'

The little girl did not reply but wept all the more.

116

'Broke something, did you? That's nothing to worry about, as long as it's not upstairs. If it's in the kitchen, I'll say I did it!'

Maggie shook her head and managed to snuffle out an answer. 'No, I ain't done nothing like that.'

'Then what? Tell us, Mags, do. We can't help you if you don't.'

'I can't... I don't know what to do...'

'About what?'

'He said we had to tell him if we knew something...'

'The constable?'

'...and I don't know what to say.'

'You don't have to say anything,' put in Ruth, relieved that, after all, nothing too awful had happened to Maggie. 'You only have to talk to him if you know something unusual about Thursday night. He won't mind if you don't.'

'But I do!' Maggie wailed.

Sally frowned.

'What do you mean, Mags?'

'I don't want to get her in trouble.'

'Who? Who'll be in trouble?'

The little girl's voice was barely audible. 'Margaret.'

'Margaret? What's Margaret done?'

Maggie hesitated, and then spoke in a rush. 'I woke up, and I saw her; saw her coming in. She'd been somewhere. I 'tended to be asleep but I was peeping. She had a stump of candle lit. She cleaned her boots on a bit of rag before getting undressed and into bed.'

'But she's always later than you into bed, Mags. That's nothing. She's got to collect all the boots and shoes for the staff and take them down to George, hasn't she. Sometimes she has to wait a bit if some of them aren't ready. Most likely she'd forgot to give him her own.'

The little girl shook her head.

'No! It wasn't like that. She'd already got into bed, before. I know because I'd woke up and had to use the pot. She was in bed then. It was later on when I woke up again.'

'So you're saying, Margaret went to bed, then got up again, and went somewhere where she got her boots dirty?'

Maggie nodded.

'What can I do? I don't want her in trouble. She's kind to me and gives me a cuddle when I'm sad. But that constable, he said...'

Sally and Ruth exchanged looks over the little maid's head, then Sally took her hand and gave it a reassuring squeeze. 'Look,' she said, 'as you're scared of the constable, me and Ruth'll tell him for you. We'll tell him what you said and say he's not to let on to any of the others that it was you, and not to get Margaret in trouble. Then it'll be all right, won't it?' Maggie sniffed loudly and nodded. 'Now, you better get up to bed. Jane said to send you. You have a good night and mind the bugs don't bite.'

*

After Maggie's departure, and Sally's return from her errand to assure Jane that the little girl was safe, the two kitchen maids remained in the storeroom while they discussed her revelation.

'Can we really ask Mr Archer not to get Margaret in trouble?'

'Dunno, Ruth. We can try. We don't want any of us in trouble, not us junior staff.'

'Where d'you think she'd been, Sal?'

Sally shrugged.

'Meeting someone, maybe? You've heard the others talking, same as me. And I did see her once, in the yard with that Michael, when I was taking their dinners over to the stables.'

118

'He looks at me funny, that one. I wouldn't want to be there on my own with him. His brother's all right, though.'

'Mr Harries says he's got a chip on his shoulder, Michael I mean. Don't know what about.'

'So you think Margaret's sweet on him?' Ruth's eyes were wide with awe.

'Maybe. We won't tell Mr Archer that though. We'll just stick to what little Mags told us.'

'I hope we're doing right, Sal.'

'We got to be, Ruth.' Sally smiled, though a little apprehensively. 'After all, we been waiting for this chance, ain't we? Won't have to bother making something up, neither. Fancy it just falling into our laps like that!'

20

At Sir John Bright's suggestion, Archer was in the yard at Rosings quite early the following day. They had agreed that it would be easier to waylay Jane on one of her many journeys to the coal shed than to make a further formal request to Mrs Flowerday to interview the gossiping house maid.

Aware that he might thus become an object of attention among the Rosings staff, Archer made a show of examining his notes closely, while still keeping one eye on the door to the kitchen quarters. However, the only person to emerge with a coal bucket so far had been the little maid-of-all-work, Maggie, who, despite Archer's encouraging smile, had scuttled away like a frightened mouse.

Soon afterwards, the two kitchen maids emerged, and – rather to Archer's displeasure – made their way over directly to where he was standing. Bright had warned him in a jocular moment that he had found two new admirers in the girls, and he was anxious not to encourage them.

'Mr Archer!' The taller of the two, whose name Archer could not for the moment recall, hissed out his name in a way which indicated that she didn't wish to be overheard. 'Mr Archer! We have some information for you.'

The other kitchen maid, whose name he did remember, was nodding vigorously and glancing over her shoulder every few seconds in trepidation.

'Have you Mrs Penny's permission to speak to me?' asked Archer. 'I'm sure you have duties to perform this morning.'

'Yes! I mean, no, she doesn't know. No-one must know, Mr Archer. We must tell you!'

'It's Ruth and... er...'

'Sally. It's Sally, Mr Archer.'

'Yes, that's right. Well, Sally, you'd better tell me what this piece of information is.' Archer's eyes were still on the doorway, in expectation of Jane's emergence.

'Not here, sir.' Sally had her own eyes on the door as she beckoned Archer over to the shelter of a storehouse wall, Ruth following them closely.

'We got to be careful, you see, sir. You'll know once I've told you.'

Archer's exasperation was increasing. Now he would not be able to see Jane, and, worse, was being made something of a fool of by the two infatuated girls. He frowned darkly at them.

Sally, however, was not deterred. 'This was told to us by Maggie, sir.' She dropped her voice to a whisper. 'But you're not to tell anyone it was her, only maybe Sir John. And you've got to stop Margaret getting in trouble.'

'Margaret?' Archer was now completely at a loss.

'Maggie shares a bed with her, Mr Archer. She's the between maid.'

Archer recalled now that he had yet to speak to Margaret; he had made a note that she was indisposed on the morning after the murder.

'Maggie says that Margaret came to bed at the normal time on Thursday night, but she must of got up and gone out, because she woke up and Margaret was getting undressed again.'

'Don't forget the boots, Sal!'

'No, Ruth. She had to clean her boots on a rag, Mr Archer. They was muddy. Maggie seen her while she was pretending to be asleep.'

121

'And you're sure all this is true? You're not making anything up?'

Sally looked scandalised. 'Of course not, sir. Why would we? Last thing we'd want is to get Margaret in trouble, like I said. You mustn't say anything to her about us, promise?'

'Why isn't Maggie telling me this herself?'

'She's proper scared, Mr Archer. We told her we'd tell you for her. She's been in a right state about it all, in tears and everything.'

Archer was silent for a few moments. Certainly, the girls seemed sincere, and Maggie's fear had been obvious when he had seen her earlier.

'Very well,' he said, 'I promise not to mention either Maggie or yourselves for the time being... and I would be grateful if you in your turn did not pass this knowledge on to any other party. Do you agree?'

The girls nodded vigorously.

'Now,' said Archer, 'I think you'd both better get back to work, or questions will be asked, I'm sure.' The two kitchen maids gave little curtsies and Archer smiled, despite himself. 'Oh, and thank you for coming to me with this information.'

For some time after the kitchen maids' departure, Archer stayed in the shadow of the storehouse, his brow furrowed in thought. Could the two girls have made the story up? They had certainly been eager to impress him. However, why would they have involved the little maid-of-all-work? He had only to consult her, and the truth would be out. He had no doubt that the making-up of stories of any description would be a task beyond Maggie's abilities. In that case, Sally and Ruth must be believed, which meant that, at long last, some real information had come his way, and a possible suspect. He shivered, partly in excitement and partly in fear. Although tempted to request a meeting at once with the elusive Margaret, he decided, reluctantly, that it would be discreet to speak to Sir John first.

*

'I think you're right, Robert. There is no reason why the kitchen maids should have invented such a tale. They would be more likely to tell you they'd spotted an intruder in the hen-house, or something of that nature. It must be remembered, as well, that Margaret was not available to see you on the day after the murder. However, how or why the between maid should be in any way involved in the killing of the rector is beyond my imagination.'

Archer shrugged in response to Bright's observation. 'I have asked myself that question again and again,' he said.

Bright frowned. 'We need to interview Margaret, and urgently. As a between maid, she would certainly have been in a position to take a paper knife if so inclined... But I feel that, for the present, we must make the procedure seem routine. If she is in some way responsible, we must be careful not to alert any accomplice she may have. It seems quite incredible that such a person as she might get out of bed, murder a clergyman, and then climb back into bed again – unless, of course, she is insane, a factor which would scarcely have escaped Mrs Flowerday's eagle eye.'

'What do you suggest, sir?'

'We shall tell Mrs Flowerday that we need to see Margaret because you were unable to interview her on Friday, and tell Margaret the same thing. It will not then appear in any way unusual. All the staff are by now aware of our methods of investigation. She may have a perfectly innocent explanation for the actions described by little Maggie, and, if so, will not conceal them when we question her regarding her movements on Thursday night. Do you agree, Robert?'

'That sounds very well reasoned, sir.'

'Good, then let us proceed.'

*

On the pretext of checking some detail of household procedure, Bright had contrived to join Archer below stairs at the time the latter had arranged to speak to Margaret, though Mrs Flowerday had made it quite clear that she regarded his request to see the between maid as quite incomprehensible.

'You will understand when you see the girl, Mr Archer. However, you must do as you wish. You are the constable... And you will please note that we are exceptionally busy here today.'

'We shall be as brief as possible, Mrs Flowerday.'

A short time later, with the two men again in possession of the housekeeper's parlour, she ushered Margaret into their presence, giving the girl a little push and glaring at her before leaving the room. The between maid was a little person, perhaps in her early twenties, with dull brown hair and a sharp nose and chin, reminding Archer of a small rodent. She stood before them, nervously clasping and unclasping her hands.

'You may sit down, Margaret,' said Bright, encouragingly.

The maid looked around with wide eyes, then perched on the very edge of the chair nearest the door, as if prepared for flight at the earliest opportunity.

'Now,' continued Bright, 'you will know that Mr Archer and myself are speaking to all members of the household here at Rosings, as part of our investigations into the most unfortunate death of the rector.' Margaret said nothing, although her expression of fear and bewilderment deepened. 'We are talking to you today because we were unable to see you on Friday. You are better, I trust?'

'I had a turn, sir.'

'Do you often have turns?'

'Sometimes, sir.'

'All right. Now, can you tell us of your movements last Thursday night?'

'The night the rector died,' added Archer, by way of explanation.

'Movements, sir?'

'Yes: what you did.'

'I didn't do nothing, sir. Nothing except what I was told. I do the boots and shoes of a night, collect them up and that.'

'Did you... go outside at all?'

'I only do what I'm told, sir.'

Bright sighed. 'We have heard that perhaps you were outside for some of the time. Could you tell us what you were doing?'

'Doing?'

'Were you perhaps meeting someone? We have heard it said that servants sometimes go out through the orangery. It's most important, Margaret. If you were out, and know something, you must tell us.'

The girl regarded them with wide eyes, remaining silent.

'How long have you been in service here, Margaret?' attempted Archer.

This was obviously safer ground. 'Thirteen years now, sir, nearly fourteen. I know that because Mrs Flowerday was saying to me only the other day. Nearly fourteen years here, she said, and you still don't know a left boot from a right! She was joking a bit, like, though I do get muddled up still.'

'Do you like it here?'

'Oh yes, Mr Archer. Lady Catherine has always looked after me.'

'Do you get on all right with the other servants?'

'Jane looks out for me and Sally and Ruth are a laugh. I get nervous sometimes with Mrs Flowerday and Mr Barker. Sometimes I don't understand what I'm s'posed to be doing. But it's always all right, like.'

'And what about the young men in service here? Do you chance to have a sweetheart, Margaret?'

The maid blushed and looked away. 'Mrs Flowerday says she don't allow followers, sir.'

'But if you were, is there anyone here you might take a liking to? What about Michael Flannery? He's about your age'.

'Michael? He's nice to me, sir. He talks to me sometimes about the horses. My dad used to have horses. He's not as good-looking as John, though.'

Archer glanced at Bright. 'So you like John best, Margaret?'

She nodded shyly.

'Have you ever been out to meet him, through the orangery? We won't say anything to Mrs Flowerday, I promise.'

Margaret bit her lip and looked away. 'Just once or twice, like.' She was blushing a deeper red than before. 'Promise you won't tell,' she begged Archer. 'He told me not to say anything. I shouldn't of said anything, should I? I've done wrong.'

Archer shook his head, trying to reassure her. 'We're not going to say anything to Mrs Flowerday. We just need to know if one of the times was last Thursday?'

The girl looked stricken. 'No, Mr Archer, I didn't see John on Thursday. Will he be in trouble, sir?'

'No, Margaret. But, you're quite sure, about Thursday?'

'You will tell us the truth, won't you, Margaret?' put in Bright, in rather a stern voice. 'It's really most important.'

The girl's face started to crumple. 'I didn't meet John Thursday night, sir. I said I didn't.' She began to weep rather noisily, wiping her nose on her sleeve.

With no more than a token tap on the door, Mrs Flowerday entered the room and frowned at the two men.

'That will be sufficient, I think, sirs,' she said. 'Margaret is too upset now to help you further.' She turned to the girl a little impatiently. 'You may go about your duties now, Margaret.'

When the maid had left them, the housekeeper sighed. 'I apologise for cutting short your interview, sirs, but I could not allow you to persist when I heard the noise that Margaret was making. It came through to us even in the servants' hall. I did try to warn you. The young woman is not the sharpest knife in the box – I must apologise for using that expression – and she is also prone to fits. I dare say that we should not have considered her for service at all, except for a tragic accident. Her father was a carter in the village and died as the result of a Rosings hound spooking his cob. The cart overturned, crushing both himself and his poor wife, who was riding with him. Their little daughter survived, and Lady Catherine insisted that we take her into useful service. However, as you can see, she is as she is. I feared at one time that she would be entirely unemployable, but she has managed, according to her limited abilities. She began here at eight years old as maid-of-all-work, and sometimes seems scarcely older now, except in years. We try to treat her gently, you understand, in order to prevent her going into one of her fits.'

'It is a sad tale.' Bright was tempted, in view of this information, to mention Margaret's confession about her nocturnal liaisons with the footman, John, but was loath to break their promise to her, and was also anxious to pursue this information with as little hindrance as possible from the senior staff.

'Will that be all now, Sir John?' Mrs Flowerday was looking at them quizzically, as if she suspected that they were concealing something from her.

'Yes, thank you, Mrs Flowerday. Mr Archer will return later this afternoon to interview your chamber maids. I believe you said that three o'clock would be convenient?'

'That is correct, sir. Though, again, I must urge you not to detain them long, Mr Archer. I am doubtful, anyway, that Eliza and Alison will have any useful information for you.'

'Be that as it may... We are most grateful for your kindness in permitting it. Now, I must briefly see Mr Harries before we depart.'

'Very well, sir. I shall claim back my parlour.'

*

Having learned from Mr Harries that the footman, John, was at present on duty in the hall, Bright and Archer made their way up the back stairs from the servants' quarters.

'Although the girl is unreliable, I cannot think her a deliberate liar. And yet there is something here which does not ring true.' Bright's face was grim as he spoke in a low voice.

'Unless Maggie was mistaken, she was out *somewhere* on Thursday night,' agreed Archer. 'Perhaps she went out to meet John, but he failed to appear because of his sickness.'

'That's a plausible explanation, of course, Robert, but doesn't this whole liaison seem quite *im*plausible? Margaret is small, simple, and very far from handsome. Why would a good-looking footman choose to pay court to such as her? Except for the very reason that she *is* simple, and therefore open to misuse. This information may not help us in our search for our murderer, but we must act upon it, I feel, as a moral duty. There are many such as her in our asylums, Robert, labelled as morally destitute through no fault but that of their abusers. I am not one of those blinkered men who concur with such treatment. Lady Catherine, through the goodness of her heart, has seen fit to act as protector to the girl, and I would not see her charity go to waste.'

Together they went through the concealed door in the panelling which gave way to the grand hall of Rosings, where they found John in conversation with the head footman, Barker.

'Ah, John,' said Bright, 'we have need to speak to you again briefly. I have obtained Mr Harries' permission.'

The footman looked surprised for a few moments before regaining his composure. 'Very well, sir. How can I help you?'

Bright glanced at the head footman. 'I would prefer this interview to be conducted privately, if you please, Barker. We have followed this procedure throughout our investigations, as you will remember.'

'As you wish, Sir John.' Barker bowed abruptly, with rather bad grace, and frowned at the under footman before leaving the room.

Bright waited for the door to close behind the head footman before turning to address John.

'Now, John, I need to speak to you regarding a serious matter which has arisen as a result of our investigations. When I questioned you previously, you were quite sure that neither you nor any other servant at Rosings were ever out of doors at night without good reason.'

'That's correct, sir.'

'However, it has come to our notice that you do indeed venture out on occasion to meet a junior female servant, the purpose of such meetings being easily guessed.'

'Who told you that, sir?'

'It doesn't matter, John. What does matter is that we understand that the servant in question, though a young woman in years, is mentally little more than a child, and, what is more, employed here through the direct charity of Lady Catherine herself. I am sure you would not wish knowledge of this unsavoury liaison to reach your mistress?'

'I don't know what you may mean, sir.' John's face was flushed. 'I stand by what I told you before. Anything else you've been hearing is just lies, though I don't know who'd want to discredit a junior footman.'

'And you still maintain that you were sick on Thursday night? Too sick to take advantage of your night off?'

'I was most ill, sir. I believe it was owed to stale faggots which I ate at midday.'

'Faggots? Were other servants affected likewise?'

'I do not believe so, sir. I have a sensitive digestion.'

Bright sighed and shook his head. 'Very well, John. We will leave you to your work. However, I want you to know that if any more rumours reach my ears, or those of my constable, concerning yourself and that female servant I mentioned, I shall not hesitate to bring the matter to the ears of Lady Catherine. Do you understand?'

John was silent and stared after them as they left by the main door.

*

Behind the panelled door to the back stairs, where he had advantageously concealed himself, Richard Barker had listened to the magistrate's words in increasing discomfort.

21

Archer was gratified, when, that afternoon, he was shown into the orangery to await the arrival of the chamber maids. The footman, Philip, explained that there was now much activity both above and below stairs, owing to the impending visit of the Bishop of Rochester.

'Mrs Flowerday felt you might be more private here, sir.'

'Thank you, Philip. Is the bishop a regular visitor here? I have not heard of it.'

'Oh no, Mr Archer. He comes to conduct the burial service for poor Mr Collins.'

'Of course. I had not thought of it. I am sure he will provide much comfort to poor Mrs Collins, and to the household here, of course.'

'Indeed, sir. I will send Alison and Eliza to you at once.'

After Philip left him, Archer strolled about the room, if room it could be called, delighting in the huge windows, glassed roof and trapped sunlight. He breathed in the smell of warm vegetation and the sharp tang of the oranges. Reaching up, he touched the waxy, dimpled fruit and wondered what it would be like to eat such a delicacy. Not for the first time in his life, he reflected that the lives of the rich were a whole world away from his own.

He was also pleased to see at last the small side door into the garden, and to find that there was indeed a key left in place in it. The room was situated at the far end of the long corridor which led from the front hall past the library and appeared to span much of the southern side-wall of the great house. He could well appreciate how, isolated as it was from the rest of the house, the orangery could lend itself to the enablement of forbidden liaisons.

The first of the two chamber maids to appear was Eliza, who, like so many other members of staff, had little to add to his store of information. She was very young and quite quiet, and was, she said, a recent addition to the Rosings staff. She told Archer that she had been suffering from a heavy head-cold and had retired well before nine on Thursday evening with Mrs Flowerday's blessing. She had blushed deeply at his question regarding nocturnal comings and goings through the door to the room they sat in but assured him that she had no knowledge of such activity.

The second chamber maid, Alison, was an older woman with a hard face and sly eyes. She entered the orangery as Eliza was leaving and watched her go.

'She'll have been about as useful as a holed butter-churn, I'll not doubt.' Alison looked at Archer, shaking her head. 'She's been here more than two month by my reckoning and still needs watching like a hawk as she goes about her work. Still... I'd wager she'll get preferment before I ever do. Mrs Flowerday does like a nicely spoken girl.'

Archer was rather taken aback by the woman's forthright approach. He cleared his throat and made a show of looking at his notes. 'We are questioning all members of the Rosings staff regarding Thursday night,' he began.

'And have any of them told you anything?'

Archer blinked. 'Any information obtained is a matter for Sir John Bright and myself. However, if you do have something to add, I would be very grateful to hear it.'

'As it happens, no. I remember Thursday evening very well because Mrs Flowerday let her Highness there go to bed early on account of a cold. That left me with the three bedchambers to prepare, and they all wanted warming pans put through. I wasn't best pleased, I can tell you, and I got myself to bed as soon as I could.'

Archer glanced over at the door in the corner and then back at Alison. 'We've been hearing some rumours,' he said, 'that servants sometimes make use of that door over there, in the hours of darkness.'

Alison laughed drily. 'Now why would that be, I wonder?'

Archer felt his face becoming warm. He frowned sternly to cover his embarrassment.

The chamber maid shrugged. 'I won't gainsay it. You'll not know what it's like to be in service, Mr Archer. Our lives are not our own. We might as well all have been press-ganged, for the amount of freedom we get. But we're still people, you understand? The young ones especially...'

Archer cleared his throat again. 'Is there anyone in particular...?'

'Now that *would* be telling!'

Archer sighed. He wished suddenly that Bright had accompanied him. However, he was alone this time and knew that it was his duty to ask, given that this woman was clearly prepared to talk plainly.

'Do any of the men ever – forgive me for asking you this, but – do any of the men in service here ever take advantage of the very young maids?'

'What a question! And how it relates to the murder of the rector, I know not. But no, Mr Archer. They'd soon hear from me if they did. We'd not let the likes of Sally and Ruth fall into the hands of men such as Barker and John. Us older ones, we have to stand in for their own mothers when they're in service.'

'That's most commendable.' He paused. 'Er... what about Margaret?'

'Margaret?'

'She is not so young in years as some of the others, but is of a disposition to be led astray, perhaps?'

'Goodness me, sir, I can see you are bent on guarding us all from sin as well as from thieves and murderers. But, as you ask, Mr Archer, I don't really think Margaret is the sort of girl to attract followers of any sort. What we have to watch out for with her is fits.' She shuddered. 'They're horrible to see, believe me.'

'I can well believe you.'

'Mind you, she's another little favourite of Mrs Flowerday's. Only the other day, she was given a cast-off cloak that used to be Miss Anne's. Crimson plush it is and only a few bare patches. Mrs Flowerday says she's of a size and that's why she had it, but honestly! Crimson plush on a between maid?'

'I understand she was left an orphan and that Lady Catherine took responsibility for her, and I suppose with her illness...'

'All that's as may be, Mr Archer. But crimson plush?'

Archer could not think of anything to say, so he thanked Alison and told her she might leave. He felt reasonably pleased with the encounter and made some notes with his pencil.

Just as he was rising to leave the orangery, he saw the small door opening, and the old head gardener, Dudgeon, appeared.

'Ah, Mr Archer,' he said, 'what brings you here today?'

'I was directed here to conduct my interviews. Apparently, they are very busy in the servants' quarters preparing for a visit by the bishop.'

Dudgeon sighed and rolled his eyes. 'Don't I know it, Mr Archer. I've had orders left right and centre today. Pounds of this and pounds of that, flowers for here and flowers for there. You'd think the man was bringing the whole cathedral close, and not just himself. I'm to see if any of the oranges will be ripe for the bishop's breakfast, if you'd believe it. I've told them it's too early, but they don't listen.'

Archer looked up at the fruit. 'What does it taste like, Mr Dudgeon?'

The old man made his way to a small tree at the far end and, after examining each fruit short-sightedly, plucked one and brought it back to Archer.

'Here,' he said, with a wink. 'You take this home, young man.' He dropped his voice confidentially. 'It's an early variety.'

*

At the same time Archer was being introduced to the wonders of the orangery, Mary Bennet was being shown into the library by Barker, the head footman. The latter's attitude seemed so disdainful that it took all her courage not to turn on her heel and depart immediately. She was quite flustered by the time the library door closed behind him, leaving her in the company of a concerned Anne de Bourgh.

'Why, Miss Bennet, you are most welcome, but I fear you are out of sorts. Are you unwell? I must send down for a reviving cordial at once.'

'Oh... No, thank you, Miss de Bourgh, I am not unwell.' Mary sat nervously in the armchair to which she was directed by her companion. 'It is just a silly fancy of mine, that's all. It seemed to me that your footman thinks me unworthy to call upon you... me being my father's daughter. You told me yourself of the gossip you had overheard among the servants.'

Anne frowned. 'Dear Miss Bennet, you must dismiss all such

thoughts immediately. My mother gave her approval of our acquaintance only last evening, and that is all that matters in this house. Please pay no heed to Barker. I fear his attitude is sometimes far from that which is desirable in a senior footman. Indeed, I don't believe he would have risen to the position he has were it not that he was favoured by my father when he lived. I think that my mother feels duty bound to respect my father's choice.'

Mary smiled gratefully, her confidence somewhat restored by Anne's kind words. She looked around the library.

'Is Mrs Jenkinson not with you today?' It was unusual to see Anne without her constant companion.

'She fell asleep after luncheon and I was loath to disturb her rest. She will no doubt be most indignant when I tell her that she has missed your visit, but I do feel that, at her age, rest is most important. We shall just have to manage on our own.'

'I am certain we shall manage perfectly.'

*

For the next two hours, Mary and Anne were absorbed in their studies, sitting one either side of the small walnut table conveniently positioned in one of the library's great windows. From time to time, Mary looked out at the rolling parkland of Rosings in its tranquil beauty, and knew that she would give everything she had if only the past few days could be wiped from history, together with the terrible burden they had brought to her father and herself. Even happy times like this one were now bordered by black despair. Mary was no philosopher, but she was becoming daily more certain that all happiness must be paid for.

Her eyes met those of Anne, who was regarding her across the table with a compassionate expression.

'You are sad still, Miss Bennet.'

Mary sighed. 'It gives me the greatest pleasure to be here, Miss de Bourgh, and I am more grateful than I can say, but I think all the time of my dear papa. Every day that passes brings no relief. Indeed, I feel more and more certain that matters must come to a head soon. I understand that the bishop is to bury Mr Collins on Thursday. I shall be glad of that, of course, but I worry that he will demand an answer as to what happened to his rector here. He may force Sir John's hand into naming my father. No-one else has motive but him. And Sir William Lucas will arrive. He is a dear family friend, but how will he think of us now? I feel that I am in one of those dreams where my legs have turned to lead, and I cannot run from the monster which is bearing down on me.'

Anne reached over and took Mary's hand in hers.

'Take courage, Miss Bennet. Your father is innocent of this deed and we must trust in the good Lord that no ill shall befall him.'

'I shall try to do as you say. I think you are my only comfort, Miss de Bourgh.'

'Then you must keep me company again tomorrow afternoon. I believe the bishop is not expected until evening, so we shall be undisturbed in our studies.'

'You have made wonderful progress, Miss de Bourgh.'

Anne smiled confidentially. 'Truth to tell, I have been pursuing my studies for a little while each night, following my Bible study. I have been quite determined. Why, one night I forgot to bring up the Addendum to my Grammar and had to tiptoe downstairs to fetch it when all were asleep... Oh!'

Mary was alarmed to see her consternation. 'Is something amiss?'

'Not really, Miss Bennet. It's just that it has now come to me

that that night was Thursday, the night when poor Mr Collins...'
She shuddered. 'To think I was abroad when all the time there
was someone nearby intent upon murder.'

'I cannot even contemplate such a thing,' said Mary.

Anne was silent for a while and then looked up with worried
eyes.

'Sir John asked me most particularly about my movements on
Thursday night. I just said I was in bed. I forgot, you see. I was
so shocked about the poor rector. Do you think I should tell him
about my visit to the library?'

'I expect as you didn't see anything important, it doesn't really
matter, does it?'

'But he did want to know every little detail so that he could
complete the puzzle.'

'Then you must tell him about it when you next see him.'
Mary thought uncomfortably of the information which she was
hiding, and found herself wondering for the thousandth time
whether she could ever contemplate revealing it to the
magistrate.

22

Seated upon the bench on Hunsford Village Green, Archer and Bright were able to contemplate the stocks, happily without an occupant on this sunny autumn afternoon.

'Do you make much use of that contraption, Robert?'

Archer shrugged. 'Rarely, sir. It can be of use when a villager is persistently inebriated and will listen to no sense. At least it stops him fighting all he meets or going home to beat his wife and children senseless. Though such men seldom learn from their humiliation.'

'A reasonable answer, as always, Robert. But I am grateful that such devices are largely falling out of fashion in these enlightened times. We who are responsible for the upkeep of the law must always have reason as our watchword, as I believe you do, my friend.'

Bright had suggested a stroll about the village while they conferred upon their latest findings and Archer had concurred readily enough in the hope that he might thus be afforded a chance encounter with Miss Smith. He still felt ashamed of his behaviour towards her on Sunday afternoon, bur hoped that, in Bright's company, his embarrassment might be lessened. He glanced over to where the draper's shop stood but could see little behind the colourful awning which protected the window display from the sun.

'Now,' said Bright, 'you told me that one of the chamber maids was more forthcoming than the other?'

'Yes, Sir John. Alison is the older of the two women and not afraid of speaking plainly. She confirmed that some of the Rosings staff do indeed make use of the small door at the corner of the orangery in order to consort with one another, though she was unwilling to name anyone outright. I also took the opportunity to question her regarding the possible misuse of the younger servants. She was most adamant that this would not be allowed.'

'What of Margaret? She gave us to understand that she has been in the habit of meeting our footman, John. Of course, she would not be considered particularly young...'

'I mentioned Margaret, yes, sir, as someone perhaps less able to take responsibility for herself and therefore in need of such protection as is afforded to the youngest ones. Alison was very clear that she did not consider Margaret likely prey for any of the men – she did mention John and Barker as examples, by the way – so if there is a liaison in existence between Margaret and John, it does not appear to be widely known about.'

'Hmm... interesting. Can the girl be deceiving herself, do you think, Robert?'

'I know not, sir. If John is unwilling to speak, then I cannot see how we shall learn the full truth of the matter, the girl being as she is.'

'You are right. At least Alison appears to regard Barker and John in the same light that we do. However, all this is rather removed from our main purpose. We have now completed our interviews, I believe, and are really very little nearer to discovering our murderer. The case is as perplexing as ever.'

Archer nodded glumly. He was beginning to despair of ever returning to his lathe, and – although his apprentices were carrying on his business as well as they could – he had already had to refer an emergency repair to another wheelwright in a nearby village.

'What will happen, sir – if we fail to uncover the true identity of the felon? Will this case simply remain unsolved?'

Bright looked grim. 'I fear not, Robert. I think that Lady Catherine would never tolerate such an outcome. We shall be compelled to name our most likely suspect in that event.'

'That would be Mr Bennet.'

'Indeed so, although I personally find it most difficult to see the man as a murderer. Yet, he had both opportunity and motive, and, moreover, had been heard arguing with Mr Collins for days before that man's death. He is clever enough to have taken and used a Rosings paper knife for his purpose. What can be said in his favour?'

'Very little, Sir John, when you put it like that. Will you then accuse him?'

'Lady Catherine has asked me to attend her tomorrow in advance of the bishop's visit, but I shall attempt to delay any accusation for as long as I can. We have no actual evidence against the man. I shall talk to him again tomorrow morning. You need not accompany me. See to your business, Robert. I have had you removed from it too often these past few days.'

'Thank you, sir. I should be grateful to you.'

'Very good. Now, I think we have concluded our discussions for today.'

Rising, the two men were about to take leave of each other when, quite unexpectedly, the object of Archer's affections, Miss Smith, appeared before them, a little out-of-breath and daintily holding her skirts clear of the path, which was still muddy after the rainfall of Sunday night.

'Oh, Sir John! Mr Archer! Please excuse my interruption. My aunt saw you talking here and has sent me to request your

141

company tomorrow afternoon at three o'clock for tea. Our shop closes early on a Wednesday, you see.'

Bright glanced at Archer, who was appearing dumbfounded, and then inclined his head gallantly. 'You must thank your mother, Miss Smith,' he said, 'but for my part I very much regret that I have to decline. I am summoned to Rosings on official business tomorrow afternoon. However, I feel sure that my constable here will be delighted to accept your kind invitation.'

They both looked expectantly at Archer, who, reddening, mumbled his thanks and agreed on the time. At which Miss Smith, with a little curtsey, turned and tripped away.

Bright clapped Archer on the back. 'You see, Robert. It wasn't so difficult. Now you are on your way! Something tells me that that young lady's aunt may have set her sights upon you as a possible match for her niece!'

Archer could hear him chuckling as he walked over to where his horse was waiting.

*

'I warned you to keep your mouth shut!'

The great hall at Rosings was silent on that Tuesday evening, apart from the ticking of the long-case clock and the occasional whirring of its striking mechanism. Replying, John kept his voice as low as he could. 'I told you yesterday, Mr Barker, I don't know why they're asking about me and Margaret. I've made sure no-one suspects, and it's got nothing to do with Mr Collins' murder, after all.'

'Maybe they think she did it!'

'They're accusing me of debauching her.'

'Well, that's more or less the truth, isn't it?'

John glared at the head footman angrily. 'All right, but what if it gets to Mr Harries' ears, or, heaven help me, Lady Catherine's? I don't see why I should lose my position and my good name. It was done for both of us, wasn't it? Just because you're too high and mighty to do your own dirty work.'

'You would have benefitted nearly as much as me. Had a bit of fun as well.'

'Fun? A few kisses and a fumble in the rose garden! She's no beauty, you know.'

'Well, it was dark, wasn't it? What do you expect? If Martha had stayed on in service here, we could have roped her in, with a bit of luck. She was game for almost anything, as you and I well know. I don't think that new chamber maid is going to be anything like that, more's the pity. Still, Margaret should have fitted the bill – with the rector, that is.'

'Should have! Seems to me she took against him.'

'Well, I still don't understand it, John. She always does what she's told, and, as you say, she's happy enough with your attentions. Besides, a man like him, it'd have been over before she knew what was what.'

'You don't think she did do it, do you? The murder, I mean?'

Barker frowned. 'We've no way of knowing, have we? I can't imagine her being violent, but I suppose you can never tell. She has those fits, doesn't she? Had one Thursday night, even. Mrs Flowerday had to excuse her from duties on Friday morning... You never know what goes on in the head of somebody like that. Maybe you've had a lucky escape, John!'

John regarded him angrily. 'It was your idea. I don't see why I should get all the blame... What do I say if they ask me again about her?'

'Keep to your original story. It's her word against yours and she's the one who's simple.'

23

It was with a heavy heart that Bright walked through the gate and up to the parsonage door the following morning. Reason told him that logic pointed directly to Mr Bennet as the murderer, but he could not prevent the feeling that to accuse him now would be an injustice; that there was, somewhere, a large piece of the jigsaw puzzle yet to be discovered.

The door was opened by the little maid, Alice, who regarded him with frightened eyes and seemed uncertain what to do with him until Mrs Parkinson appeared and showed him into the study. 'I'll find Mr Bennet for you now, Sir John,' she said.

As he waited, Bright found himself sending up an unspoken prayer for something to be said today, or some evidence to be retrieved, which might allow him to be absolutely certain that he had uncovered the murderer of Mr Collins and put to rest the doubt which afflicted him increasingly painfully. He had never borne lightly the burden of his office, with its ultimate power to deprive a man of his very life.

'Sir John.' Mr Bennet, though never a large man, seemed smaller than before. His eyes were dull and bloodshot. Behind him, before he closed the door upon her, Bright caught sight of Mary Bennet, a horrified expression on her face.

'Good morning, Mr Bennet,' said Bright. 'I fear that my visit causes consternation to your family and servants.'

Mr Bennet shrugged. 'Your visit was only to be expected, sir.

Please take a seat. We must rest when we can… I take it you are come to accuse me.'

Bright was exasperated by the man's passivity. Such a path could lead only to the gallows. 'No, Mr Bennet. I am not… Or I am not here with that primary intention. But I must ask you, as an honest man, which I believe you are, did you kill Mr Collins?'

'I did not.'

Bright sighed. 'Then you must help me to prove that, Mr Bennet. You must tell me all you can about Mr Collins and your dealings with him. Is there anything at all which can exonerate you? Any small detail which you overlooked on our previous interview? Otherwise, you must agree, the finger of guilt must point only at you.'

Mr Bennet frowned and rose from his seat to pace the room. 'As I told you, I came here to plead my case with my cousin regarding the entail on Longbourn. I sincerely wish now that I had left well alone, but there, what's done cannot be undone. The matter had been preying on my mind more and more of late. The years are passing, and I was desperate to secure the future of my wife and remaining unmarried daughters. All right, I believe Kitty would be perfectly content to divide her time between Mrs Bingley and Mrs Darcy, and not be too much of a burden to those households – she does this for much of her time, even now – but as for my wife and Mary… Mrs Bennet is a proud woman, Sir John. It would break her to have to fall back upon the charity of others. And Mary is a very special young lady, with her own interests, but not well suited to being out and about in society, even such as that enjoyed by her aunt and uncle Gardiner in London. So, I came to Hunsford.'

'But you argued.'

'Yes, sir, we did. I could find no means to convince Mr Collins to agree to delay that time when, after my death, he would take possession of Longbourn. For a clergyman, he was little swayed by considerations of charity. If I were to be honest, I might say that he valued his own worth highly and was intent upon taking what he felt he deserved.'

'Are you able to give me any more information as to why the rector should have been abroad in the grounds of Rosings so late at night?'

'As you will have heard, Mr Collins was in the habit of walking in the gardens there. He said that it helped to concentrate his mind when composing his sermons. Also, I believe he was much disturbed by the new baby's crying, and, indeed, by his own wife's indisposition following the baby's birth six months ago... Forgive me, Sir John, it is wrong to speak of indelicate matters.'

'No, please do, Mr Bennet. Believe me, I must know everything if I am to help you.'

'Very well. While Mrs Collins has been unwell, Mr Collins has been obliged to sleep in one of the smaller bedrooms, alone. He remarked to me that he was finding such an arrangement extremely inconvenient and that... he was desirous of resuming the comforts of the marital bed. I believe his walks in the cool of the evening were an attempt to divert his thoughts.'

*

Mary Bennet, distraught at the arrival of Sir John Bright, was still weeping when she saw, from the window, a familiar carriage drawing up before the parsonage. Opening the front door, she rushed into the arms of Sir William Lucas, who had just alighted.

'Why, Mary!' he said. 'Whatever ails you so, my dear?'

'Oh, Sir William,' she cried. 'Dear Papa is to be arrested and hanged!'

'What? That cannot be true, Mary. What has put such a grim idea into your head?'

'Sir John Bright is now in the study with Papa, Sir William. I know he means to accuse my dear father. I heard him saying that Papa was the one who would gain from my cousin's death and was most likely to have killed him!'

'Look,' said Sir William, 'I am only just arrived from Hertfordshire and know nothing of all this, save that my son-in-law is dead. Let us ask Mrs Parkinson for tea in the parlour and you can tell me all about it. I take it that Charlotte is not yet risen... No?... Then I must wait a little longer to comfort her.'

It was a great relief to Mary to be able to talk to Sir William Lucas about the grim events of the past few days and to share her own fears for the future. Their families had long shared a close friendship, and Sir William was so kind and reassuring that she felt as if a great burden had been lifted from upon her shoulders. For some time, she had looked forward to Sir William's arrival with foreboding; she had worried that he would surely blame her father, as many people seemed to, for the death of Mr Collins, which had left his daughter a widow and their children fatherless. However, these fears had lasted no longer than the time it took her to open the door to him.

'Thank you so much for listening to me, Sir William. I have felt myself so alone in recent days. My father has been distracted, and I have not been willing to trouble Charlotte when she is so frail.'

'What of Mrs Bennet and your sisters, my dear? Have you not written to them? I am certain they would come to your aid immediately.'

'My father has forbidden it. He will not have them troubled. I am... I am to write to my uncle Gardiner if my father is arrested.'

'Forgive me, Mary – this means that your father has considered this possibility?'

'Yes. He has. Even he cannot deny that he, of all people, has reason to be guilty. I am increasingly of the opinion that he is resigned to his fate.'

'Well, we cannot permit that. I have known your father for many years, Mary, and I am perfectly sure that he is incapable of committing such a deed. I shall see this Sir John Bright immediately to vouch for his character. Now, I hope you are a little cheered.'

'I am better, Sir William.'

'Good. I must say, I feel quite angry to think that a young woman such as yourself should have received so little support from the people here. You will be relieved to return to Hertfordshire, I don't doubt.'

'Indeed I shall – provided my dear father is with me.' She hesitated and regarded him shyly. 'I must mention, though, that – apart from Charlotte, of course – there is one young lady here who has proved a true friend. It is Miss Anne de Bourgh.'

'Anne de Bourgh?' Sir William frowned as he recalled the young heiress of Lady Catherine. He had dined at Rosings several times during visits to his daughter and son-in-law but could not remember even hearing the young lady speak. Although she had seemed nervous and lacking in confidence, he had concluded that she was probably too proud to make conversation with a provincial squire and his family.

'She has been most kind to me, Sir William. I have kept company with her at Rosings and she has expressed the warmest affection towards me and my father. I am to visit her again this afternoon.'

'Well, well. How extraordinary! You are fortunate indeed, Mary, to have found such preferment. Though it is no more than you deserve. Your support for your father is exemplary.'

No, thought Mary, though she did not speak the words aloud. I could and should do more.

*

Sir William Lucas spent a considerable time with Sir John Bright but, on taking leave of each other, their faces were grim. Seeing this, Mary knew that there was only one course of action left to her and she consequently hurried outside to waylay the magistrate as he waited for Parkinson to fetch his horse.

'Sir John,' she began, 'I am sorry to delay you like this, but there is something I must tell you.'

'Miss Bennet! If you have remembered something, I should be very grateful to hear it... But, come, you are shivering. You must let me escort you back into the parsonage.'

'No! I mean, no, thank you, Sir John. I cannot speak inside. I... I cannot be overheard, you see.' She frowned and looked away. 'This is most difficult for me. It is something that was told to me by a member of the parsonage staff, in confidence, you understand. It does not have a connection with the death of my cousin that I can see, but I am somehow convinced that it is important. I am loath to break a confidence, but I must save my father!'

Bright inclined his head gravely. 'I assure you of my discretion,' he said.

Haltingly, Mary recounted the tale told her by the children's nurse, after which Bright was silent for several moments.

'Thank you,' he said. 'I have much thinking to do, but I agree with you that this unfortunate episode may well have some bearing upon the rector's death. In the meantime, Miss Bennet, keep your spirits up. I assure you that I shall endeavour to do all I can to get to the truth of what happened on Thursday night.'

As he rode away, Bright's brow was furrowed. An idea was forming in his mind which was so unwelcome as to be almost unthinkable, but which might at last begin to shed light upon the rector's final hour.

24

'Please come in, Mr Archer.'

Mrs Smith showed Archer to a pretty room in their living quarters above the draper's shop. There were flower-upholstered chairs and frilled curtains at the window.

'It is a pleasant room,' he said. 'I fear that it puts my own establishment to shame.'

Mrs Smith beamed. 'We are fortunate to have our choice of all the fabrics at our disposal. And you are a single man, Mr Archer. You cannot expect the same home comforts as are enjoyed by your married acquaintances.'

'That is true, Mrs Smith. Though Mrs Teale looks after me very well.'

'I am sure she does. I have heard that she is a very capable cook.'

'Is it time for tea, dear?' Mr Smith patted his stomach. 'I have cut three coats today. I have need of something to revive me.'

'How you exaggerate, Mr Smith! I'm sure Mr Archer here could teach you a thing or two about hard work. How is your business, Mr Archer?'

'It continues to thrive, although I have been obliged to assume my role of constable rather too often this past week.'

'And are you nearing a resolution?'

'No, Mr Smith, not yet. It is a most troubling crime.'

'Indeed it is, Mr Archer,' put in Mrs Smith. 'We have not felt safe in our own beds since the news of it reached us. Who could have imagined that anyone would attack a man of the cloth in such a way?'

'Especially not in Hunsford,' said Mr Smith, 'and at Rosings, of all places. I can only think it is the curse of the age. Perhaps there are revolutionaries among us. France is too close for my liking.'

'That is something to think about, certainly,' replied Archer. 'Though we are still of an opinion that our murderer is someone closer to home.'

The door opened and Miss Smith appeared with a dish of scones, followed by a young maid with a tray of tea things. Mrs Smith put her forefinger against her lips. 'Here is Sarah, Mr Archer. We must cease all this talk of murder. The young are so sensitive. Thank you, Meg.'

Cups and plates were duly handed around and Archer was helped to a scone.

'Sarah baked these herself, Mr Archer,' said Mrs Smith proudly. 'She is most accomplished in the kitchen.'

'I'm sure they are delicious,' said Archer.

In truth, the scone was a little too dry, but – unwilling to disappoint the cook – Archer took a second, and even a third. He smiled encouragingly at Miss Smith and sought around for something to say to her. He was relieved to spy a sketch book on a nearby table.

'Are those your sketches, Miss Smith?'

'Yes, Mr Archer. Would you like to see them?'

'I should be most interested.'

The sketches were, as Miss Smith had suggested on their previous meeting, mainly of plants and flowers. They were competently done and nicely coloured, and Miss Smith had written in the names of some of them in a neat hand.

'You have not named them all,' said Archer, in an attempt to find something to say.

'No, Mr Archer. I am afraid I have yet to learn the names of all the plants. I was brought up in the town and was not much in the countryside. My uncle and aunt tell me they are too busy to accompany me on my walks to study nature.'

Mrs Smith laughed. 'Indeed we are, Sarah. But perhaps Mr Archer might accompany you one Sunday afternoon? He has younger legs than us and I'm sure he knows the names of all the wild flowers.'

They all looked at Archer expectantly, and, reddening a little, he confessed that nothing would give him greater pleasure.

*

At Rosings, Sir John Bright was also seated with a teacup before him, but that was where the similarity with Archer's situation ended. He faced Lady Catherine across the rather chilly drawing room. She had dismissed the maid who had come to make up the dull fire until a later hour, confiding in Bright afterwards that she found the day unduly warm.

It had not taken long for Bright to outline their findings to date, unable, as he was, to mention any of the information he had been given that morning at the parsonage, let alone, for the present at least, his suspicions regarding the activities of the footman and the between maid. Lady Catherine looked at him sternly.

'For all your questioning and interviewing, Sir John – which has been a source of great inconvenience to myself and my staff – you still appear to be as much in the dark about the identity of Mr Collins' killer as you were on Friday morning.'

'As I told you, Lady Catherine, we still have some threads to follow up.'

'Threads! Jigsaw puzzles! This whole investigation seems to be a game to you. It has been nearly a week now, the place has been turned upside down, and it seems you have no answers of any kind. Poor Mr Collins is to be buried tomorrow. I expect the bishop within two hours. What, pray, am I to tell him? It was most inconvenient that such a crime should have taken place at Rosings at all, but now we are being told that there is no felon to be brought to justice. This is too bad, Sir John, too bad.'

'We shall discover this man's identity, I assure you, Lady Catherine. But I fear we must be patient.'

'Patient! Tell that to Mrs Collins, if you will, and her poor fatherless children.'

Bright seized at a straw. 'As regards Mrs Collins, Lady Catherine, I am pleased to inform you that her father, Sir William Lucas, is today arrived from Hertfordshire. He will, I am sure, be of the utmost comfort to her and to his grandchildren. I was at the parsonage this morning and was pleased to witness their reunion. Mrs Collins seemed much revived at seeing him.'

'I don't doubt it. He is an affable gentleman and devoted to his family, I think. Will Mrs Collins return to Hertfordshire shortly?'

'I believe she is still too unwell for the present, but Sir William mentioned that he will return to Kent together with his wife before long, to supervise packing and so forth. They are anxious not to prevent the speedy installation of Mr Collins' successor.'

Lady Catherine nodded grimly. 'I will be obliged to give that matter much thought in the very near future. It really is all most unsettling.' She glared at Bright, as if everything were actually his fault. 'So, Sir John, how are you to proceed? I cannot stomach another week without result. You are, of course, the magistrate, and I must respect that, but it does seem to me that there is one person who had both opportunity and reason to murder Mr Collins.'

Bright sighed. 'You speak of Mr Bennet, of course.'

'I do. Have you confronted him, Sir John?'

'I did so this very morning. He acknowledges that he must appear guilty but is adamant that he is not. Indeed, Sir William Lucas came to speak to me on this very subject; he wished most sincerely to vouch for Mr Bennet. He says that he has been a friend of his for many years and cannot, in any circumstances, see him in the role of killer. I have myself found him to be a mild-mannered man.'

'Be that as it may, there are wayward elements in that family, which, it seems, has been sent by God to plague me. Miss Mary Bennet is at this moment at study in the library with my own dear daughter. They are learning Greek, if you will! For some unaccountable reason, Anne has taken to the creature.'

'Miss de Bourgh is a most Christian young lady. You must be proud of her.'

'I shall be more pleased when Miss Bennet returns to Hertfordshire. Meanwhile, I must suffer her company for my daughter's sake... Now, I believe you mentioned that you were looking into the possible involvement of poachers?'

Bright had indeed said this, though his intention had merely been to flesh out the too-bare bones of his report. He had mentioned no-one by name.

'It is a possibility, Lady Catherine. A man was seen by one of your footmen in the grounds of Rosings on Thursday evening.'

'Then he must be sought out as soon as possible. You have my permission to enlist the help of my keepers in this work. You must inform the constable.'

'Thank you, Lady Catherine.'

'Now, if that is all you have to offer, I shall bid you farewell. I must prepare to greet the bishop.'

Bright rose hastily as a footman appeared at his side to escort him out.

*

'Procurement!' Archer's eyes widened in surprise.

'Not so loud, my friend,' said Bright, looking cautiously around them at the motley crowd of labourers and yeoman farmers who made up the early evening clientele of The Three Crowns, 'we do not want to be overheard.'

Archer lowered his voice. 'But *procurement*! At Rosings? How can that even be possible?' In his mind's eye, he suddenly had an appalling picture of Lady Catherine being denounced by county society as a madam.

'It is merely my own interpretation of information so far obtained. I may be shooting a long way from the centre of the target, of course, but I cannot ignore the feeling that we are nearing the truth.'

Archer frowned, another unwelcome thought filling his mind. 'You surely cannot think that... that *Margaret* has been so ill-used?'

'I fear very much that that is the case.'

'But she is simple, sir, and prone to fits as we have been told!'

'Exactly, Robert. She is available for such abuse for that very reason. Someone stronger in the mind would, of course, be better equipped to object. Remember what she said, that John had been paying court to her? We thought at the time, didn't we, that she seemed an unlikely object of such attention. And from your conversation with the chamber maid, Alison, this was not suspected by her fellow-servants.'

'I can recall Margaret telling us that she does what she is told,' said Archer slowly.

'Precisely so. My theory is that she was flattered by the footman and invited to meet him after hours, which she then did on several occasions. However, this was done on his part not for reasons of affection but for his own cynical ends. Servants' hall gossip knows no bounds, in my experience, and it is very probable that word had come to his ears of the rector's temporary estrangement from his wife's bed and the gentleman's consequent impatience with that state of affairs. After all, Mr Collins had not shrunk from complaining of it to Mr Bennet. My idea is that John approached Mr Collins with a proposition, and, in return for some sum of money, arranged for Margaret to meet the rector in the grounds of Rosings.'

'How would she agree to that, Sir John? She believes herself in love with the footman.'

'I cannot know that, Robert. Suffice it to say that he had done enough to inspire her loyalty, and had broken her in, as it were, to the ways of the flesh.'

'If you are right, it was a most vicious crime. Mr Harries must be told of it at once.'

'Not quite at once, Robert. It is merely surmise, as of yet. I shall need proof but have no idea how to get it. Also, although it was, as you say, a vicious enterprise, I cannot see how it relates to Mr Collins' murder. However, I do feel certain that it must, and to speak too soon might alert our murderer and allow him to evade capture. We must be circumspect.'

'So, how are we to proceed?'

'I must set my mind upon that. In the meantime, Robert, I have a task for you.'

25

The following day being that of Mr Collins' funeral, Archer had been able to spend time again in his workshop. The tolling of the bell had reached him clearly as he turned his lathe. He pondered on the strange turn of events which had caused the magistrate to cast his net in a different direction. But for that, he knew, it would have been Bright's intention to arrest Mr Bennet straight after the funeral.

Now, seated upon a fallen tree-trunk, he pulled his woollen cape a little closer around his shoulders. A cool wind had sprung up; he could clearly hear it rustling the leaves high above his head. It was late evening, and the light was gone. He had so far made several circuits of this part of the wood but had surprised only a few pigeons. In other parts of the estate, he knew, the Rosings keepers had been patrolling their previously agreed patches. Now, it was too dark to walk far from the paths and he was relying upon his ears and the instincts of his dog to alert him to the presence of a poacher.

He had not been pleased by Bright's request to arrange a watch in the woods. It caused him to think only too bitterly of the events of Sunday evening last and his humiliation by the young stable lad. However, it was Lady Catherine's will, so must be done. He was slightly cheered by the prospect of perhaps apprehending Michael Flannery, after all; this was a well organised watch, and he had no doubt that of poaching, the man was guilty.

Archer's mind wandered to the subject of Miss Smith. He had been greatly cheered by the events of the previous afternoon, and it had been agreed that he would accompany her on an expedition to study the local flora this coming Sunday afternoon. He was looking forward to it most eagerly, although he was still worried that he had yet to master the art of conversation with the fairer sex. When he had mentioned the arrangement to Bright, the latter's eyes had twinkled mischievously, and he had brought the blood to Archer's face with his comments about how far the two might take their study of nature. However, he had promised to furnish Archer with a herbal from his own library, so that the latter might impress Miss Smith with his knowledge, not only of the names in current usage, but also with their Latin equivalents. 'You will need to supervise the young lady very closely as she writes those in!' he had said, with a smile.

If their walk were a success, reasoned Archer, then more would surely follow. He found himself wondering how soon he might broach the subject of marriage. He had reason to hope that her family would approve of such a match. His business was thriving, he had a ready home to offer her, and his role as constable gave him some standing in the community. He was concerned that he would be unable to find the words with which to approach the young lady herself, but perhaps when he was more familiar with her company, that problem would be resolved.

In the distance, he recognised the shrill squeal of an animal in distress, followed by the barking of a dog and a faintly heard human shout. His heart beat a little faster and he stood up and looked all around him, his eyes straining in the darkness. Could it be that one of the keepers had indeed apprehended someone? It had been agreed that, in this event, a whistle would be blown to alert other members of the watch and that all would then converge on the boundary of the wood, so that the culprit might be handed over into the safe keeping of the constable.

When no whistle-call came, Archer sat down again. Presumably it had been a false alarm. He felt disappointed. In his mind's eye, he had seen Michael Flannery being hauled before him by one of Lady Catherine's burly keepers, and his eventual despatch to the village lock-up, there to await the assizes. Now it seemed that this evening had constituted yet another wasted use of his time. No doubt there would be more such watches to come, as, according to Sir John Bright, Lady Catherine was convinced of their value in apprehending Mr Collins' murderer.

The faint chiming of his timepiece announced to Archer that it was the hour when he and the keepers had agreed to abandon the watch and make for their beds. He rose again, stiffly, and struggled for some time to light his lantern, the wick of which had become damp during his long vigil. He was determined not to repeat the wetting of his boots, such as had occurred on Sunday evening. Eventually, he had a light bright enough to see his way, and started to plod gloomily back towards the village, the dog, Peter, following behind.

Breasting a small rise in the ground, he suddenly came face to face with a man walking in the opposite direction. He was surprised to see that it was the very man who had been so recently on his mind.

'Michael Flannery!' he exclaimed. 'What business do you have in these woods at such a late hour? I have heard no nightingales tonight!'

The man glared at him and made no reply. Archer swung the lantern closer to him. 'Why,' he cried, 'your shirt is covered in blood, and I'll wager that I can see it on your hands as well. Now what have you to say for yourself?'

'I found a kitten entangled in the briars at the edge of the wood nearest the village. The poor creature was likely to rip itself to pieces in its efforts to escape. I am sure that even you would be unwilling to leave it there.'

'And where is this *kitten* now?'

'I wrapped it in my neckerchief and left it in the care of a kind lady.'

'What *lady*?'

'That I cannot say.'

Archer frowned in exasperation. 'What *I* can say is that it's far more likely that you caught a nice fat rabbit and left it in the hands of someone who rewarded you for it.'

'As God is my witness, Constable, it was a kitten.'

'So why don't you prove it to me? Tell me where this woman lives, so that I may see for myself.'

'I cannot. It must not be known that she is friendly with someone like me. You understand, Constable? A stable lad, and Irish into the bargain. That's all I'm saying.'

'Well, that's very convenient for you, isn't it?' Archer was overcome with fatigue following his long evening's watch. His patience snapped. 'But it's not good enough for me,' he said. 'You're out in the woods at midnight, you've blood on you, and only a fairy tale for an excuse. I'm taking you to the lock-up. You can stew there for the rest of the night and I'll hope to have a better story from you tomorrow.'

He half expected the man to take to his heels, but he just shrugged wearily and allowed Archer to lead him back to the village.

26

The following day, Archer rose early and made his way to Rosings, where he notified the head keeper of Michael Flannery's detention, and also informed the head groom. Both were surprised that Flannery was suspected of poaching.

Archer, who now slightly regretted his hasty decision of the night before, explained his reasons for apprehending the young man, and made it clear that he had not, as yet, charged him with the crime. 'I shall make investigations today,' he said, 'and if it so turns out that the lad is telling the truth, there will, of course, be no charge to answer.'

He had not long returned to the village when an out-of-breath Patrick Flannery appeared in his yard, with a request to speak to him urgently.

'Excuse me, Mr Archer,' he said, 'I have run all the way from Rosings, and I must not be gone long, or Mr Kirkwood will have my guts for garters! I must see my brother, sir. I believe I have the answer for you – about his doings last night, I mean – if I can just talk to him first.'

Archer regarded him wearily. 'For God's sake, what is it now? I am thoroughly sick of you two, I can tell you. I suppose you have another fairy story for me – a stray dog run down by a cart, perhaps, and rescued by your saintly brother.'

'Mr Kirkwood told me Michael's story of the kitten, as you recounted it to him this morning. I am sure it is true, sir, and I will prove it to you, if only I might just see my brother.'

'Can you not tell me directly, if you already know what he was about last night?'

'No, sir, I need to get things clear. I promise it won't take more than a few minutes. Will you allow me that?'

Archer's patience was again beginning to run thin. He was most unwilling for these brothers to get the better of him but could feel the situation slipping from his grasp. Could he trust Patrick any more than the brother whom he had imprisoned? Perhaps the two would simply concoct some story which would again make a fool of him. However, he was tired after the late watch in the woods, anxious to return to his workshop, and most reluctant to spend his day on a wild goose chase after an apocryphal kitten. He had promised the head groom that he would not detain Flannery if his innocence could be proved, and if there was a possibility that Patrick could help do this, then his work would be done for him. He disliked Michael, that was true, but his conscience would never permit him to send someone for trial unjustly.

'Come with me,' he told Patrick. 'I shall open the cell for you. Knock upon the door when you are finished, and the old man who watches it for me will let you out. Will you then return to me with more information?'

'No, sir,' said Patrick, 'I think not. But if my plan works, then someone else may well be here to see you. I have high hopes of it, sir.'

'If this is some game, I can tell you that I won't stand for it...'

'No, no! It's not, sir. I promise you.'

Archer raised his eyebrows and shook his head as he walked with Patrick towards the lock-up.

*

Archer had only just set out his tools when his work was disturbed yet again, this time by Sir John Bright.

'Robert,' he said, 'I wanted to thank you for arranging the watch with the keepers last night. Tell me, did it bear fruit? I fear that Lady Catherine will not let me rest until I assure her that I have acted upon her instructions.'

Sighing, Archer recounted the events of the previous night. 'I was impetuous, Sir John, I know it. Though even you may agree that a person with a shirt soaked with blood must arouse suspicion.'

'Especially in the woods in the middle of the night,' agreed Bright. 'But do you think there is any chance he is telling the truth?'

'His brother seems to think so. But then, he would, wouldn't he? I don't know, sir. It seems to me to be the sort of tale which would seem possible in the light of day, but at that time of night? And who on earth can this "kind lady" be? Someone of dubious reputation, I don't doubt, if she receives stable boys at her door when most honest folk are in bed.'

'Or a married woman, perhaps, who must keep their liaison a secret. Such things do happen, you know, Robert, even, I imagine, in a village like Hunsford!'

'You could be right, Sir John. I should not be surprised to know that Michael Flannery was guilty of a dishonest relationship like that.'

'What, then, are your plans for the young man?'

'Well, according to Patrick, I am to expect a visitor who will shed light upon Michael's actions last night.'

'It is all very mysterious, Robert!'

'Mysterious, certainly, and somewhat unlikely, I fear. If this person – who, I imagine, must be the married woman of whom we spoke – does not present herself by the afternoon, I shall be forced to go from door to door in the village, enquiring about an injured kitten.'

'Not the best use of a constable's time. I do sympathise with you! Meanwhile, as you await your visitor and go about your work, could you concentrate your mind on how we might find out the truth of what happened between Margaret and John on the night of the murder? I have been racking my brains for hours at a time and have yet to reach any sort of conclusion. And yet I am convinced now that such knowledge would be the key to this whole confusing puzzle.'

'Do you think John could be our man, sir?'

'It's possible, I suppose. He is strong enough, and, I surmise, not particularly honest. However, why would he do it? If my supposition is right, though it galls me to think of it, then Mr Collins was a source of ready extra income for the man. And why would an under-footman be carrying a paper knife?'

'Surely not Margaret!'

'Surely not, Robert. She is so small and frail that I cannot imagine her capable of violence of any kind.'

'Unless she was frightened, sir. I have heard that fear can lend people extra strength sometimes.'

'That is certainly so. I have seen it myself in battle.'

'And she does have fits, Sir John. She possibly would not know what she was about.'

'Possibly not, possibly not. But why would Margaret have a paper knife? She is a between maid. I doubt she can even read... We have much to consider, Robert.'

*

For the rest of the morning, Archer worked at his lathe with an increasingly heavy heart. He knew that he could not detain Michael Flannery indefinitely without charge, and that he would soon have to apply himself to investigating his story. It was a pleasant autumn day, and his work was congenial. He had no wish to abandon his tools yet again in order to assume his role as constable.

At eleven o'clock, he helped himself to a tankard of ale and sat in the sun to collect his thoughts. Mentally, he made a list of all the houses and cottages in the village, and then excluded those where there were no female inhabitants – such as his own, he realised. There still remained the majority of houses to visit. He sighed. This past week had been a trying one. Initially, he could not deny that the notion of investigating a murder had caused him some excitement. It was far removed from his usual experience. However, their general lack of progress had proved more frustrating than he could have imagined, and there was still no obvious way out of the maze. Now he had to enquire after a probably fictitious kitten!

He set down his tankard and prepared to return to his work. Mrs Teale, his daily woman, would have his meal ready at midday, and he would wait until after that to start on his tour of the village. He cheered up a little when he realised that he would of necessity have to call upon Mr and Mrs Smith.

27

At the parsonage, Mary Bennet's mood varied between relief and trepidation. She had been more grateful than she could have explained to see Mr Collins' coffin finally taken out of the house. It had seemed to cast an atmosphere of gloom over the place, and even Charlotte Collins appeared relieved that her husband's body had been at last laid to rest, so much so that she had risen from her bed and seemed more animated than she had for days.

Sir William Lucas had now departed, having pressing business to attend to at home. He assured them that, failing any deterioration in Charlotte's condition, he and Lady Lucas would be in attendance well before the end of the month, to lend any assistance they could to their daughter and grandchildren as they prepared for the move back to Hertfordshire.

Mary was grateful for the company of Charlotte, as her father's mood was as taciturn as ever. She was not to go to Rosings that day, as the bishop was still visiting there, so she sat in the parlour with the anticipation of a long day ahead of her with little to lighten her spirits.

Her main fear was that, now that the rector was finally buried, her father would become the object of ever more intense scrutiny and suspicion. Sir John had required him to remain in Hunsford as long as his investigations continued, and he had readily acquiesced. But what, pondered Mary, would happen now? Plans were already afoot to move the family out of the parsonage, and those arrangements did not include her father and herself. Yet the felon was still undiscovered. They could scarcely stay there once Lady Catherine had appointed a new rector, and she could not envisage a time when they would be welcome to stay at Rosings. Notwithstanding Anne de Bourgh's assurance that her mother looked favourably upon their friendship – which, in her heart, Mary somewhat doubted – she was sure that Lady Catherine was far from satisfied of her father's innocence, and, ultimately, her antipathy to Lizzy and consequently to their family in general, remained.

Mary had just begun the third chapter of a book of Greek history, which she had found in the parsonage collection, when the eldest of the three Collins children began to pester her for the piano, and, although she expected Charlotte to discipline the girl, the former merely smiled indulgently and told Mary how pleased she was that her daughter was so interested in music. Mary found herself wishing fervently that she could look forward to another afternoon in the library at Rosings, instead of the prospect of enduring more time with the children. Sighing, she put down her book and moved to the piano, where she humoured the girl by playing some nursery tunes. However, it was not long before the second-eldest child – who was still very young indeed – took it into her head to bang the lowest keys of the instrument, causing severe discord, and making the eldest girl burst into loud wails. It was into such a scene of disarray that Mrs Parkinson appeared at the parlour door, ushering in Lady Catherine, Anne, Mrs Jenkinson and the bishop.

Lady Catherine glared at Mary as the two little girls scuttled away timidly to hide in their mother's skirts. 'Mrs Collins,' she said, perching in a very upright fashion on the edge of the settee, 'we are come to offer you our condolences, but did not expect to enter Bedlam! This is most unlike a house of mourning. I might suggest that the place for young children is the nursery.'

'I must apologise, Lady Catherine,' said Charlotte, hastily ringing for the nurse. 'My daughter was anxious to hear Mary play. I did not want to disappoint her at this sad time.'

'She was obviously disappointed anyway, to judge by the noise she was making. It is a mistake to indulge children, Mrs Collins. You must be extra firm with them now that they have no father to discipline them, just as I have been with my own daughter.'

Everyone looked at Anne, who blushed.

'And I think that music has no place in a bereaved household. Miss Bennet would do well to remember that. When I was widowed, we had the clavichord covered with a black cloth for quite six months. Respect is the key... Do you not agree, Bishop?'

'Certainly, Lady Catherine.'

Lady Catherine continued to speak at some length on correct procedures for mourning, while the bishop and Charlotte nodded in agreement, although the latter appeared progressively more weary. Mary remained seated on the piano stool and hoped to attract no more attention, a course of action which seemed to be successful, although Anne de Bourgh smiled at her when her mother was not looking. Mary wondered whether her father would come out from the study to join them, though she was not certain he would be well received.

Soon Mrs Parkinson arrived with tea, followed by the little maid, Alice, who carried plates for biscuits. However, as soon as Alice caught sight of their guests, she flung the plates down upon the table, breaking several, and ran from the room with a look of horror. Lady Catherine looked after her in amazement.

'Extraordinary! This household is most unsettling, Mrs Collins!'

'You must excuse her,' said Charlotte. 'She has been very upset since my husband's death.'

'She is a servant, Mrs Collins,' replied Lady Catherine sternly. 'Her personal feelings are neither here nor there. You must not tolerate indiscipline among the servants. I trust her wages will be stopped until the breakages are paid for?'

'She receives very little, Lady Catherine. I fear that she would be paying for many years to come. Mainly, she has her bed and board here while she learns her duties.'

'She shows very little promise, I must say.'

'She has still much to learn. She has been something of a protégé of mine... I took her from the poor-house, out of charity, you know.'

'Charity is all very well, Mrs Collins, but it does not have a place in an establishment such as this one. You will have to be thrifty now that you are a widow. Anyway, you will be moving to Hertfordshire very soon, I understand, and I don't doubt that the girl will be returned to the poor-house. I cannot foresee Mr Collins' successor wishing to employ her.'

At this, Charlotte shook her head. 'Oh, I wouldn't expect him to, Lady Catherine. I intend to take Alice back to Hertfordshire with me. My father assured me, before he left today, that he is happy to employ her in his house in Meryton.'

Lady Catherine sniffed. 'He must be generous indeed, Mrs Collins.'

*

To Mary, the time seemed to be passing at half its normal speed. If only Anne had been able to visit without the rest of the party from Rosings, it would have been of such comfort to her. However, before she left – and with her mother some paces ahead of them – Anne de Bourgh turned to Mary and patted her hand.

'I hope you'll be able to call upon me tomorrow afternoon, Miss Bennet,' she said quietly. 'It will be wonderful to resume our studies.'

Mary accepted with gratitude, and felt her spirits lifting a little, though her good mood lasted only until she caught sight of her father at the study door, with the blackest of looks upon his face.

*

Robert Archer, his meal now eaten and cleared away, was preparing to set out on his tour of the village. There had been no sign of the mystery woman promised by Patrick Flannery. He shook his head as he thought of the brother, still incarcerated in the lock-up. Had he needed to make his own duties more complicated than they were, at this troubling time? He ought to have permitted the young man to return to Rosings and then questioned him in the morning in the company of Mr Kirkwood and the head keeper. He would not then have fallen into the trap of allowing a petty grudge to colour his judgment. However, he was now obliged to go from door to door, with, he realised, no real guarantee of an honest answer if he did come across the woman in question – if indeed she existed. Anyone who revealed intimate information to such as himself would be likely to become the subject of village gossip, and, if she were married, would thus incur the wrath of a husband, and, perhaps, violence from that quarter. Yet he had to do something, and so, after giving orders to the apprentices, he called to his dog and was unlatching the gate to his yard when a familiar voice called to him.

'Mr Archer!'

He looked up to see the diminutive figure of Miss Smith, all alone and a little flustered. 'Miss Smith!' He coloured with surprise and searched for words. 'You are all well, I hope?'

'We are quite well, thank you.'

He noticed a sketchbook under her arm. 'You are out to do some drawing, I see. It is a lovely afternoon.'

'I complained to my aunt of a headache, and she suggested that some sketching in the open air might benefit me. We have had a busy morning.'

'And are you quite recovered?'

'It was a ruse, Mr Archer. I... I wanted to see you.'

Archer felt his heart leap. He had not thought of Miss Smith as a forward young lady, but, given his own shyness, he considered that would not be a bad thing. If only he did not have to make these enquiries! Why, he wondered, must their encounters always chance to happen when he had some work demanding his attention?

'I am delighted to see *you*, Miss Smith.' He remembered their meeting in the woods on Sunday and hated himself for having to repeat his incivility. 'It would give me the utmost pleasure to accompany you on your walk today if only I were free to do so. I very much regret that I must carry out some official duties this afternoon. I have a young man in the lock-up who must be investigated.'

Miss Smith was now herself blushing. 'No, Mr Archer, I...'

'Of course,' Archer blundered on, 'I am greatly looking forward to our agreed walk on Sunday. I have been studying the names of the plants and...'

Miss Smith shook her head. 'No, Mr Archer! I am here to see you as constable. It is... it is about the young man you mentioned.'

Archer stared at her, not understanding. 'Michael Flannery? What do you mean? How can you know anything of him?'

'His brother came to see me this morning. He managed to catch me as I returned from an errand to a customer.'

173

'His brother? But... I still cannot understand how you are acquainted with the stable lads at Rosings! They are not to be trusted, Miss Smith. Certainly not by a young woman such as yourself. I have had to have words with them on several occasions at The Three Crowns. Whatever can Patrick Flannery have had to say to you?'

'He asked me to speak to you on behalf of Michael, Mr Archer.'

Archer frowned in disbelief. He felt that he must have stepped out of the real world altogether – seemingly into a nightmare.

'You'd better explain yourself,' he said, sadly.

'I... I met Michael one evening in the spring when I was walking in the woods. I was not long arrived from the city and I had no knowledge of the countryside. He told me the names of the birds and showed me where they nested. Where there is a badger sett. I had never met anyone like him. Before I went home, we arranged to meet again, on a Sunday, which is his evening off. As the days grew longer, we met at night sometimes, after my uncle and aunt had retired to bed. They could not know that I was meeting him... You must not tell them, Mr Archer!'

Archer was too shocked to speak. A sudden picture came into his mind, of Miss Smith in the wood on that previous Sunday afternoon, and the uneasy look on her face when she first had sight of him. He shrugged and waited for her to continue.

She blushed a deeper colour. 'After a while we became... more than friends. Oh, there was nothing... improper, please believe me. Mr Archer, I was with Michael last night, and it was to me he gave the injured kitten. It is at home at this minute, in a little box before the stove. I told my aunt that I had found it in the morning outside our gate.'

Archer stared at her for a few moments, his mind reeling ever more wildly in his bitter disappointment.

'You may visit us to look at the kitten, if you wish. My aunt and uncle would be pleased to see you. I believe you know what they have in mind... I'm sorry, Mr Archer... to disappoint them and you.'

Archer was silent for a long time, then recovered himself sufficiently to answer. 'That will not be necessary, Miss Smith. I do not doubt the truth of your story. I... I will go immediately to release the young man from the lock-up.'

Miss Smith smiled. 'Thank you, Mr Archer... And I would be grateful to you if you could keep what I have told you to yourself – regarding my friendship with Michael, I mean.'

Archer bowed. 'That is your business, Miss Smith,' he replied, coldly.

*

At the lock-up, Archer handed a few pennies to the old man he employed as an occasional gaoler, and instructed him to set the prisoner free. He had no wish to face the young stable lad himself. But as he started on his way home, he was surprised, and annoyed, to hear Michael Flannery calling his name. No doubt he intends to gloat over my mistake, he thought, and plodded resolutely on. However, it was not long before Flannery caught up with him.

'Mr Archer,' he said, 'I wanted to say something to you.' Archer frowned at him and remained silent. 'I do not intend to thank you, if you're thinking that. I should not have been put in that place, as an innocent man. Still, I would be willing to make a trade with you, if you're willing.'

'Trade? What in hell are you talking about, man?'

'Sarah, through the goodness of her own heart, has seen fit to tell you the truth of my account. That was what my brother was to arrange, and the fact that I am free means that she has done so. I expect she has also had to reveal the fact that we are walking out together. Now, it wouldn't do if her uncle and aunt were to hear of this; not yet, anyway. For her sake, Mr Archer – I know you won't do it for mine – will you promise not to tell them? In return, I'll tell you exactly what I know about the night the priest died.'

Archer shook his head in exasperation. 'We've questioned you about this more than once, Michael. Why have you suddenly found something to tell us? It'll be another fairy tale, I don't doubt.'

'I never lied to you, Mr Archer. Maybe I just didn't tell you everything. It was not a lie about the kitten, was it?'

Archer closed his eyes and sighed deeply. 'Go on, then,' he said. 'What is it you know?'

'Well,' began the young man, 'I went to meet Sarah that night. It was moonlight, and bright enough for her to see the road from the village. That was me on my way, that your man saw from the window of the big house.'

'About half-past nine,' said Archer.

'I have no timepiece, but that would be about right. After the hour when the lights are put out. We did not meet for long. I saw the clouds coming over and I did not wish her to struggle home in the darkness once the moon was hidden.'

'Ever the gentleman,' said Archer sourly.

Ignoring the comment, Michael continued. 'I was walking round towards the stable block when I heard a scream, and, soon after, I collided with someone small, a woman. She was running.

It was quite dark by then and it was only when she screamed out again that I realised it was Margaret. I asked her what had happened, but she seemed frightened and did not reply. She ran off to the orangery.'

'Have you spoken to her since that night? Has she said anything about it?'

'I have spoken to her once or twice, yes. She was in the yard when I had the horses out. She likes them. But I didn't think it fitting to ask her about Thursday night. It's none of my business, is it? And Margaret gets worried if people ask her questions. I had no wish to bring on one of her fits. As far as I could see, she was her usual self, not hurt or anything, and I concluded she'd been out a bit late and got scared of the dark, and I didn't help by walking into her... So that's it, Mr Archer. Make of it what you will.'

With a curt nod, he turned and walked away in the direction of Rosings.

28

'So,' said Sir John Bright, 'Michael Flannery's mysterious woman friend turned up after all. Were we right in our suppositions?'

Archer regarded him gloomily. He felt himself to be doubly stupid, firstly for arresting Michael Flannery without more thorough investigation, and secondly for agreeing to keep silent on the matter of the lad's courtship of Miss Smith. He could not decide whether it would be more dishonest to break his word to the pair and inform her uncle and aunt, or to keep it and risk the young woman's honour. Either way, he would scarcely live up to the good opinion of Sir John Bright. He set down his tankard of ale and took a few moments to compose himself.

'It was no married woman,' he said, quietly. 'I very much regret, sir, that the woman in question is Miss Smith.'

Bright frowned at him and shook his head. 'I find that most difficult to believe, Robert... How could that young woman have become acquainted with Flannery, of all people?'

Sadly, Archer recounted Miss Smith's story, together with his subsequent conversation with Michael Flannery. He would rather, at that moment, have been anywhere but in the company of the magistrate, especially when he reached that part of his tale where he had to describe the bargain he had made with Flannery.

Bright, however, was sympathetic. 'It must have been a severe blow to you to see your ambitions dashed in such a way... I suppose there is no accounting for where Cupid's dart will strike, but I cannot imagine a more unlikely pair. You will have to be philosophical, Robert.'

Archer sighed. 'I care not for myself, sir. What concerns me is that I gave my word to Flannery and Miss Smith without due consideration for her reputation.'

'You hoped to further our investigation. It was a worthy aim. As I see it, you faced a most difficult dilemma and did what you believed best. You must not berate yourself too severely.'

'But, in the end, Flannery's account of the night when Mr Collins died has only confirmed what we already knew.' Archer's voice was bitter. 'We are no further ahead than we were two days ago.'

Bright regarded him thoughtfully. 'I suppose the one thing we do now know,' he said, 'is that Margaret's flight into the orangery must have been at a time very close to that when Mr Collins was murdered. Either she saw something happening or...'

'Or she is our felon,' said Archer.

Bright shook his head. 'I still cannot see it, Robert. But I think we shall have to talk to Margaret again, without a doubt.'

'Mrs Flowerday will not be happy.'

Bright shrugged. 'I fear that we shall have to incur her wrath. Lady Catherine is becoming ever more impatient to see this affair brought to a conclusion, especially now that your suspected poacher has been found to be blameless. Will she be told of your suspicions of last night regarding her stable lad?'

'I have informed Mr Kirkwood of his innocence. Whether he has brought any of this to Lady Catherine's ears, I know not... I still believe the man to be guilty of poaching, you know, Sir John.'

'But not on that Thursday night. He was otherwise engaged... I am sorry, Robert... Meanwhile, we must concentrate our energies on finally bringing this murderer to justice. Which we shall do now, with another visit to Rosings and a second interview with Margaret. The day is drawing to a close, I know, but I feel that the matter is too urgent to delay it for yet another day.'

*

'Margaret? Most certainly not! She is about her duties, and I shall not interrupt her in order that she may be upset further.'

Bright nodded at the housekeeper. 'I do appreciate how you feel, Mrs Flowerday, but I assure you that I would not be making this request without good reason. My constable and I are as desperate as I am sure you are, to uncover the identity of the man who attacked Mr Collins, and it has come to our attention that Margaret may just be able to help us further.'

'I fail completely to see what help the girl can be, Sir John. Can you enlighten me?'

'For the moment, I cannot. It is most important, for the present, that we maintain our policy of confidentiality. We are hoping to make all clear in the very near future.'

'Then I shall insist upon sitting with the girl while you speak to her. It took quite some time to calm her after your last visit, I might say.'

Bright sighed. 'Again, I fear I must refuse, Mrs Flowerday. You must agree with me, do you not, that a junior servant would be unlikely to... admit to some action which she fears might be frowned on, in the company of the housekeeper?'

'Hmph! I believe you over-estimate the girl, Sir John. She is exceptionally dutiful, where her intellect allows it, and it would not enter her mind to be otherwise. What you think she can have done is beyond my imagination... However, I suppose I shall be

180

obliged to agree to your request, though I shall tell Margaret that if you upset her, she is to come to me immediately.'

Mrs Flowerday left the room with a stern backward glance at the two men, and some minutes later reappeared with the between maid.

'Remember what I told you,' the housekeeper said, as she closed the door.

It had been decided that Archer, having been better received by the girl on the previous occasion, would commence their interview.

'Sit down, Margaret,' he said, smiling. 'There's no need to be nervous. We just need to know the answers to one or two more questions.'

'I get muddled with questions,' said Margaret, looking from one to the other in trepidation.

'Don't worry. I'll go slowly. It's about that night when Mr Collins died. You told us you didn't meet John that night. Is that right?'

'Yes, sir.'

'Now, we've been talking to a friend of yours, Michael Flannery. He told us that he saw you outside on that very night. He bumped into you as you were running towards the orangery.' The girl looked anxiously around her, as if seeking help from some invisible source. 'Michael said you seemed frightened of something.' Again, Margaret remained silent. She started chewing at one of her fingernails. 'Margaret, were you outside that night because you were meeting someone else?'

The maid jumped, as if startled by a loud noise. She shook her head vehemently. 'I can't say nothing, sir. I haven't done wrong, but I can't say nothing.'

'Why, Margaret?' asked Bright. 'Has someone told you to keep quiet? Perhaps John doesn't want you to say anything.'

'I don't want to get him in trouble, sir.'

Archer noticed the tears gathering in her eyes and glanced sideways at his superior, shaking his head slightly. They could not risk causing the girl to weep in earnest.

'We don't want trouble for anyone, Margaret,' he said, lightly. 'We're not going to mention anything to Mrs Flowerday or Mr Harries. It's just that we need to know everything ourselves, to catch Mr Collins' attacker. I'm sure you want that too, so that everyone can feel safe again.'

Margaret nodded a little uncertainly.

'Now,' continued Archer, 'it's all right to tell us what happened, isn't it?'

Margaret nodded again, blinking the tears away. 'If you say so, sir.'

'Very well. So, did you go out to meet someone that night? It wasn't John, was it?'

'No, sir. I didn't meet John. He said... he said... someone wanted to see me. He didn't say who, just that I wasn't to tell nobody, and then it would be all right. And I wasn't to mind if the person I was meeting wanted to... kiss me, and that. He said I like it well enough with him, don't I, and I do. I like it a lot.'

Archer found it difficult to retain his composure. 'So, you went out...' he prompted.

'Yes, and it was very dark. I was a bit scared, to tell you the truth. It was quite hard to see where I was going, and then there was this man, right in front of me. He was quite big, and he started to touch me, you know... where he shouldn't... and he wasn't gentle, not like John, and I screamed, sir. I shouldn't of, I know. I'd promised John I'd be quiet, but I hadn't expected that. I wouldn't of minded a few kisses. He... he had my dress up, and I was trying to push him away, and then someone else came and

182

grabbed the man and shoved him off me, and I ran. I ran as fast as I could back to the house. That's when I bumped into Michael. I wanted to tell him, but I couldn't. I'd promised John. And mostly I just wanted to get back to my bed and cuddle little Maggie. Then in the morning I had one of my turns.'

Archer and Bright looked at each other. Both felt unable to speak for some moments after the between maid had finished.

'Thank you, Margaret,' said Bright, nodding gravely. 'You have been of the utmost help to us, and I think you're very brave. There's just one final question.'

'Yes, sir?' Margaret seemed more confident now that her tale was told.

'Can you tell us what the second man – the one who saved you – looked like?'

'It was pitch dark, sir.'

'Was he tall or short?'

'He was quite short, I think, sir, and not very big. I can't say nothing else about him.'

'That's good, Margaret. Now, you may go. I shall tell Mrs Flowerday how helpful you have been – though I promise not to say anything else.'

Margaret gave a little bob and left the two men alone.

'Well,' breathed Bright. 'That was quite a story.'

Archer looked at him angrily. 'It makes my blood boil, sir. The sheer wickedness of that footman, little better than a whoremonger.'

'Indeed, Robert... And we must not overlook the similar wickedness of the footman's client. A man of the cloth, no less, who no doubt preached about sin, week in week out. Is he not equally to blame?'

'I suppose you're right, Sir John,' replied Archer, after a few moments, although, to his mind, such a sentiment was a novel one.

The two men were silent, and then Bright stood, a determined expression on his face. 'Right,' he said, grimly, 'we must now interview John once more. The girl's testimony has proved to me that he is a blackguard of the worst kind, and I would like to hear what he has to say for himself when we confront him.'

*

With dinner not far off, Mr Harries was very reluctant to allow the footman time away from his duties to speak to Bright and Archer, but at length, after much persuasion, he agreed to a short interview. He frowned at all three men as he closed the door behind John.

Bright did not offer the footman the luxury of a seat. He drummed his fingers upon the table for a few moments before regarding the man with an angry glare. 'When I last spoke to you, John, you assured me that there was no truth in our supposition that you were guilty of an improper liaison with a young maidservant here... No, I do not wish to hear your protestations of innocence. I have now heard enough to convince me that you have not only contrived to seduce this maidservant but have also sunk so low as to attempt to... hire her out – I cannot bring myself to use a coarser term – for your own monetary gain. Have you anything to say at all, to redeem your character? It will be no use to you if you lie to me again.'

'Who told you that, sir?' John's face was pink with indignation. 'They've no right to blacken my name like that! If the person you're talking about is who I think it is, she's got no more sense than a flea.' Calming, he looked ingratiatingly at the magistrate. 'Besides, you know how it is, sir. These young girls, they get ideas in their heads.' Here he paused and turned to look at Archer. 'They like to think a man has a fancy for them... You should hear what our kitchen maids have to say about the constable here.'

'I care not what the kitchen maids think about Mr Archer!' Bright's patience was swiftly becoming exhausted. 'I am perfectly certain that the young woman in question would be incapable of concocting the story she told us, were it not the truth. And she is not accusing you, John. Far from it. She thinks that you and she are walking out together, and she speaks of you with affection. As to the other matter, again she does not accuse you. But from what she has told us about her meeting that night with Mr Collins – and I have no doubt that it was he – I can only deduce that you have made use of her in the most wicked way. Tell me, how much did you charge him?'

At this, the footman began to bluster, but Bright raised a hand to stop him. 'Remember, John,' he said, 'that this is an investigation of a murder, and the path of murder leads only to the gallows... Perhaps the rector was tardy in paying you, or you thought you might extort a little more while you were at it.' He turned to Archer. 'I think we may have found our felon,' he said.

'I believe you may be right, Sir John,' agreed Archer.

They both looked hard at John, who was silent and breathing fast. Eventually, his eyes flicking from one to the other, he shook his head vehemently. 'No! You're wrong!' he cried. 'You cannot think of accusing me of the murder of Mr Collins! I did not set foot outside the house that night.'

Bright shrugged. 'You may say that,' he said, 'but all the evidence points to you... Constable, I think you may escort John to the lock-up tonight, and I shall arrange for him to be taken to

Maidstone gaol tomorrow... Goodness knows what Mr Harries is going to say...'

'No! It's not fair!' Although uninvited, the footman sank down onto a chair, his face in his hands. 'You can't arrest me, Sir John. It wasn't even my idea!'

Bright glanced at Archer. 'All right, John,' he said. 'Perhaps we may start again. Please tell us all you know about this reprehensible affair – and make it the truth this time.'

John stared at the floor and spoke in a dull monotone. 'It was a couple of months ago,' he began. 'Our head footman, Mr Barker, was talking to Mr Parkinson from the parsonage. He'd come over to Rosings with a message for Mr Collins, who was visiting her ladyship. He was saying that his master was always in our grounds at night, walking around, because he wasn't getting the exercise he was due in the bedroom.' He looked up a little sheepishly. 'You understand what I mean, sirs? Anyway, Mr Barker had this idea. He asked me to help him, me being the one the women seem to go for... Not that I want to sound proud, Sir John.'

'Heaven forbid that you should!'

John frowned at him, uncertainly. 'Anyway, he said that it probably wouldn't be difficult for me to win the favour of one of the young maids and get her to meet me outside after dark... It wouldn't be the first time in this house, believe me, sirs, that such an arrangement has been made... Anyway, we thought the person most likely to accept my attentions would be Margaret. She'd always seemed to like it when I talked to her, and most of the others are either too young or too... worldly, I suppose you'd say. She's simple and more...'

'Gullible?' said Bright, grimly.

John nodded miserably. 'I met her a few times. She liked being with me and... what we did. She really liked it... After a bit, Mr Barker said he thought we were ready for the next part of the plan. He would approach Mr Collins with... with a proposition. He'd tell him he'd heard tell of his wife's illness and ask him if he'd like a bit of female company. After all, it's a man's right, isn't it? He'd say there'd be a bit of money to pay for the woman's... services, but that he would arrange everything. I said he was sticking his neck out, especially with a clergyman and all, but he said it was all sound. He'd done it before, when he was younger. There's always some lonely people around, even in the ranks of the aristocrats – though I think, in the past, the women servants he got to help him were more... knowledgeable, as it were, and had a share of the proceeds.'

'But you weren't going to give Margaret any money, were you?'

John frowned. 'She wouldn't have understood, Sir John... Anyway, we thought she'd be all right with it all, but, when we heard about Mr Collins being stabbed, well, we didn't know what to think. For a bit, I honestly thought she'd done it, stabbed him. I didn't see her until hours after we all learned about Mr Collins, and then it turned out she'd had one of her fits. She came up to me and said she was sorry, but she'd screamed and run away. She was worried I'd be angry with her for not letting the man... do things to her. She had no idea it was Mr Collins, I don't think. I'm not sure she does even now... It surely wasn't her that stabbed him, Sir John. I'm not saying that at all. And it wasn't me nor Mr Barker. We were inside all evening.'

'But you were not unwell, were you?'

'No... no, sir... I am sorry. I was not. Mr Barker and I were at cards together. It is frowned on by her ladyship.'

Bright rubbed his brow. 'It is a most despicable tale, John, and I shall have to consider most carefully what punishment you, and your unworthy senior footman, deserve for it – and also, whether either of you may be responsible for the rector's death. However, it is time for dinner, and you have duties to attend to. I promised Mr Harries that we would be brief, and we have been anything but. I would not risk his good opinion of me by detaining you further.'

After the footman's departure, Bright and Archer sat for some time in shocked silence. Finally, Archer said, shaking his head, 'It would be almost impossible to believe in such goings-on at Rosings, were it not for that man's testimony.'

'I agree,' replied Bright, 'but, believe it we must.' He cast a weary look at Archer. 'I'm very grateful to you for supporting me in my ruse, Robert – I mean, accusing John of the murder. It certainly drew the truth from him, but, of course, it cannot be anything but false. John – and Barker, for that matter – are both tall, well-built men, and our killer has been described as small... Whichever way we turn the wheel, it always returns to point at the same man.'

'Mr Bennet.'

Bright nodded. 'Why he would be there, we can't tell. Did he go to dispute further with his cousin out of the hearing of the parsonage household? And then come to the aid of a young woman in trouble? It's a possibility, I suppose – though the man denies most emphatically that he had any part in it. Nevertheless, I shall have to put it to him again, in the light of what we have discovered. I shall visit him tomorrow.'

29

The day after Lady Catherine's visit, Mary was pleased to note that her father at last seemed a little brighter. He chatted to Charlotte and herself at the breakfast table and ate more heartily than he had of late. He even went so far as to compliment Mrs Parkinson on the smoked herrings, although she acknowledged the compliment a little coolly. Mary frowned at her; the housekeeper obviously still doubted her father's innocence, just as the Rosings servants did. She hoped that her cousin Charlotte would remind Mrs Parkinson of her place, but the former merely looked a little anxious and asked the housekeeper how little Alice did.

'She was, of course, most upset by the breakages,' replied Mrs Parkinson. 'I cannot think what came over her. She is usually very careful.'

'I hope you weren't too stern with her,' said Charlotte.

'As much as I needed to be, Mrs Collins. I understand that the rector's death has affected her deeply. She is also very worried about the future, I think... I understand that you have not yet told her of your intention to take her back to Hertfordshire with you. I have tried to reassure her that all will be well, but I think she will only believe it if it comes from your own lips.'

Charlotte shook her head. 'No, I have not spoken to her, what with all that has occurred, and my illness. It is very remiss of me, and I will put it right this very day. Thank you for reminding me, Mrs Parkinson.'

The housekeeper nodded. 'I'm sure Alice will be much more herself when she knows what you intend, ma'am.' She smiled as she remembered something. 'The poor little lass has also been upset by the loss of her kitten. It has seemingly run away.'

Charlotte smiled in return. 'I did not know, Mrs Parkinson. I'm sure that cannot have helped at all.'

After the housekeeper had left them, Mr Bennet turned to Charlotte with raised eyebrows. 'A kitten, Charlotte? I must say, I have never heard of domestic servants keeping pet animals!'

Charlotte blushed. 'Alice found the creature in the stable. I believe it was abandoned by its mother. She asked me if she could have it in her room. As she sleeps in the little box-room next to the back door, it did not present a problem. I think she saves scraps of her own food for it and lets it out as necessary.'

'An interesting arrangement. Though perhaps it is fortuitous that it has escaped in time to spare itself the journey to Hertfordshire.'

'I *had* been asking myself what my father would have said about it.'

'You are leaving at the end of the month, I understand?'

'That is what my father plans, yes, Mr Bennet. I feel I am now sufficiently strong to make the journey, and I shall be pleased to see my mother and my brothers and sisters again. This has become an unhappy place since my husband's death... Will you and Mary be accompanying us?'

Mr Bennet smiled grimly. 'I am afraid Sir John Bright requires that I remain here until his investigations are completed, which, please God, will be soon. Meanwhile, if necessary, I shall take a room at the local hostelry.'

Charlotte frowned. 'I have heard tell that The Three Crowns has not the best of reputations. My husband was reluctant to cross its threshold – though I believe his predecessor, the Reverend Vaughan, was a more frequent visitor.'

'Ah well, my dear, it will have to suffice for a short time. I am certain that the excellent Sir John Bright will not be much longer in discovering his prey... Of course, Mary will be free to go back with your party if that is convenient to you.'

'Oh no, Papa!' Mary was horrified at the thought of abandoning her father, and was especially upset to imagine him all alone at The Three Crowns, which Charlotte obviously considered unsuitable. 'I cannot go home until you are able to accompany me. We shall move to the village together if we have to.'

Mr Bennet smiled at her. 'Your loyalty does you credit, Mary. But, with any luck at all, this terrible situation will be soon resolved, and we shall *all* travel home by the end of this month. It wouldn't surprise me to know that Sir John is at this moment poised to capture the felon. I have the utmost faith in his abilities.'

*

'Mr Archer! Mr Archer! Oh, you must help us! Mr Archer!' Mrs Smith's voice could be heard even before she had arrived at the gate to the wheelwright's yard, and came so suddenly that Archer's chisel slipped, causing him to curse loudly in front of his apprentices. He hastened to the door of the workshop, where Mrs Smith appeared before him in a state of obvious distress, shortly to be joined by her husband, who was red faced and breathing hard, having obviously struggled to keep up with her.

'Mrs Smith! Whatever can be wrong?'

'Oh, I can hardly bring myself to tell you, Mr Archer. It is our dear niece, Sarah. She has disappeared!'

Archer caught his breath. 'Disappeared, you say? When did this occur?'

'She did not come to breakfast this morning... She is usually so reliable, and is often up well before I am, but today she was nowhere to be seen. I imagined that she was perhaps unwell, and so I went to tap upon her bedroom door, and it was ajar, Mr Archer. She was entirely gone! We searched all over the house and workshops, but there was no sign of her, none at all.' She wept a little into a large white handkerchief.

Mr Smith patted her back. 'We have to tell the constable the worst thing, my dear... You see, Mr Archer, we found a note.'

Archer felt suddenly chilled. He could imagine only too well what such a note might contain.

'She'd left it on the mantelpiece,' continued Mr Smith, 'hadn't she, dear? It was just a few words. It said, "Don't worry about me. I shall be looked after".'

'And that was all?'

'That was all. What shall we do, Mr Archer?'

'We promised her parents that we would take good care of her,' put in Mrs Smith. 'They were worried about bad influences in the town. We said she would be safe here.'

'And so she should have been.' Archer was cursing again, inwardly this time. Why had he been so stupid as to agree to Michael Flannery's request that his dalliance with Miss Smith be kept secret? His information had not really furnished them with new evidence, after all. Now he would have to confess to the kindly couple that he had concealed vital knowledge regarding their niece. He looked at them miserably. 'I have an idea where Miss Smith may have gone,' he said, 'but I think I must act swiftly. If you will excuse me, I shall saddle my horse and proceed immediately to Rosings.'

'Rosings! Why should our niece have gone there?' Mr Smith's face betrayed complete bafflement.

'There is no time to explain. Forgive me... I only hope I will not be too late.'

'I shall come with you.'

'No, please... I really must go now, and I have no other horse broken to the saddle. Please return home and wait there. It is possible, after all, that Miss Smith will think twice about her adventure and will need to find you both there.'

'That's true, husband,' said Mrs Smith eagerly. 'I'm sure the constable knows what he is about, even though it is beyond our comprehension. Oh, I do hope that we shall discover dear Sarah waiting for us at the shop!'

*

As he approached the great house, Archer reflected bitterly how much he had come to hate the very sight of the place. It had been bad enough that he had been forced to spend so much of his time there, away from his rightful trade – and all entirely without recompense of any sort – but now he had put himself in a position which no decent man should occupy. How was he ever to explain to the Smiths that he had willingly allowed their niece to fall into danger, that he had even been an accessory to her deceit? The only small crumb of comfort available to him was that Sir John Bright was also party to the secret.

He rode into the stable yard and searched around the outbuildings until he found Patrick Flannery, cleaning tack. The latter regarded him with an unfriendly expression. 'Ah, Constable. I had a feeling it wouldn't be long before you came calling... My brother is gone, thanks to you.'

'What? Where? For God's sake, you must tell me! He has abducted a young woman from the village. Where can I find them?'

Patrick shrugged. 'On the road... Halfway to Wales, probably. They left well before dawn. But you'll not find them, Constable. They will not be travelling by any established coach. My brother begged a ride from a carter who owed him a favour, and, at the end of that, he will find another, until they reach an inn for the night, where he will work for board and lodging. The next day, it's on their way again. It is how we came here.'

'Wales? Why on earth are they going to Wales?'

'Why, to find a boat for Ireland. My brother, thanks to you, is going home.'

'Thanks to me? Why do you say that?'

'Well, wasn't it you that arrested him yesterday and cost him his job? It was all I could do to hang on to mine, though I'll get precious little pleasure out of it without Michael. But it's well paid, and my mother and sisters need the money I send them. They'll be without Michael's, now, as it is.'

'I told Mr Kirkwood that I had no charge against him.'

'Yes, but Lady Catherine will not tolerate even the hint of a misdemeanour among the staff. It was sufficient for her that Mike had been arrested. He got his marching orders yesterday afternoon, and quite without testimonials. There'll be no more permanent positions for him in England.'

Archer frowned angrily. 'And he went straight down to the village to persuade a young and impressionable woman to go away with him. That certainly isn't my fault. Her uncle and aunt are beside themselves.'

'I am sorry for their grief. But there was nothing I could do to persuade him, Constable. He is in love, you see, romantic fool

194

that he is. Believe me, the last thing my ma needs is two extra mouths to feed, though she will treat Sarah as one of her own. Don't worry yourself on that score... Perhaps you could tell her uncle and aunt that, too. She is the kindest woman on God's earth.'

'He should not have taken her! He had no right.'

'She did not exactly need persuasion, Constable. I can tell you that without a shadow of a lie. When Michael went to her to tell her he was having to leave, she would not hear of remaining, even though he assured her that he would send for her somehow, some day, when his fortunes were a bit brighter.'

'And he let her go with him, without the permission of her uncle and aunt, without even telling them of her intention? It was typically irresponsible of him.'

'They would have said no, so. Sarah is over twenty-one years old and made her own decision. As did Mike. There is nothing any of us could have done.'

Archer shook his head. 'But what of Miss Smith's reputation? However well she's looked after – if there's any truth at all in what you say – will not make up for the fact that she and Michael are not married.'

'My brother assures me that they will be married as soon as they arrive home, if the priest will agree to give the new bride instruction in the faith.'

'Oh, my good Lord! This is a sorry mess, indeed. How I am to deliver this news to Mr and Mrs Smith, I cannot tell.'

Patrick picked up his rag and bottle of oil and turned to the saddle on the bench before him. 'I have helped you all I can, Constable,' he said, sourly.

*

Bright waited uncomfortably in the study at the parsonage while Mr Bennet was fetched from the parlour, where, to judge by the cheerful voices he had overheard, the family was enjoying a happier morning than had been usual of late. He inwardly cursed the mission he was set upon.

'Ah, Sir John!' Mr Bennet smiled as he entered the room. 'I was talking of you only a short while ago. I told my daughter that you were surely on the brink of discovering the man you seek, and that we would be travelling home in no time at all. She does worry so, you know...'

'Mr Bennet... your faith in me is most touching, but I fear that it is misdirected... I am here to ask you further questions. We have received some information which throws new light upon your cousin's last minutes.'

Mr Bennet regarded him eagerly. 'This must be good news, surely? Can you tell me what you have found out?'

Bright looked away, disturbed by the note of hope in the man's voice. It seemed to him totally illogical that someone guilty of a felony should be glad when details became known, and yet this person remained the one most likely to have committed the crime. 'I cannot divulge everything we know,' he said, 'but I can tell you that a female servant at Rosings was... accosted by Mr Collins in the gardens on that night, and was rescued from him by the person who, in all probability, went on to stab him.'

Mr Bennet frowned in incomprehension. 'You amaze me, Sir John. How can that be? My cousin was... tiresome, yes, but of a violent disposition? And why on earth would he attack a servant?'

'As I said, Mr Bennet, I cannot give you all the details at present. Suffice it to say that I am satisfied that this account is a faithful one. What I must ask you now is whether you were that person who went to the aid of the servant... I can well understand how you might have denied all involvement, in the light of your cousin's reprehensible behaviour, but, as this has become known to us anyway, I am wondering whether you may now feel able to confess. I can tell you that this person has been identified as a small man.'

Mr Bennet sank down onto a nearby chair, frowning at Bright as he did so. 'Your revelation has floored me, Sir John. It seems that there must be something in the air here which turns all things upside down and inside out, so that they lose all reason. And perhaps you have yourself succumbed to these vapours, in that you persist in assuming me capable of the murder of my cousin.'

'As you say,' responded Bright, 'the unthinkable has been happening.'

Mr Bennet was silent for some moments, eyes closed as if in prayer. Eventually, he shrugged and, shaking his head, looked resignedly at Bright. 'I have given you the answer to your question,' he said, 'and this new information cannot change that. However, I can *prove* nothing. And neither, I would say, can you... Though I can understand that the circumstantial evidence is weighted against me. You are the man of law, Sir John. If that evidence is sufficient, in your eyes, to accuse me, then so be it. There is nothing I can do.'

*

Bright's expression was solemn as he waited outside the parsonage for his horse to be brought to him. The day had suddenly turned colder, as if in sympathy with the chill he felt inside. There was a stiffening wind from the east and he watched as some leaves began to fall at his feet. The sound of rustling in the shrubbery made him turn his head, and he fully expected to glimpse a red squirrel at work on its winter store, but saw instead the small maid, Alice, creeping among the bushes and calling out some name he couldn't catch. He was still watching her with curiosity when Parkinson appeared, leading his gelding.

'Is someone missing, Parkinson?'

'Oh, no, sir! Well, not *someone*, exactly. Alice is looking for a kitten.'

'A kitten?'

Parkinson looked a little sheepish. 'Yes, Sir John. You see, Mrs Collins has been a little... indulgent with the girl, you could say. She allowed her to take charge of an orphaned kitten, and now the silly girl has gone and lost it. I think it has upset her more than the death of her master.'

'I was concerned that one of the children had wandered off.' Despite himself, Bright found his mood lightening a little. 'Well Well, a kitten you say... I believe I might be able to help Alice with that, if she can just wait a little longer. Meanwhile, Parkinson, please tell her that the creature will not be found in the shrubbery.'

'Yes, sir,' replied Parkinson, confused. He shook his head in wonder as the magistrate rode away from the parsonage.

30

Mr Bennet was still and silent for a long time after Sir John Bright left him. For the first time, it seemed to him that the magistrate was becoming seriously convinced of his guilt; there had been an additional gravity in his demeanour this morning.

He put his head in his hands as he thought of the family. If he were to be accused, how could he ever tell them of his plight? Or, to be precise, how was he to tell Mary? She had the misfortune to be at hand and would thus have the unenviable task of writing to her mother and sisters. And, firstly, to her uncle Gardiner, who would necessarily have to be involved from the outset in the day-to-day arrangements for his wife and daughters. He was under no illusion that, as the family of a convicted killer, they could possibly continue in any semblance of the genteel life which they had so far enjoyed. As for his two eldest daughters, married, as they were, into families of note, he could not imagine the shame which they would surely suffer.

Seated thus, and distracted by the worst kinds of thoughts, he did not hear Mary's gentle tap upon the door and was only made aware of her presence by her voice calling him.

'Papa! We heard Sir John leaving, but I was quite unable to catch him up. Do tell me that he brought good news, as you hoped, and that we may all soon go home together. Charlotte and I have been in the best of spirits, thinking of it.'

Mr Bennet closed his eyes and shook his head slowly. 'You had better sit down, please, Mary. Sir John has received some new information which is not... helpful to me.'

Mary gazed at him without understanding. 'You mean that you and I shall be obliged to take rooms at the inn in the village? It will not be too bad, Papa. We shall be together, and...'

'No, no!' said Mr Bennet in despair. 'What I mean is that I fear Sir John intends to arrest me... I am sorry, my dear, but I cannot help but think it... Oh, he has not said it to me in so many words, but, from what he *has* said, I can only conclude that my detention is imminent.'

Mary's face blanched in horror. 'It cannot be true, Papa!' she cried. 'You have mistaken his words in some way. You said yourself that Sir John is an able and intelligent man who would not accuse you unfairly. You are innocent, as anyone may see. You must ride after him at once, so that this misunderstanding may be put right!'

Mr Bennet shook his head again, sorrowfully. 'There is no misunderstanding, Mary. A witness has come forward who has identified me as the felon for whom they have been searching, or, to be more precise, I am the only person who fits the description supplied by this witness and who also has both motive and previous access to the weapon involved.'

'But how can that be, Papa? There must be another man just like you.'

'I cannot tell, my dear. I know only what Sir John has seen fit to tell me.'

By this time, Mary was weeping. She reached out with a damp hand and grasped that of her father. 'I cannot let you be accused, Papa! You would be taken to some terrible place! How could you bear it? We must go away, tonight, though we cannot go home, or they will find us. As soon as it is dark, we shall escape. We shall make for the coast – it is not far – and secure a passage on a ship.'

Mr Bennet smiled gently. 'You forget, Mary. We are still at war with France. We should be no safer at sea than we are here – and considerably less comfortable.'

'Then we must find somewhere else to go. We could live in London, change our names. No-one would find us.'

'But what about your mother, my dear? And your sisters? I could not leave them grieving in ignorance as to whether we lived or died, and neither, I am sure, could you. No, I must accept whatever fate awaits me and trust that justice will be done.'

'But they will take you to prison, Papa, and you will be murdered in your sleep!' sobbed Mary.

It was on the tip of Mr Bennet's tongue to reply that this might, after all, be preferable to the gallows, but he refrained for the sake of his daughter's sensibilities.

'I have heard it said that, as long as a prisoner has cash to pay his gaolers, he will be kept safe,' he said. 'But come, Mary, I am not accused yet. We must not grieve for what may never occur.'

*

In the parsonage kitchen, there was a certain air of self-satisfaction about Mrs Parkinson as she rolled out the pastry. 'I am certain that Mr Bennet will soon be arrested,' she said. 'He was all sweetness and light this morning, and now, after Sir John's visit, he's shut himself up in the study again, and Miss Bennet is weeping in the parlour... It will be a grave disappointment for poor Mrs Collins, of course, but it will be a relief in the long run – knowing that her husband's attacker has been brought to justice, albeit a person whom she has considered a friend.'

'Do you really think so, dear?' replied Mr Parkinson. 'He would have to have been a desperate man to have committed such a deed... I mean, being a relation, and all. I can scarcely bear to think upon it.'

'I think we are all aware of the strength of his feelings,' replied his wife. 'Remember all those arguments! We could hardly fail to hear them. It was a black day in this house when he crossed the threshold. It makes my skin crawl now, to think that the man is still under our roof. If Sir John does believe him guilty, then he should have made sure that he was removed immediately. I shall not sleep until he is gone. Who knows what he might do if he suspects that he will be caught? He may try to silence all of us – we are witnesses, after all.'

'Hush, dear – you will frighten little Alice! I'm sure we don't have to worry on that score... I do feel concerned for Mr Bennet's daughter, though.'

'His daughter! Yes, I'm sorry for the girl, odd fish though she seems. What will become of her, do you think, if he is arrested?'

'Probably she will return home with our dear Mrs Collins and the children. But after that – who knows? She and her mother will very likely end up at the mercy of the parish. Mr Bennet's savage deed will have ensured that they will now never inherit his estate, just as if he had done nothing at all. Which all goes to show that crime will never pay.'

Mrs Parkinson nodded sagely. 'You are right, of course, husband. And we must think as well of Lady Catherine. What a terrible source of shame it will be, that the de Bourgh family is connected to the family of a murderer! If only Mr Darcy had married Miss Anne as was intended... Chop that turnip finely, Alice!'

The little maid, who had listened in silence to the conversation, now looked up at the housekeeper with fear-filled eyes. 'What will happen to Mr Bennet if he is arrested?' she said, in a small voice. 'Will they 'ang 'im?'

'Of course they will!' replied Mrs Parkinson. 'He's a murderer.

I daresay we'll go along there, on the day, if we can have time off – it's been a long while since there was a hanging, what with the thieves and robbers getting sent to Australia instead... You'll be gone by then, though, so you'll miss it.'

'Come now, wife,' said Mr Parkinson, in mock disapproval, 'don't you think maybe it would be a bit much for a young lass like Alice? Might give her nightmares. Look, she's gone dead white already.'

Alice looked from one to the other. 'I'll really be going with Mrs Collins, won't I? To 'ertfordshire?'

Mr Parkinson beamed at her. 'You really will, Alice. It's all arranged. You're such a lucky girl. You must always be grateful to Mrs Collins.'

'She won't change her mind, will she? What if I said something she didn't like?'

'Have we ever known Mrs Collins to change her mind once her word is given?' He patted the little maid's arm. 'And whatever could you possibly say to her that she wouldn't like? Now... you and Mrs Parkinson must get on and finish this pie, or we'll have no supper for her tonight.'

*

Soon after this conversation in the kitchen, Alice was sent on her regular tour of the house, refreshing the fires and refilling the coal buckets as necessary. On opening the parlour door, she was deterred from entering by the sight of a tearful Mary Bennet, whom Mrs Collins was attempting to comfort. 'Maybe later, Alice,' said the latter softly.

Going instead to the study, she was equally startled by encountering Mr Bennet, still seated, head in hands, at the desk.

'Sorry, sir,' she mumbled, 'I didn't know you was here.'

Mr Bennet looked at her with a tired expression. 'No need to be sorry, Alice. You're just doing your job. This fire could do with a bit of brightening. I am feeling suddenly chill... Thank you so much... Oh, a moment, Alice!' The little maid paused, regarding him fearfully. 'Here, hold out your hand,' said Mr Bennet.

Alice did so and was rewarded with a silver sixpence. She looked at it with wide eyes before managing to mumble her thanks. Mr Bennet patted her hand.

'I heard about your kitten, Alice. I'm sorry it's lost. This may help to cheer you up a little... Now, in case I don't see you again, I wish you a happy future with Sir William and his family. They are good people, you know.'

To his surprise, the maid burst into tears and ran from the room, quite abandoning her coal bucket.

*

Archer's face was red with embarrassment as he entered the draper's shop for the second time that day. He'd spent a most uncomfortable half hour there earlier, attempting to explain why he had not informed the Smiths immediately of their niece's unsuitable attachment to the stable lad. Of course, he had not been able to make any mention of the deal he'd made with Michael Flannery, and so had had to keep stressing the fact that he'd given his word to Miss Smith. It had been obvious, however, that Mr and Mrs Smith by then considered him morally reprehensible, and had barely been civil to him as he'd taken his leave the first time. Shortly afterwards, he'd seen Mr Smith's horse galloping past his yard, in obvious pursuit of the runaway pair.

Now, to rub salt into the wound, he'd been asked by Bright to retrieve the unfortunate kitten from the draper's, and deliver it to the rectory. Earlier, he had been about to recount to the magistrate the sorry tale of Miss Smith and Michael Flannery. But Sir John had seemed in a bad mood and unwilling to listen, with the result that Archer had had no opportunity to explain the awkwardness of his request. 'I shall see you later this afternoon,' Bright had said, as he turned his horse's head to the road. 'Meanwhile, I have some thinking to do.'

In the shop, Mrs Smith took her time displaying fabric to the two female customers who were already there and made a show of not looking in Archer's direction. Eventually, after about twenty uncomfortable minutes, the customers left, and Archer was able to approach her.

She looked at Archer disdainfully. 'I thought we had said all we had to say this morning, Mr Archer. Unless you are here to offer assistance to my poor husband, of course. He has taken to the roads in an attempt to bring back my niece. An additional horseman would be of utmost use. My husband is not a well man, you know.'

'I saw him riding past,' said Archer glumly. 'I'm sorry, Mrs Smith, but I have come here on quite another errand, to collect the injured kitten.'

Mrs Smith's face took on the colour of the crimson cloth she was holding.

'The kitten! Do you mean to say that you are concerning yourself with a *kitten* at such a time as this? Really, Mr Archer, I did not think my opinion of you could sink any lower, but you have quite proved me wrong.'

'I know what you think of me, and I've said I'm sorry,' replied Archer miserably. 'Believe me, Mrs Smith, if I could change what has occurred, I would do it gladly... As to the kitten, it is at Sir John Bright's request that I fetch it. He asks that I deliver it to the parsonage.'

'Oh, I see,' said Mrs Smith, slightly mollified. 'If it belongs to poor Mrs Collins, then she must have it back at once. Anything to cheer the poor lady in her time of mourning... I shall fetch the creature from the kitchen.' She glanced coldly at Archer as she went out to the back.

Fortuitously for Archer, another customer now entered the shop, a stout woman with three young girls in tow, so that he was spared any further conversation on Mrs Smith's return. She handed him a small box from which came a mewing sound, and then turned away without any salutation. Archer hurried out, pursued by the curious stares of the children.

*

At the parsonage, he was surprised, and not altogether pleased, to be received by Mr Parkinson with loud guffaws of laughter when he was made aware of the purpose of Archer's visit.

'Well,' he said, his round face creased with merriment, 'that takes the biscuit, Mr Archer, it really does. I've never heard of an officer of the law concerning himself with lost pet animals. Though Sir John did say he could help find the kitten for us... The constable *and* the magistrate! They'll be calling out the militia next!'

Archer frowned at him. 'Where do you want me to take the creature, Mr Parkinson? Shall I give it to you, or shall I hand it over directly to Mrs Collins?'

'Mrs Collins? Oh, no, Mr Archer. It's not her kitten. It's little Alice's. I'll fetch her directly. She'll be so pleased!'

Archer fumed inwardly. What could Bright have been thinking, sending him on such a mission for the sole benefit of a serving maid? Silently, he relived his humiliation in the draper's shop.

'Here she is, Mr Archer.' Parkinson pushed the girl forwards, beaming. 'The constable's got your kitten, Alice. What do you say to him?'

'Thank you, sir,' said Alice dutifully. She timidly reached forward and took the box which Archer was holding out to her. With a small glance at both men, she lifted the lid and peeped inside. 'Oh,' she said, 'it *is* Kit, but she's so thin, Mr Parkinson, and something's cut her.'

'Don't worry, lass. She's bound to be thin after being gone that long, and most probably some dog took a dislike to her. She'll be right now, sure enough, with you to take care of her. Don't you think so, Mr Archer?'

'I believe the kitten was discovered caught in brambles,' said Archer, stiffly.

'That would explain the injuries, then... Look, Alice, you take her down to the kitchen and Mrs Parkinson will give you a bit of milk for her, if you ask nicely... Now, will you excuse me, Mr Archer? I have some tasks to see to.'

The little maid smiled shyly at Archer and started to walk slowly along the passage, stroking the kitten and talking to it as she went. 'Oh, Kit!' she was saying. 'You've led me a dance! Why did you go off after the master like that? You was so fast, I couldn't catch you...'

Archer's mind, which had, up to that point, been fogged by his feelings of resentment, suddenly cleared. He hurried after the girl.

'Alice!' he called. 'Would you mind talking to me for a few

minutes? It won't take long, then you can get the milk for your kitten.'

She looked up at him fearfully. 'Am I in trouble, Mr Archer?'

'Not at all! It's nothing to do with anything you've done... Could we go out into the garden? You can bring the kitten.'

'All right, sir.'

Archer chose a spot where they could not easily be observed from the house, not wishing to spark the interest of either Mrs Collins or Mrs Parkinson. It suddenly occurred to him that he had never, in fact, interviewed Alice – that that small part of the jigsaw had remained missing until this moment.

'I heard you talking just now,' he began, 'to the kitten. Can you tell me what day it went away?' Alice looked more fearful than before and was silent. 'Was it the night when Mr Collins died, perhaps? You won't be in any trouble, Alice... If you can tell me, it might be of help to Mrs Collins. I'm sure you'd want that.'

Alice nodded. 'It was that night, sir.'

'You said that the kitten followed the master. Did you see where it went?'

Again, a nod.

'But you haven't mentioned this to anyone?'

She whispered, in so low a voice, that Archer had to strain to hear her. 'I was scared, sir. I thought they'd send me away, if they knew what I seen... But Mrs Collins is taking me with her now, sir, and Mr Parkinson says she never breaks her word.' She paused to wipe a few tears away with her grubby handkerchief. 'And... and I don't want Mr Bennet to be 'anged, sir. He won't be, will he?'

Archer felt his heart beating more swiftly. With an effort, he remained as calm and reassuring as he could. 'You'd better tell me what happened, Alice,' he said. 'Start at the beginning.'

Alice looked at him fearfully. 'You won't let them send me away? You promise?'

'I promise,' said Archer, at that moment willing to take the girl into his own employ, if necessary, if only she could help him arrive at the truth.

Alice took a deep breath and continued in her small voice. 'It was the night Mr Collins died,' she began. 'I'd gone to my bed, but Kit was scratching at the door, wanted out.'

'The kitten?' asked Archer.

Alice nodded. 'I went to let her out, and I saw somebody walking off, down the path to Rosings. It was Mr Collins, on one of his walks. Then Kit goes and follows him, and I didn't want to lose her, so I went after. It was dark, but I'm used to seeing in the dark, there wasn't no light in the poor-house. Anyway, she goes all the way to Rosings and I still can't catch her. After a bit, he stops, and I think, now I'll get her, but she's in the bushes behind him, and I can't let him see me in case he gets angry. He didn't like me 'aving the kitten, only Mrs Collins made him say yes... Then I see this woman coming along, and I don't know what happens, but suddenly she screams and then there's this other person there and the woman runs away. Then... I see the new person's arm jabbing at Mr Collins and he falls down.' Alice shudders. 'It was 'orrible, sir. I didn't know what to do. I ran back to the parsonage and I had to leave Kit. I didn't say nothink to nobody. I was afraid I'd be sent back to the poor-house. Till Mrs Collins told me I'd be going with her. Even then, I was scared, though I wanted to tell, honest I did.' She raised pitiful eyes to Archer's. 'But then, you've got Kit back for me and this morning Mr Bennet give me sixpence. He was kind, and it isn't right to see 'im 'anged. And now you've asked me, so I've told.'

Archer gazed, perplexed, at the maid and spoke his next words with the utmost difficulty, at the same time sending up a silent prayer. 'You've been very brave, Alice, to tell me all this. But there's just one thing more – do you have any idea who this third person might have been? The one who... stabbed Mr Collins? Any detail which might help us to identify this man? Was it one of the servants, perhaps?'

Alice, more confident now, almost smiled at him. 'Oh, yes, sir,' she said. 'You see, the moon came out, just for a little tiny bit – after it happened – and you couldn't see their face because they had their back to me, but I could see what they was wearing, sir, and they wasn't no servant, nor no man, neither. It was one of the fine ladies from Rosings!'

31

The midday meal was already long over when Mary recalled that she had been invited to Rosings that afternoon. Her mind had been so preoccupied with her father that, for once, the delights of the library had been forgotten. Hurriedly, she put on her bonnet and cape and trotted down the path, mentally composing excuses as she went. She didn't feel that she could devote time to books – or even to Miss de Bourgh – while her father was likely to be taken away at any moment.

In the library, the fire was bright and welcoming, and Anne de Bourgh was already seated at the small table at the window, a number of volumes in front of her. Mrs Jenkinson occupied one of the armchairs at the side of the fireplace. Anne looked up as Mary was shown into the room and smiled happily.

'Ah, Miss Bennet! I am so pleased to see you. I was afraid that you were unable to come... Look, I have found some books of history for you to look at. I remember you mentioning the one you are reading from the parsonage collection. See, one of them has drawings.'

Mary looked sadly at the lovely book which Anne was holding out to her. 'Oh, Miss de Bourgh, it is so beautiful, and you are so kind.' She sat down suddenly, raising anguished eyes to her friend's, and continued in a low voice. 'But I fear that I must return to the parsonage immediately. My dear father now thinks that his arrest is imminent, and I cannot leave him alone.' She wiped away the inevitable tears. 'I am come merely to give my excuses.'

Anne reached over and took Mary's hand. 'Is he so sure, then? Has Sir John told him such a thing? Surely it cannot be true.'

Mary shook her head. 'Sir John has received a description of Mr Collins' attacker, and it fits my father. He cannot see how he can now escape accusation.' She wept quietly. 'I cannot bear it, Miss de Bourgh!'

Anne's own eyes filled with tears. 'And I cannot bear to see you like this, Miss Bennet.' She grasped Mary's hand a little tighter. 'I just wish I knew what to do. It would be so wrong to accuse your father unjustly... I think I must go to Mamma immediately. She will know how to resolve this situation, surely.'

Mary gave her a watery smile. 'You are so kind,' she said again, returning the pressure on her hand, 'and I would be so grateful for any help you can give me.' She sighed. 'I am just afraid that Lady Catherine's goodwill towards our family may have been thoroughly drained by my sister Lizzy!'

'Nevertheless,' said Anne, 'I shall go to her without delay.' As Mary stood up to leave, she reached out impulsively and embraced her friend. 'Please don't distress yourself, Miss Bennet. We shall find some way.'

Mary nodded dumbly and made for the library door, watched all the way by the old lady, Mrs Jenkinson.

*

Lady Catherine de Bourgh looked at her daughter's eager face and shook her head in exasperation. 'I warned you not to become close to this person, and now it seems my intuition has been proved correct. I have believed for some time in Mr Bennet's guilt, though it has taken Sir John all these days – and much inconvenience to this household – to reach the same conclusion.'

'But it cannot be true, Mamma! Miss Bennet has become my dear friend, and it is simply not possible that her father could be in any way guilty. You must send for Sir John immediately!'

Lady Catherine's face darkened. 'I *must do* nothing of the sort! You forget yourself, Anne, and I am most displeased... I had begun to think that you had reached some level of maturity... But it is that stubbornness of spirit again, which you have learned from the Bennet girl. Now, you may return to your studies until tea-time.' She turned to Mrs Jenkinson. 'I understand that Mary Bennet is gone?'

The old woman nodded.

'Then I shall hear no more about this matter. The sooner the father is arrested, and the daughter returned to Hertfordshire, the better. I do not wish you to contact her again, Anne.'

'But she is my friend!' repeated Anne. 'She needs my support at this terrible time. I shall go to her at the parsonage.'

'You will do no such thing!' Lady Catherine rose from her chair in anger. 'This is utter wilfulness and disobedience. I wish to see no more of it, do you understand?'

Anne stood before her, frowning, and made no reply. Mrs Jenkinson watched her anxiously.

'Very well.' Lady Catherine turned her head away. 'You may go to your room... Now! And do not think of making your way to the parsonage. I shall ensure that one of the footmen will prevent you if you attempt to do so. You will go *now*... Go!'

'Miss Bennet will be heartbroken!' cried Anne. 'And my heart will break too in thinking of it!'

Scarlet-faced, she turned away sharply and rushed from the room, bursting into tears as she went. Mrs Jenkinson rose to follow her, but Lady Catherine shook her head.

'No, leave her.' she said, 'Anne does not deserve your company.

213

She can think upon her behaviour alone and, I trust, come to regret it. It makes my blood boil to see how far astray she has been led by the Bennet girl. She has never spoken to me in that headstrong way, never!'

The old lady looked at her worriedly. 'I hate to see her so miserable,' she said. 'Dear Miss Anne has such tender sensibilities. And she *has* been so very happy in Miss Bennet's company. I have seen it myself. You could say that she has *blossomed* at those times.'

'Hmph! As you say, my daughter has seemed to enjoy the company of that girl, and I allowed the friendship for that reason. Be that as it may, the girl is the daughter of someone soon to be convicted for murder. Any further association with her would now be entirely inappropriate.'

'But if Anne's heart should break?'

'Then break it must.' Lady Catherine sighed. 'There is nothing you nor I can do to prevent it.'

*

When Anne did not appear at the tea-table, nor, later on, at the dinner table, Lady Catherine's mood worsened considerably. She became increasingly silent, and her thunderous expression warned all who approached her to disturb her at their peril. Mrs Jenkinson, for her part, became more and more agitated as the afternoon turned to evening, and made frequent visits to Anne's room, partly to assure herself that the young lady had not, as she had threatened, somehow escaped from Rosings and made her way to the parsonage. After each visit, she returned to the drawing-room with a more tragic expression than before, and, eventually, could contain herself no longer.

'Dear Anne is overtaken by grief,' she said, in a shaky voice, ignoring the look on Lady Catherine's face. 'She refuses to open her door to me, or even to speak very much, except to say that she wants no dinner... I do so fear that she will make herself ill.' She shook her head in sorrow. 'What shall we do, Lady Catherine? Another fever might be the death of her! We cannot forget the turn she took after her dear father left us.'

'You surely cannot be equating the fate of this... murderer with the demise of my most illustrious husband!' Lady Catherine was scandalised. 'Even for you – and I make allowances for your advanced age – even for you, Mrs Jenkinson, that is a *most* inappropriate comment.'

The old lady's response was to whimper like a small whipped dog. 'But it is all so *wrong*!'

'Wrong? What can you mean?'

'I mean that you are... *We* are wrong to accuse Mr Bennet. Poor Anne is distressing herself unnecessarily.'

'Ah, so you now know more than Sir John Bright, merely because my daughter has been hoodwinked by the manipulative Miss Bennet and has convinced you in the same way. Really, Mrs Jenkinson, I am seriously of the opinion that your wits are softening.' Lady Catherine stared hard at her aged cousin. 'You should perhaps go to lie down, in the hope of some restoration.'

Mrs Jenkinson wrung her hands in despair. 'No! No! You do not understand, Lady Catherine! I *know* that Mr Bennet is innocent of the attack upon Mr Collins, because I know what happened that night.'

Lady Catherine cast her eyes upwards as if seeking help from the Almighty. Then, resignedly, she settled more comfortably in her chair and nodded to Mrs Jenkinson. 'Very well. I am listening. I can see that you will not settle until you have told me your story – although I am certain that it will turn out to be the product of some feverish nightmare resulting from one of your headaches. As it is, you had better sit down.'

32

Sir John Bright gazed at Archer, his brow furrowed in perplexity. 'This is a most extraordinary tale, Robert,' he said. 'It has completely taken the breath from me.'

The two men were seated at the kitchen table in Archer's cottage, the two apprentices having been despatched early to their homes in preparation for the Sabbath. For this discussion, they had deemed The Three Crowns too public a place. Earlier in the afternoon, Archer had succeeded in persuading Alice to recount her story again in the presence of the magistrate. He had managed to convince Mrs Parkinson that it was necessary to interview her properly in order to fulfil the obligations of their investigation, although his request to do so had been received with much the same scepticism as Mrs Flowerday's, when they had asked to see Margaret.

'Do you think it is true, Sir John? Surely the girl must be mistaken. I have thought of nothing else since her revelation, and cannot see any of the ladies as a murderess. Miss Anne is far too gentle, and the old lady is so frail that she must be hard pressed to hold a knitting needle steady, let alone a knife, and dim-sighted to boot. And as for Lady Catherine...'

Bright shook his head helplessly. 'The girl was quite adamant. She is convinced of what she saw.'

'But what can we do, Sir John? We cannot go to Rosings and inform Lady Catherine that we must choose between Miss Anne, Mrs Jenkinson and herself – God forbid – in order to find our killer.'

'Hardly. And yet, if we are to believe little Alice – and I can see no reason why she would lie to us – then that is exactly what we have to do.'

'I suppose she cannot have imagined it all, can she? People of her age often seem to have vivid imaginations.'

'Well, no, I really don't think so, Robert. Remember that her account of the happenings of that night chime very closely with Margaret's. Alice merely tells us the next part of the story, after Margaret ran away. It is most unlikely that the two maids have ever even met, given the restrictions imposed on them by their respective domestic duties in different households. No, I think we must believe the girl.'

'But do you think she could have mistaken what she saw? All right, she saw a woman, but could it have been one of the servants?'

'I asked her that, and she was most emphatic that the person was a lady – lace-trimmed nightdress and cap, thick velvet cloak. People in service are very well able to recognise a lady by her clothing.'

'The ladies' maids have access to their mistresses' wardrobe. One of them could have borrowed a cap and a cloak.'

'But how could they have known what was to happen? Such an action would have required premeditation, not to mention the collusion of someone party to the footmen's unscrupulous plan. Margaret herself would not have told anyone else. She was desperate not to break her promise to John, whom she loves... No, an accusation has been made, and I shall need to interview the three ladies in more detail, though I shall have to consider my words very carefully. It is a thorny prospect indeed, Robert!'

Archer stared at him in consternation. 'It is impossible to think upon, sir,' he said, with a shudder. 'I fear that all three will be most unwilling to allow any weight to be put on an accusation made by such a junior servant.'

Bright frowned. 'Exactly so,' he said.

*

By the time that he and Archer had finished their deliberations, Bright had deemed it too late to visit Rosings that day. Instead, he rose especially early the following morning, in order to make some time to ponder the questions he might ask to finally discover the truth. Sabbath or not, he could delay no longer.

Approaching the door of the great house, he hesitated. What he was about to do was so shocking that he fully expected Lady Catherine to question his authority, if not his sanity. However, he was the magistrate, and he took his duties with the utmost seriousness. High-born or lowly, a felon was a felon, and, if found to be guilty, must be dealt with accordingly. He pulled the bell-cord and waited in some trepidation.

He was greeted by Mr Harries, though with none of his usual good cheer.

'Ah, Sir John! This is a coincidence, sir. I was about to despatch one of the footmen to ask you to attend us.'

'Really?' said Bright, a little comforted to know that his visit would not be entirely unwelcome. 'Is something amiss, Harries?'

'We have a... situation here which is most unfortunate. You must accompany me to the presence of Lady Catherine, who will explain it to you.'

Bright's heart sank a little. He was about to make whatever situation existed at Rosings a good deal worse. He followed the butler to the morning room. There he found Lady Catherine, together with Anne de Bourgh and Mrs Jenkinson, the two latter showing signs of recent tears.

'Sir John!' Lady Catherine regarded him with some surprise. 'You are most prompt, I must say. I have but three or four minutes ago ordered my butler to summon you.'

'Lady Catherine,' began Bright, 'I was, of course, on my way here anyway. I have some new information – of a most disturbing nature – concerning the death of Mr Collins. I must beg your forbearance while I recount it. It is… distressing in the extreme.'

At this, Anne de Bourgh began to sob. Her mother frowned at her, although, for once, she did not admonish her daughter in any way. She sighed deeply.

'As you see, Sir John, we are already distressed enough. I learned something yesterday evening, regarding the death of Mr Collins, which, when you hear it, will, I am completely certain, quite surpass the new information which you have for me, and in the worst possible way.' She paused and put her hand to her brow, as if suppressing an ache. 'I have slept upon the matter, but the light of day brings no peace to me. I am quite lost for words… I would that God could wipe away these past hours and allow us to start this day again, in innocence… But He cannot, and, as magistrate, you must now learn this… abominable secret too.'

Bright moistened his lips. He was aware of the ticking of the mantel clock and the crackle of the fire. At length, Lady Catherine, not looking at her subject, said, in a dull voice, 'Mrs Jenkinson, if you will…'

There was again a silence, during which the elderly lady appeared to be muttering to herself. Then, she cleared her throat and spoke in a small but clear voice.

'That night… that night, I was restless and did not sleep. I could see the light in Miss Anne's room – we leave the doors open, you see – and then, after a while, I heard her getting out of bed. I was worried, of course, as she had been a little out of sorts earlier – nothing much, I don't think so, just enough to need a posset before sleep. She's so delicate, you see, Sir John... Well, she went downstairs, so I followed her. She was quite quick, I must say, and my old legs don't cope with the stairs so well now, but I was just in time to see her going towards the passage, the one that goes to the library and the orangery. I couldn't think what she wanted down there. I would have rung for a footman, if only she'd said,' she regarded Anne with an affectionate frown.

The latter stared at her old companion with fearful eyes. 'The Addendum to my Greek grammar!' she said. 'I went down to fetch it.'

Lady Catherine shook her head despairingly.

Mrs Jenkinson, looking a little bewildered, continued with her story. 'I could see Anne going into the orangery. She'd put on her crimson cloak by then, so I knew she was set upon going outside. My eyesight is not so good, Sir John, but I'd have spotted that colour anywhere. It's a bit worn, you know, but still so bright!'

Here again, Anne appeared to be on the verge of interrupting, but was shushed by a stern Lady Catherine.

'I followed her out, as best I could. It was very dark, but I could just make out her moving shape and the swish of her skirt on the grass, which was overlong. My poor slippers became quite soaked! You must send word to Dudgeon on the matter, Lady Catherine... Then... What was I saying?'

'You were following Miss Anne, Mrs Jenkinson.'

'Oh, yes, I recall. I followed Miss Anne and then – oh, Sir John! – I recall it now only too well. I heard her scream, and I feared for her life. Perhaps she had met with a cutthroat, or... or worse... I had not even a walking cane to protect her. Then, in my panic, I felt in the pocket of my dressing-gown, and discovered, to my joy, a paper knife. I had been earlier slitting the pages of a notebook, in my room, you know. Sometimes I find it helpful to jot things down, to help me remember.' She paused, bewildered again. 'What was I saying, Sir John?'

'You heard a scream,' he replied.

'Oh, the scream... It was terrible, Sir John! I heard her scream, and when I came closer I could just make out the shape of a man attacking her. I don't know how I got there in time, but I did, and I came between them. I pushed my dear Anne to safety, and she was able to run away, unharmed...'

'And you used the knife...'

'Yes, Sir John! The moon came out then, just for a few seconds, and I was able to keep the man at bay with the knife... He fell down, and I escaped. When I got back upstairs, Miss Anne was safely in bed. Her door was just ajar, so I did not see her, nor she me, but I could hear her turning the leaves of her book. She does love to read! I must confess that I felt a little dizzy by that time, not myself at all, so that I just took off my wet slippers and got into my bed – even though my skirts were still damp from the dew, and the sheets no longer reflecting the heat of the bed-warmer. In the morning, I could only think it all a bad dream.'

'But the next day, when the body of Mr Collins was discovered...?'

The old lady frowned at him in confusion. 'But that was the rector, Sir John! The man I fought off in the garden was a wicked felon, out to attack my dearest Miss Anne. I have cursed myself repeatedly since that time for leaving the paper knife behind me. It is obvious that this cutthroat must have picked it up after rising and accosted dear Mr Collins with it. He must have been a desperate man indeed to have attacked an innocent girl and a reverend gentleman all in the same night!'

'May I ask why you did not tell me all this when I made my enquiries?'

Mrs Jenkinson looked scandalised. 'It would not have been seemly, Sir John. You would have had to question Miss Anne, and we couldn't have that, could we? Even I have not enquired as to why she thought fit to venture outside in the dark... It was just lately, when she was so deeply affected – even mortally wounded – by the thought of Mr Bennet's arrest, that I knew that I must come forward with my information. Of course, I am certain that Mr Bennet, as an innocent man, would have been completely exonerated, but now I am able to prevent him being arrested at all, and ensure that Anne is quite restored to good spirits... I must assure you, by the way, that the felon in the garden was a good deal taller than Mr Bennet.'

A period of silence ensued, during which Mrs Jenkinson dabbed at her forehead with a scented handkerchief. 'If that is all, Sir John,' she said, 'may I be excused? I fear that I am over-tired and must retire to my room.' With that, she made her way slowly from the room, patting Anne's shoulder as she passed.

Lady Catherine raised her eyes to meet Bright's. 'So,' she said, 'our conundrum is at last solved, Sir John, a fact which causes me no joy whatsoever. Now, perhaps you should tell us your own reason for calling on us today.'

Bright shrugged. 'The new evidence to which I am privy merely confirms that which has been supplied by Mrs Jenkinson. A witness has come forward – the little maid at the parsonage, Alice. She can testify to having seen Mrs Jenkinson attacking the rector that night. She was afraid that, if she told tales on any of the ladies from the great house, she would get into trouble and be returned to the poor-house. However, her own conscience with regard to Mr Bennet – and Mrs Collins' assurance that she would be employed in Hertfordshire – proved stronger than her fear. She related her story to Mr Archer and myself yesterday afternoon.'

Lady Catherine nodded slowly. 'That would explain why the creature saw fit to break the crockery when we called at the parsonage. She saw the face of... the murderess.'

'Oh, Mamma!' Anne de Bourgh burst into tears afresh. Bright thought it best not to disclose the fact that he had come to Rosings with no clear idea as to which of the three ladies might have murdered Mr Collins.

Lady Catherine sighed. 'Much as I would wish it, I cannot shield you from the truth, my dear...'

'But Mrs Jenkinson thought she was protecting me, Mamma! She must have seen Margaret – who, as Mrs Flowerday will tell you, has been given my cast-off crimson cloak – going into the garden and thought she was me.'

'Margaret?' Lady Catherine frowned. 'In heaven's name, what part could that creature have to play in this appalling drama?'

'I know not, Mamma.' Anne shook her head in confusion.

Bright considered his words carefully. 'As it happens, ladies, my constable and I have already been informed that Margaret was, indeed, abroad in the gardens that night. I imagine that Miss Anne's surmise is most perceptive.'

There was a period of silence, and then Lady Catherine nodded sadly. 'That would seem to be what happened, certainly. For some reason, that addle-brained between maid took it into her head to walk in the grounds after dark and was surprised by Mr Collins. She screamed in fright – perhaps even started to throw a fit – and the rector, attempting to restrain Margaret, was assumed by poor Mrs Jenkinson to be attacking her – or, rather, attacking Anne. I believe our friend had no notion that she was stabbing Mr Collins. It is all a most dreadful misunderstanding.'

'What will become of her, Sir John?' asked Anne, tearfully. 'She was attempting to protect me, as she has always done.'

Bright gazed at them both, his brow furrowed.

'You are both correct, of course,' he said. 'Mrs Jenkinson was acting purely upon the necessity, as she saw it, to protect Miss de Bourgh. I cannot, in all honesty, attribute any degree of malice to her action that night. However, misguided though her thoughts were, I fear that she may still be guilty of manslaughter in the eyes of the law.'

Anne gasped in horror.

'But she is sometimes bewildered, Sir John. Increasingly so, these past few years.' Lady Catherine frowned at the magistrate. 'I do not believe that she would have acted as she did if she were in her right mind.'

'That too is true and is most unfortunate.' Bright paused, sighing. 'And I have no doubt that a wise judge will take all these circumstances into consideration when assessing her case.'

'You cannot mean to commit her for trial, Sir John!' Anne's voice was shrill with desperation, and she rose from her seat as if to attempt to restrain the magistrate. 'She is my oldest companion and I know she would never have intended to harm Mr Collins. You cannot send her away!'

Lady Catherine reached forward to place a hand on her daughter's arm. 'Anne, I beg of you – please sit down. You must try to be calm, as must I. This is a most distressing situation, but it is happening, and we must find some means of dealing with it... I am very much afraid that Sir John has no option. Mrs Jenkinson has caused the death of another, and must answer to the law. No-one – even a member of a family such as ours – must be seen to be above the law, or it would mean nothing.' She frowned at Anne, who looked back at her bleakly. 'It is a matter of honour.'

Bright inclined his head. 'Thank you for your understanding, Lady Catherine... I shall not remove Mrs Jenkinson from your care just yet. It is not long until the Michaelmas Assizes, and I have no qualms about leaving her to your guardianship until then.' He rose to take his leave, then paused. 'And I feel that, owing to her age and disposition, Mrs Jenkinson's punishment may well be no more than some spell of time in an asylum.'

With another gasp, Anne de Bourgh ran from the room.

33

Unwilling as he was to disturb the Sabbath at the parsonage, Bright felt duty bound to visit Mrs Collins as soon as possible, to inform her that her husband's killer might finally be named. He looked forward to her reaction with some trepidation, but, as it happened, the widow listened to his account with equanimity.

'Thank you, Sir John,' she said, quietly. She shook her head. 'It is a strange tale, indeed... I must confess that I can only feel sorrow, rather than anger, towards poor Mrs Jenkinson. She has always been so devoted to Miss de Bourgh.' She sat in silence for some minutes, and then rose. 'If you will excuse me, I think I would like to spend a little time in contemplation.'

Bright nodded and hurried to open the door for her. 'You are most gracious, Mrs Collins.'

Afterwards, he turned back towards the other two occupants of the room. Mr Bennet and Mary both appeared to be struck dumb by his revelation. Eventually, Mr Bennet shook his head in perplexity. 'You have quite taken my breath away, Sir John, I must confess. My cousin died as a result of some sort of misunderstanding, you say. Well, well. So it was a sort of accident, in the end. A tragedy, indeed, though better, perhaps, than deliberate murder by one of evil intent.'

Bright inclined his head. 'It is easier to contemplate, certainly, Mr Bennet. We are none of us happy to think that real evil may be present among us.'

'Indeed not, Sir John. And I am sure that this will be of some comfort to poor Mrs Collins... But, tell me, must the old lady be punished for her unwitting assault upon Mr Collins? As his cousin, I would not wish it, and you have heard Mrs Collins' opinion of her.'

Bright sighed heavily and reiterated his words of earlier in the day at Rosings, at which Mary Bennet blanched and covered her face with her hands.

'Oh,' she cried, in muffled tones, 'poor Miss de Bourgh! She will be beside herself with grief in thinking of her companion! How will she endure a trial?' Rising hurriedly from her chair, she went over to the writing desk, where she gathered paper and pens with fumbling fingers. 'Please excuse me, Papa, Sir John,' she said, in a trembling voice. 'I must write to Miss de Bourgh at once. I shall go to the dining room to gather my thoughts.'

Mr Bennet's brow furrowed as he watched his daughter leave the room. 'I am sorry, Sir John,' he said. 'I fear that Mary's affections are much engaged by Miss de Bourgh. It is most unfortunate that all this has had to happen. Deeds and misdeeds never occur alone, do they? Their consequences spread out, like ripples in a pond from a thrown stone, in ever-widening circles, and eventually touch us all.'

*

Later, as they waited in the parsonage garden for their horses to be brought to them, Bright regarded Archer with a tired expression.

'You have told all Mrs Collins' servants, then, Robert? It is important that misleading gossip does not make this case worse than it is.'

'I have, Sir John... Though I think Mrs Parkinson is having

difficulty in accepting the truth of my account. I believe she is still convinced of the guilt of poor Mr Bennet.'

'Let us hope that her husband will convince her otherwise.' Bright sighed and smiled weakly at the constable. 'Well, it looks as though this case is finally ended, Robert. It has been an uphill struggle, and, although I am not happy with the conclusion, I am in no doubt that we now know the full truth of what happened.'

'I still cannot believe that an old lady such as Mrs Jenkinson should have been responsible, sir.'

'Nor I... And the worst of it is, that the whole sorry thing could have been avoided. If... if... if... If that scheming footman had not hatched his evil plan to make money. If Mrs Collins had not been so unwell, or her husband so impatient. If Miss de Bourgh had made sure she had all her wretched books with her when she went upstairs. If the maid had not been given a cast-off cloak...'

'And if Mrs Jenkinson had not retired to bed with a paper knife.' Archer shook his head in disbelief. 'You are right, sir. There is no rhyme nor reason to it... Sometimes you wonder what the Almighty can be thinking, really you do.'

The two men could hear, from within, the chatter and laughter of the children.

'They're all right, though, Robert. They're young enough to forget all this. They'll soon be in Hertfordshire, in the heart of Mrs Collins' family, and I believe Mrs Collins will find peace there too... I am grateful that the true purpose of Mr Collins' excursion that night need not come to light. I would not have poor Mrs Collins shamed by such knowledge.'

'But what of the footmen, sir? I do not attach much blame to Margaret. She was an innocent party in that foul plan. But John and Barker – well, that's different, is it not? They should be brought to book in some way, surely.'

Bright smiled grimly. 'And so they will, Robert. Before I left Rosings, I spoke to Mr Harries, in strictest confidence. The result was a confrontation between the two of us and the footman, John. He admitted to Harries his part in the seduction of poor Margaret for his evil ends. Furthermore, he also informed him of the part played by Barker. Mr Harries lost no time in dismissing the two of them without testimonials. He will tell Lady Catherine that they were suspected of trying to sell Rosings property for their own gain. It is not without a grain of truth.'

'Will she not expect their case to be brought to the assizes, sir?'

'He intends to make it clear that they were discovered before any real theft could occur. And, in the current unhappy circumstances, both he and I agree that any further unpleasantness at Rosings would surely be unwelcome to her.'

'And what of Margaret, sir? Will she be disciplined in any way?'

'We decided that Margaret has been put through enough already. Mr Harries will watch over her as best he can, to make sure that she is not exploited again, but the knowledge of her part in this episode will remain his, and his alone. Lady Catherine believes she was merely startled by the rector – she has not questioned why such a girl would be out of doors well after the time she prefers her staff to retire... For once, it may be a good thing that, in the eyes of a great lady such as she, domestic servants are not possessed of personal motives.'

Archer stretched suddenly stiff limbs. 'With your permission, Sir John, I shall make my way home now.'

'Certainly, Robert. There is no news of your little Miss Smith, I suppose?'

'No more news than we already know, Sir John.' Archer sighed. 'Mr Smith was not long upon his quest. I think he is not a very willing horseman. According to public gossip this morning – of which there is much – it seems that her uncle and aunt are now resigned to the idea that she will marry Michael Flannery. They merely await a letter from Ireland.'

'Bad luck, Robert!'

Archer shrugged. 'It was partly my own doing – bringing matters to a head like that – and I am sorry for it. I let my feelings get the better of me. It was not an action worthy of a man chosen to be your constable.'

Bright clapped him on the back. 'You must not be too hard on yourself, my friend. Everyone has to learn from his mistakes. And, from the sound of it, the young lady's heart was already given... You have been of invaluable help to me in this investigation, and I look forward to many more collaborations in the future.'

Secretly, Archer hoped that such collaborations might be few and far between. However, he nodded and thanked his superior officer. Then, breathing a sigh of relief, he mounted his horse and set off at a canter towards the safe haven of his cottage.

*

It was some days later that a messenger arrived at Sir John Bright's door with the news that his scheduled visit to Rosings at Michaelmas would not now be warranted: Mrs Jenkinson had, that day, been discovered dead in her room.

Lady Catherine, who had penned the letter personally, made

it clear that the end had been a peaceful one. 'I believe that my cousin's heart finally succumbed to its great age,' she wrote. And then added, archly, 'We would not want you to embark upon another of your investigations in this case.'

Bright folded the letter, and then spent a few moments in quiet contemplation. He felt that the weight of the past weeks, which had been pressing heavily upon him, had all at once been lifted, and he suddenly remembered Archer's comment about the opacity of the Almighty's motives. He reflected that, sometimes, it seemed that God was not entirely without compassion for mankind.

34

As the month's end neared, the parsonage became a place of bustle and preparation, as Sir William and Lady Lucas helped their daughter and grandchildren pack their possessions in readiness for the move back to Hertfordshire. In truth, as it turned out, there was not as much work as had been feared. Most of the furnishings were part and parcel of the parsonage itself and would be passed on to the next incumbent. When it came to Mr Collins' personal effects, his wife chose to retain very little. His clothes – apart from the clerical vestments – were given to the poor, and Charlotte decided to allow his books to become part of the parsonage's collection.

Mr Bennet and Mary had decided to travel back with the rest of the party. Mrs Bennet was still in Newcastle, and would be for some time to come, so there was no need for haste. Now that the threat of arrest had passed, Mr Bennet was increasingly able to make light of the fate which had almost befallen him, and often chuckled to himself when he considered what his wife's reaction would be, should he ever tell her the full details of the past days' events. He did not intend to do so, given her weak disposition, and trusted that Mary would be similarly disinclined. All in all, Mr Bennet was now more content than he had been for some years. He intended to visit his solicitor shortly after returning to Longbourn, but was confident that the entail on his property could now be overturned, allowing it to pass to his daughters as he had always desired.

Mary Bennet was rather less content. While overjoyed at her father's exoneration, her pleasure, already tempered by her knowledge of Mrs Jenkinson's part in Mr Collins' fate, was further reduced when the news reached her of the old lady's death. She could imagine only too well how her friend must now be feeling at the loss of her companion, and her heart was heavy as she watched the removal preparations being made.

Mary had, on several occasions, attempted to visit Anne at Rosings, but, each time, she had been informed that Miss de Bourgh was unable to receive her and had been turned away at the door. Now, just a few days before their scheduled departure, Mary was becoming increasingly afraid that she would not be able to see her friend again. Disconsolately, she decided to try just once more, and, mentioning her intention to her father, took up her cloak and bonnet.

Mr Bennet regarded her with compassion.

'Do not be too disheartened, my dear,' he advised her. 'These people – the upper classes, you know – they have their own ways of doing things, probably not for the likes of us to know. Just remember that Miss de Bourgh was a good friend to you when you needed her but may not be in a position to accept your ministrations now that *she* is in need... thus displaying weakness, as it were.'

Mary frowned at him and, pulling on her bonnet with unnecessary firmness, left without another word.

The autumn air was chilly and dank, and the late-flowering roses in the gardens at the big house had begun to lose their colour. Looking down towards the orchard, which adjoined the walled kitchen garden, Mary could make out the red and green apples now almost ready to pick, and, further round towards the stables, the stacks, all thatched and secure against the winter to come. Normally, winter was a season which Mary anticipated with eagerness; it was a time for sitting by the fire with her books and without the dread of her mother planning some unwanted expedition to the village. And this year her mother's absence meant she would be alone at Longbourn with her father for at least some weeks more, if not months. She should have been thoroughly happy, especially given that her recent fears on his behalf had come to nothing. She sighed, thinking of these things. Life's gifts never seemed to chime at once with her desires.

Remembering her father's words, she did not go to the door, as she had intended, but remained instead in the gardens, sitting down upon a cold, stone bench near to an ornamental fountain. She supposed that this would be her last visit to Rosings, and she sank into a melancholy reverie.

'Miss Bennet!' Anne de Bourgh was suddenly before her, snugly wrapped in new dark blue velvet. She was smiling hesitantly. 'I saw you from my window,' she said, 'and I had to speak to you. I hope I don't disturb you.'

'Not at all!' replied Mary, surprised out of her daydreams.

'I have been hoping that you might call,' continued Anne, 'after our... our unpleasantness, you know – but I had begun to think that you must have already departed for Hertfordshire. I am so pleased to find that you are still in Hunsford.'

Mary gazed at her. 'But I *have* called,' she said, 'on three or four occasions, but, each time, the footman has told me that you are not receiving visitors. I have been most concerned about you, dear Miss de Bourgh.'

'Ah.' Anne nodded. 'I... was not aware of that, Miss Bennet. I should have liked nothing better than to have seen my friend at this time. I must apologise for my mother's sensitivity. I fear that she may be embarrassed that something of which your father was accused has turned out to be the work of our relative – though I am certain that Mrs Jenkinson truly believed that she acted to save my own life. She was misguided, I am afraid...'

Mary looked at her earnestly. 'I am sure you are right, Miss de Bourgh... You must miss your companion so much... I have so dearly wished to be of comfort to you, as you were to me so recently.'

'I miss her more than I could ever say. I come down every morning and expect to see her at the breakfast table, and the nights... the nights have been quite unendurable, knowing that her room is empty, you know.' Her voice broke, and she wiped away the tears. 'I have... I have quite given up on my study of Greek, of late. It seems I cannot concentrate my mind upon anything.'

Mary reached out and touched her hand. 'I have been quite distraught in thinking of you,' she said. 'I only wish I could help you in some way.'

Anne seated herself next to her friend, gathering her cloak around her. 'It means so much to me that you are here today,' she said. 'I have been so lonely. Mamma has had so many things to attend to, you know... It has been so difficult for her to accept... what has happened, and then there has been the funeral to arrange. I wish we could turn the clock back to that time when we first started to study together.'

'I too, Miss de Bourgh.' Mary's eyes were welling with tears of her own. 'I have never been so happy as during those first days with you in the library.'

Anne's hand closed around Mary's. 'Well, at least you are here now. I cannot express how much better I feel for that fact... although you have not chosen our nicest seat from which to admire the garden!'

They both laughed together, albeit a little weakly, and, afterwards, were able to talk at length in comfortable companionship, until Mary at last rose to take her leave. Her face became sad again.

'We are travelling to Hertfordshire the day after tomorrow,' she said. 'I do not expect to return... I have valued our friendship more than you can know, Miss de Bourgh.'

Anne looked stricken. 'I too, Miss Bennet.' She reached out and grasped Mary's hand again warmly in her own. 'I knew you must go, of course, but hoped it would not be so soon. I wish that there were some way that we could continue our friendship.'

'Oh, if only we could!' Mary's eyes began to prickle with tears. Acting upon a sudden impulse, she leant forward and enclosed Anne in a clumsy embrace, and then, afraid that she had acted improperly, scuttled away with a muttered farewell.

*

It was with some surprise that Mr Bennet rose from the breakfast table the following day, to be told that Lady Catherine de Bourgh had just been shown into the parlour.

'She is asking to speak to you alone, sir,' said Mrs Parkinson.

Mr Bennet sighed, and, despite a fleeting whim to make his escape via the back door, duly made his way along the passage.

Lady Catherine regarded him sternly. 'Mr Bennet,' she said, 'I shall not beat about the bush. We have not always seen eye-to-eye.'

Mr Bennet agreed that this was possibly quite true.

'But now,' she continued, 'I have a proposition to put to you.' She frowned. 'It is not of my making, not at all.' There was a pause, and Mr Bennet cleared his throat and examined his clasped hands. He could not imagine what she could possibly want of him but could not avoid the feeling that it was probably something unpleasant. 'It is my daughter's idea... You must understand that she is very precious to me, and I have, therefore... agreed to sound you out on the matter.' Mr Bennet looked at her expectantly. 'You will know that Anne has spent some time recently with your daughter. I cannot say why, but, apparently, she has become very attached to the girl, plain though she is. You will also know that, a short time ago, she lost her lifetime's companion in... difficult circumstances.' Mr Bennet nodded gravely. 'Anne has been grievously affected – she has always been most sensitive – and I have been very concerned for her welfare. However, she came to me yesterday evening with this idea, and it is one which seems to cheer her greatly. I have spent some hours since then, considering the matter, and I have come to the conclusion that for the sake of Anne's future happiness, I must concur with her wishes – if only you will agree to it as well, Mr Bennet.'

'It would give me the greatest delight to be of cheer to Miss de Bourgh... but I cannot agree without first hearing the proposition, Lady Catherine.' Mr Bennet was now completely perplexed.

'Very well. My daughter requests that Miss Bennet be allowed to live with us at Rosings as her companion.'

Mr Bennet, who had remained standing, in the hope that this might encourage Lady Catherine to make her visit a short one, sat down rather suddenly on the piano stool. For once, he was completely lost for words. Lady Catherine gazed at him expectantly. 'Well,' he said, finally, in rather a weak voice, 'I must confess, Lady Catherine, that you have quite taken me by surprise... Has Mary already been approached on this matter?'

To Mr Bennet's ear, 'allowed' seemed to indicate that his daughter had expressed a wish to take up the position.

'As of yet, no. I thought it best to talk to you first. But I cannot imagine that she could have any objection. It is a chance which any young woman of her class would leap at.'

'I see,' replied Mr Bennet. 'You may be right, of course, but I think that I should ask Mary's opinion first. I shall do so immediately and will call upon you this afternoon with her reply. For my part, well, like yourself, I only want what will make my daughter happy.'

Lady Catherine inclined her head. 'I am in your debt, Mr Bennet... although, given the nature of... previous exchanges between my family and yours, it pains me somewhat to say it.'

'I believe we shall all be happier now if we can look to the future rather than the past,' replied Mr Bennet, gravely.

After Lady Catherine had left him, Mr Bennet found himself reflecting on her earlier promise – all that time ago, it now seemed – to place his daughter with a family, although he felt he could say with some certainty that she had never intended that family to be her own.

*

And so it was that, within a month's time, Mary Bennet was again in Kent, but, on this occasion, the carriage had brought her to the front door of Rosings. She had returned home only to sort out and pack her few belongings and to say goodbye to friends and acquaintances in Meryton, which were fewer. Charlotte Collins had insisted upon taking her to the dressmaker's in order that she should have some decent gowns to befit her new role, and she had waited with impatience while these were made up.

Now, she watched as her trunk was unloaded, and then turned to her father with shining eyes.

'Thank you for coming with me, Papa. I still can't believe that this will be my home.'

Mr Bennet smiled a little sadly. 'I can't say I'm pleased to part with you, Mary,' he said, 'but as long as you're content, then so am I... Though I had hoped that, when I gave you away, it would be to a husband. Are you quite sure that you will be happy here, Mary?'

'Miss de Bourgh is dearer to me than any husband might be! This is all I could ever want. And I shall visit you frequently, Papa. It is not as if I am in service here. Miss de Bourgh insisted upon that, and you have made sure of it by arranging my allowance. We shall be equals. And we shall have such times together! Lady Catherine is to engage a tutor for our Greek. Think of that, Papa!'

'Well, it all sounds wonderful... I don't know what your mother will say when she comes home. To think that we have now lost three daughters to such prominent families... I daresay she will never get over it!'

Mary kissed his cheek. 'Farewell, Papa,' she said. Then, turning towards the great front door, she saw the small figure of Anne de Bourgh, waiting for her. Holding her skirts free of the gravel, Mary ran over to her, and turned just once to wave to her father. Then, hand-in-hand with her friend, she entered the house to begin her new life.

'I'll show you to your room,' said Anne excitedly. 'It adjoins mine!'

Acknowledgements

With grateful thanks to my editor, Lindsay Ashford, and to all the lovely people at Honno who have enabled this book to become a reality. And, of course, to Jane Austen herself for creating the characters in the first place.

About the Author

Photo: Rhiannon Haf

Annette Purdey Pugh grew up in Flintshire and graduated in English from Lancaster University. In a varied career, she has worked as a medical librarian, an optical assistant, and a milkwoman, bottling and delivering milk for almost twenty years to customers in Ceredigion. A writer from childhood, she has won awards for her short stories and poetry at the National Eisteddfod of Wales but was inspired to take up her pen more regularly following an Open University course in Creative Writing. *A Murder at Rosings* is her first novel, and has its roots in a lifelong love of Jane Austen. She lives on the family farm in West Wales with her husband and three hundred sheep.

ABOUT HONNO

Honno Welsh Women's Press was set up in 1986 by a group of women who felt strongly that women in Wales needed wider opportunities to see their writing in print and to become involved in the publishing process. Our aim is to develop the writing talents of women in Wales, give them new and exciting opportunities to see their work published and often to give them their first 'break' as a writer. Honno is registered as a community co-operative. Any profit that Honno makes is invested in the publishing programme. Women from Wales and around the world have expressed their support for Honno. Each supporter has a vote at the Annual General Meeting. For more information and to buy our publications, please write to Honno at the address below, or visit our website: www.honno.co.uk

Honno, D41 Hugh Owen Building, Penglais Campus,
Aberystwyth University, Aberystwyth, SY23 3DY

Honno Friends
We are very grateful for the support of all our
Honno Friends.
For more information on how you can
become a Honno Friend, see:
https://www.honno.co.uk/about/support-honno/

Why not take a look at one of our Austen inspired short story collections?

Dancing with Mr Darcy

Wouldn't every girl like to dance with Mr Darcy? The 20 original stories in this collection have been inspired by the novels and characters of Jane Austen, or Chawton House Library, a place she knew and loved

Beguiling Miss Bennet

Beguiling Miss Bennet reveals the secret lives that continue behind the scenes at Pemberley, Mansfield Park and elsewhere in England once Jane Austen puts down her pen...

Wooing Mr Wickham

'When a young lady is to be a heroine... something must and will happen to throw a hero in her way.' Or perhaps, if she's unlucky, a villain with a treacherous heart... The twenty original and contemporary stories in this collection have been inspired by the some of the more – or less – admirable characters that inhabit Austen's fictional world.

"Entrancing collection of Austen-inspired stories."
Jane Austen's Regency World

"take(s) the Jane Austen we all love and admire and cannot get enough of and creates something new and lovely in her wake."
Janeite Deb, Jane Austen Society of North America

honno

Gwasg Menywod Cymru
Welsh Women's Press

The Mysterious Death of Miss Austen
by Lindsay Ashford

Miss Anne Sharp holds the position of governess at the Godmersham home of Edward Austen. She becomes friendly with his literary sister, Jane, when the latter arrives for an extended stay. When Jane dies at the age of just 41, Anne is devastated. But was it natural causes or murder? Even after more than twenty years, Miss Sharp is determined to get to the bottom of the mysterious death of the acclaimed Miss Austen...

"I actually couldn't put it down... beautifully written and wholly believable..."
Jane Odiwe, janeaustensequels.blogspot.com

"...a gripping, page turning, toxic sugar plum unlike any other Austenesque novel I have ever read.
Laurel Ann Nattress, Austenprose.com

"Ashford borrows the "mischievous spirit" of Austen herself in this thoroughly entertaining mingling of fact and fiction."
Anna Scott, Guardian

honno
Gwasg Menywod Cymru
Welsh Women's Press